'Captivating' *Wall Street Journal*

'There are plenty of threads for Frankie and her team to tie up in this thoroughly tidy police procedural' *Sunday Sport*

'Olivia's skill in writing ensures the plot is well delivered throughout' *Woman's Way*

'Frankie Sheehan is a wonderful creation and I loved her second outing. The locations, characters, and scenes in *The Killer in Me* are vivid and fully realised. The plot intense, intellectual and intriguing. This was a very satisfying read and I loved it' Amanda Reynolds

'Completely gripping – an intelligent, beautifully written thriller which kept me guessing. Frankie is such a great, complex lead and this is another brilliantly knotty case for her to unravel' Phoebe Locke

'An outstanding, thought provoking and gripping police procedural which kept me guessing. Exquisite writing, brilliant characterisation and thought provoking to boot. Highly recommended!' Claire Allan

'Tana French fans are a ready audience for the second in Kiernan's series, which unravels murder cases undertaken by Dublin detective Frankie Sheehan . . . She paints a rich picture of contemporary Dublin life, its social pretences and nothing-to-lose characters both crashing against the justice system. Readers will watch for more from Kiernan' *Booklist*

'A sophisticated, immersive and layered police procedural which knocks it out of the park' Fiona Cummins

'Olivia Kiernan has done it again. DCS Frankie Sheehan is fast becoming one of my favourite investigators and I was with her every step of the way in this, her second case in the series. Expect sharply observed details, a gritty, compelling plot and note-perfect dialogue' Jess Kidd

'An excellent police procedural, which will keep you reading well into the wee hours' *Meath Chronicle*

'This multi-layered police procedural is packed with intricate details, twisted trails and great characters . . . A clever, well-written page turner' *Choice Magazine*

'The heir to Tana French's throne' *Irish Times*

Olivia Kiernan is an Irish writer living in the UK. She was born and raised in County Meath, near the famed heritage town of Kells and holds an MA in Creative Writing awarded by the University of Sussex. *The Murder Box* is the fourth book in the acclaimed Frankie Sheehan series.

Also by Olivia Kiernan

Play Dead For Me
The Killer in Me
If Looks Could Kill

THE
MURDER BOX

Olivia Kiernan

riverrun

First published in Great Britain in 2021
This paperback edition published in 2022 by

riverrun

An imprint of
Quercus Editions Ltd
Carmelite House
50 Victoria Embankment
London EC4Y 0DZ

An Hachette UK company

A CIP catalogue record for this book is available
from the British Library

PB ISBN 978 1 52940 116 5
EBOOK ISBN 978 1 52940 117 2

10 9 8 7 6 5 4 3 2 1

Typeset by CC Book Production
Printed and bound in Great Britain by Clays Ltd, Elcograf S.p.A.

Papers used by Quercus are from well-managed forests and other responsible sources.

For Louis

'Whatever the objective in life, so often, success is not dependent on knowing how to play but knowing how to win.'

Camille Forbes

CHAPTER 1

Some murder cases come in quietly. They ease you in, allowing you to enter from the shallows, to take your time before wading in deep. Each investigation leaves its stain, its scar somewhere, either on the body or the mind but, by the time they begin to make their cuts, you're halfway there to expecting it. Then, once in a while, a case lands on your desk and immediately the tiny hairs on the back of your neck stand on end. These are the cases that, despite all your experience, all your skill, you find yourself asking, am I cut out for this?

The Box arrived at the Bureau yesterday. It was wrapped nicely, an unsigned card stuck on the front. The box itself is of high quality, finished in a glossy red. Inside, the contents are arranged like games pieces – each item slotted into its own cubbyhole. There is a case file, a bus ticket, two pieces of card, each covered in protective plastic. On one, a strand of hair. On the other, an earring – a silver knot from which hangs a shimmering tassel. There is a brown envelope. Inside the envelope, a blue plastic case containing a glass slide, of the kind you view with

1

a microscope. There are six round pins, their tops like drops of crimson blood. And lying beneath it all a fold-out board, a miniature case board, on which to fix my findings.

Welcome to The Murder Box, the addictive murder-mystery game, says the introductory letter. And you might think that with my day job being actual murder I would've set that sucker aside, but I didn't. The headache of a case the Bureau is working on, finds me craving diversion. It's a case that's been kicking my backside for a month. The disappearance of TV personality Teddy Dolan. No leads, the foot of my superior digging so far into my back I can taste shoe leather, and half my team paralysed by apathy.

Or perhaps the box grabbed my attention because the contents look so convincing that if I were to remove the case file from within, I could drop it alongside all the other real-life cases in my filing cabinet and it would be right at home.

This box contains everything you need to begin cracking this case, the letter goes on. *Inside, you should find: a case file including a post-mortem report, victim details and an envelope containing crucial pieces of evidence.* It tells me there's an online community, a website, where, should I need to, I can share my findings with other detectives. Other players. *As you investigate, enter your progress into our online portal to unveil more vital pieces of information. But don't dally. Life and time are short. And this killer respects neither.* I felt a prickle of adrenalin at that.

The PE, the post-mortem examination, is dated, 11th of August 2013. The state pathologist's address stamped at the top. Whitehall, Dublin 9. A satisfying flourish of authenticity. The report shows the external auditory canal – the ear – was sliced off.

Blacklight picked up traces of ink on the back of the victim's right hand. A rupture of the left cornea, fractured orbital floor. Stab wounds, seven inches deep through the lower chest bilaterally. Pneumothorax, collapsed lungs. Cause of death: heart failure. Manner of death: homicide.

In the end, it was Baz, who got the game started. Detective Baz Harwood became my partner just over two years ago. I wouldn't say I'd to be dragged kicking and screaming to the idea of working with a partner, but I wasn't begging for one either. I've spent years dragging my forearm across the desk of life, pushing anything from the table that might clutter up my career. I guess to some that makes me the lone wolf. The maverick. Laughable, really, when there are few people outside of my work who can say without a breath of hesitation they'd put their life in a colleague's hands. But I would do it. I have done it. Particularly Baz's. Jack Clancy, my boss, must be laughing at that one. I remember that day in Whitehall, peering down on the corpse of another victim. Feeling the need to prove myself, drinking coffee to rinse the bile from my mouth, desperate just to get through the autopsy. Jack, friend and stranger in the same moment, telling me I needed a partner and my response: I prefer to work alone. And I have to wonder whether that was ever true. I felt sure about it back then. But time has ways of showing us to ourselves.

Now, I can't imagine a case without Baz by my side. It's not that I couldn't get the job done without him. That's not it. I'm good at what I do. But we work well together. Where one of us acts the other reacts, like a Newton's cradle.

Late last night, Baz and I were still in my office, off the clock, the guts of a bottle of wine down, the eyes bleeding out of our heads from going through witness statements, emails and calls from the public on Teddy Dolan. It was coming up on eleven by the time we gave up for the day. I tidied up my notes, closed the case file and took up my wine. Baz did the same and we sat quietly for a bit.

The Bureau for Serious Crime is the brainchild of Assistant Commissioner Jack Clancy. Designed to bring together the best of the best, across all ranks. No point in accruing all the bells and whistles that come with experience for those skills to grow mouldy behind a desk. In my view, a case is never well managed from afar. That's one of the benefits of leading a department like ours. I can get up close and personal with all our investigations. We're a multidisciplinary team who tackle Ireland's most complex and often most headline-grabbing crimes. But if you're only as good as your current investigation, then we are falling desperately short.

'There's more to this Dolan case,' Baz said, casting his eyes down at the bundle of papers. 'The wife must know something.'

'We've questioned her twice. Everything checks out her end,' I said. He knew that. He was there with me. 'What are you thinking?'

He ran a hand through his brown hair, leaving it standing up at the back. 'Don't know. Mightn't be anything major. Could well be something she hasn't told us because she doesn't think it's important.' He unbuttoned his cuffs, rolled up his sleeves and stretched his arms above his head. 'My mam used to have this habit, still does, to be honest, where she'd cover stuff up. Stupid things like where she was off to for a night, like if she were off to a fancy bar instead of the local. Or it'd be, "Don't be mentioning

4

this to so and so." And it'd only be about where she'd bought the sausages at the weekend, and you'd find yourself telling a different story on her behalf over a pack of sausages when no one could've given two shites where she got them.'

I sipped my wine, gave him a grin: 'Some people might call that lying.'

A half-smile, then, 'I reckon there's something like that here. We're not getting the full picture and it's not that I think there's malice at the other end of it, but it could be important all the same.'

I let out a sigh, sick to the eye teeth of the puzzle of Dolan's disappearance and placed my wine on the desk. 'Let's give it a rest for tonight.'

'Happily,' he said. Then his eye caught on the red box in the corner of my office, 'What's that?'

I got up, retrieved the box. 'Birthday present, I think.'

'It's your birthday today?'

'Tomorrow. Don't get sweaty-palmed. It's not in your job description to remember my birthday. It's a murder-mystery game.' I said.

'Let's have a look then.' He held out his hand and I passed it to him. He opened it, looked the contents over, straightening in his chair. 'Who's it from?'

'There was no signature on the card.'

'Huh! Secret admirer, then?' He emptied the box onto my desk and laid out the clues. The strand of brown hair, the histology slide. The earring. 'Looks unnervingly realistic,' he said.

I picked up the earring, examined it through the protective covering, rubbed at a rust-coloured smudge on the earring post.

Dirt. Old blood, my mind said. Then I remembered it wasn't real.

'I would've gone with flowers myself,' Baz said, 'but these young buckos nowadays certainly know what to get the detective who has everything.'

'Funny.'

He unclipped the glass slide from its casing and held it up to the light. 'What are you doing for your birthday?'

'Working.'

He raised his eyebrows at that.

'We've a high-profile case,' I said, a touch defensively.

He tilted the slide to and fro, squinting up at the fragment of tissue trapped on the surface. 'Larry, on front desk, whose tweezers can't even find that giant nose hair that's been curling out of his left nostril since time immemorial has more chance of finding a lead in this case than you do tomorrow. Take the day off.'

'And do what?'

He returned the slide back to its case. 'I don't know. Contemplate your mortality or something. Have fun. Isn't there someone—' he began, scanning the desk innocently.

'Don't even think about finishing that question.'

He held up his palms. 'Alright. Alright. Just saying. I know a couple of blokes—'

'Good for you,' I interrupted.

He laughed again, then passed me the bus ticket. 'Here,' he said. 'Reckon that's a good first step. The ink on the back of her hand mentioned in the post-mortem report. It's probably the stamp from a nightclub.'

6

I looked it over. Timed, dated. Route 8a. A tantalizing starting point. I found myself opening up a search engine to track the route of the bus. We spent some time, writing down the stops, Baz commented on how convenient it would be if our real cases gave up their answers so readily.

The victim was found clothed but dead in the basement of a nightclub. But the case notes don't provide the club's name or address. In the file, there were labelled photos of each item of clothing. They were stained in places. Mud and blood. She'd been dressed in open-toe heels, tight jeans, a diamante detail along the seams, a pale pink one-shouldered tank top.

The bus stopped close to Temple Bar. A quick search online gave me the clubs in the area. Three within a block of each other. Two closed for renovations on the night our victim was murdered. I typed in the web address provided with the game, created a username and logged on. We fed the name of the club into the site and I felt the glow of satisfaction when I discovered we were right. In seconds, we were rewarded with another clue. A witness statement and a digital receipt. A local corner shop employee who said she came in for cigarettes and a tooth cleaner.

There were no real victims here. No grieving family who we'd have to tell we'd found their daughter's body. But what was most appealing was that I knew there was an answer. There would be a solution at the end of this. Our killer would not slip away into the grey mists of the cold-case archives, out of my hands, away from justice. Someone had put The Murder Box together to be solved. That was the point, right? To play the game. Unmask the killer. To win.

The Dolan case, active for a month, had sucked us dry. In every sense. Over a thousand calls and messages from the public. And nothing yet to give us an idea of what's happened to him. All other cases, as directed by the commissioner, Donna Hegarty, to be sidelined, passed to other departments until we find him. And, as if pressure wasn't bad enough with Teddy being the nation's sweetheart, he's also our commissioner's nephew. Every day, Dolan's face in the papers. And just when it looked like the press were inclined to give a different story a spin, Dolan's amputated finger turned up in his wife's post and back he was again, more headlines, more press briefings and still nothing.

And so, The Murder Box was the perfect distraction. It never crossed my mind to think about which one of my family or friends would've sent it. All I knew was that when I read the invite to solve the murder of a twenty-two-year-old woman, like a sighthound entranced by the flashing tail of a rabbit, I couldn't help but go after it. It was fun. Safe. That's what I thought. And I did think that, right up until twenty minutes ago, when Neve Jameson walked into my office and began to tell me about her missing friend.

CHAPTER 2

I drag a line through another potential witness's name. Wrong dates. Wrong times. Teddy Dolan could be a turn of a page away, but I can barely make myself look. Outside my office door is the collective murmur of the distracted. The odd laugh, a phone left ringing too long. The hum of the coffee machine. When this case came through, we grabbed at it. I could feel the team, mentally stretching out their limbs, cracking knuckles, ready to show the force what the Bureau for Serious Crime could really do. But each day brought us further into nothing.

To my right, on the wall above my desk, I've pinned a picture of Teddy. It's a PR head shot provided by his wife, Monica. When we asked her if she had another, more natural-looking photo, she said: 'When this is over, I don't want some shitty photograph haunting Teddy for the rest of his life.'

In the picture, his hair is cut short with a little length at the front which he styles to the side in a high quiff. Short forehead, a good nose, straight. His smile is showbiz wide and as white. Some might be surprised to learn that he's a small build, barely

9

hitting five seven. In the photo he's wearing a black T-shirt and even though you can't tell, I know he's wearing black trousers and a pair of thick-soled white trainers.

Teddy Dolan is the face of Irish TV. His most recent gig being a quiz show on Saturday evenings. He hosts the easy-listening slot on Sunday radio and if there's a presenter needed to step in for morning TV or for fringe shows, you bet that it's Teddy who'll be called on first. There's not a wine bottle opening in the city where he's not cutting the ribbon. But because he's risen from one of the people, the public eat him up. Can't get enough of him. The problem for us being that despite Teddy Dolan's recognisable get-up on TV, in reality, he has a very ordinary face, a less than striking physique and once removed from the glow of celebrity, I'd say anyone would be hard put picking him out of a crowd.

On the night he went missing, he was at an art exhibition on Cope Street near Temple Bar. The exhibition had a guest list but the curator confessed that after nine-thirty, it was open doors. Anyone could've come in off the street. Teddy, as far as the curator knew, seemed grand. Happy enough. 'But how would you know, really?' he'd said. 'I'd say he has to hang up his smile at the end of an evening like it were a piece of clothing.'

The last people who saw him were a group of smokers who noticed him outside the gallery. He kept his distance, cigarette in mouth, phone pinned between ear and shoulder, while he cupped his hands around the cigarette to light it. Dolan was still on the phone when the other smokers went back inside. No one saw him re-enter the building. Phone records tell us, he'd been on the phone to his wife. The call lasted three minutes and thirty-two seconds. Monica Dolan said she'd been booking flights. Teddy was planning a golf trip in Wales for the following week. He and his mates go once a year, she explained. It had become a thing. Boys only. At first, I thought she was covering up an argument. One that cemented Dolan's decision to make a getaway. Leg it from whatever it was his wife was covering for but with no sightings since, his phone not in use and his passport still at his home, now I'm not so sure. His bank account has not been used, which is never a good sign.

There was no CCTV inside the exhibition, but a camera captured Teddy's last known movements and shows him outside, on the phone. There's a heaviness to his movements that suggests he's had a few. He hangs up, drops his cigarette to the ground, taps it once with his foot, but just as he turns to go back inside, he pauses. He looks out on the street. Then he walks unsteadily away. Towards what? We don't know. There are times I imagine him straightening, closing his eyes, crossing his hands over his chest and vanishing into a cloud of smoke.

Then at the end of August, the amputated finger arrived in the post. Cleanly excised; as delicately as if by an artisan butcher for a Michelin-star restaurant. 'See how they've gone in along the joint, followed it precisely,' our pathologist had said. Sharp knife with patience and a lot of finesse. Unease had curled in my stomach. It was addressed to Monica Dolan. No traceable sender. The best of forensics studied envelope, print, tissue and flesh, but apart from confirming that the finger was Dolan's, that was it. We waited for a ransom note. None came.

Despite what Dolan's wife thinks, we have followed every lead. All necessary resources have been expended, expanded and then some. If it had been any other misper, the case would have been filed by now, albeit Dolan's celeb status would've ensured we kept a candle in the window for the public's sake. We've no leads, we've nothing to work on and there are plenty of cases waiting in the wings for our attention. But the commissioner is insistent we can't let it go. Regardless, if or when Teddy Dolan appears, dead or alive, we'll be facing a review. I rub a hand against an ache in my chest. Someone will pay for either a finger or a life. I remind myself that one of the reasons I wanted the challenge of the Bureau was this. To be the one armed with just enough power to push against the system. The downside? The system demands a price for that.

Detective Helen Flood, one of the Bureau's best assets, knocks at the open door of my office.

'Sorry to disturb you,' she says. 'There's a woman here. Young. Well, compared to us.'

I shoot her a look.

'You know what I mean. You get to a certain age and everybody under thirty looks like a teenager. Sorry.' Worker bee to the core, Helen wears her hair scraped back into a tight bun at the back of her head, clothes and shoes of the no-frills variety. She's everything you want in a detective: innovative, problem-solving, thorough – if a bit too much at times. But she's not a risk-taker. The rules are the rules. Her flair for investigation doesn't take her beyond even the most hazy of lines in procedure.

'Isn't there someone on the floor who can talk to her?'

'She wants someone senior. Said she's already made a report and no one's done anything.'

'With us?'

'No. Her local station. Although, I couldn't get anything on the system.'

A headache is threatening at the base of my skull. If I'm honest with myself, another case is exactly what I'm longing for – anything to justify a break away from the static nature of the Dolan investigation. I'm halfway to believing that he actually did lop off his own finger to escape his charmed life. Opening the drawer beside me, I find a blister pack of paracetamol, pop two into my hand and swallow them down.

Closing Dolan's file, I hold out my hand and Helen passes me the check-in sheet showing the woman's name: Neve Jameson; age: twenty-four; address and relationship to the missing woman: friend. The friend's name: Lydia Callin.

'Security checked her over?'

'Yes,' Helen replies.

I read the name again, unsure why it sounds familiar. 'Okay.'

'You'll see her?' Helen asks, surprise registering on her face.

'If I've to read about one more sighting of Dolan at a shopping centre, golf course or taking a stroll down the fucking M50 at three am, I'll lose my mind. Send her in.'

'Yes, Ma'am,' she says. 'More coffee?'

'Please. Strong. Two sugars.'

A minute later, coffee on my desk, dark as tar, the scent of the roast setting my mouth to water and Neve Jameson sidles into the room. She's tall. Five ten easy. Long-legged, athletic, but her posture is apologetic, her shoulders rounded inwards, as if she was trying to make herself smaller. She's dressed casually, blue jeans and a navy checked shirt, her brown hair pulled back into a ponytail. A pale green satchel is looped across her chest.

13

I stand, put out a hand. 'Detective Frankie Sheehan.'

She waits for Helen to close the door, then edges forward, reaching out over the desk to shake my hand, as if afraid to get too close. 'Thank you for agreeing to see me,' she says.

I gesture to the chair across from me. 'Take a seat.'

She creeps closer, pulls the chair back from the desk. As she sits, her gaze slides up to the photo of Teddy Dolan.

I look down at the report. 'You're worried about a friend? Lydia Callin?'

'Yes. My flatmate,' she says, skipping ahead. 'She's been missing almost a month.'

'You filed a report with your local station?'

'Yes. At Kilmainham station.' She slides a business card across the table. It shows the station's logo and a series of numbers and letters is written across the back. 'Here's the reference number.'

I pick it up, put it to the side. 'How long have you known one another?'

'We've lived in the same flat for almost a year now.'

'Where?'

'On South Circular Road.'

'Just the two of you?'

'Yes.'

'You've tried her mobile or messaging her, I take it?'

'Yes. I mean, I did at first. But when she didn't respond, I didn't see the point.'

'When did you see her last? Date? Time?'

'Tenth of August. She was going out. She didn't come back, which has happened before, but when she hadn't come home after a day, I began to get worried.'

14

'Did she say where she was going?'

'She just said "out".'

'And you stayed in?'

'I wasn't feeling great that night.' She pauses, bites down on her lip, then presses the back of her hand against her mouth. 'Sorry.' Eyes squeeze shut. 'I just keep thinking that if I'd gone out with her, she'd be okay.'

I reach for the box of tissues on my desk, hold it towards her.

'Thanks.' She takes one and dabs at her eyes, turning her face to the ceiling and blinks rapidly.

'Are there any items missing from her room? Coat? Clothes? Her bag, money?'

'I didn't want to touch too much but I checked and her phone charger is still there. Her laptop. No sign of her purse that I could see, but as I said, I didn't want to search too hard.'

'Okay. How about work?'

'She was working in a bar in town, The Hanamaran on Reuben Street.'

'Could she be staying with one of the staff?'

'She stopped working there at the start of last month. She'd applied for teacher training. She was due to start this week.'

'Do you have the name of the college she was going to attend?'

'Oh yes, sorry, hang on.' She pulls her bag onto her lap, opens the front. It takes her a few seconds but eventually she extracts a slip of paper and hands it to me. 'Here you go.'

'Thanks,' I make a note. 'What date was she due to start?'

'Today.'

I look over the college details. 'Have you tried to phone them? To see if she showed?'

'I didn't think to. Should I?'

'We can take care of that. What about family?'

She looks at her hands. 'I'm not sure. I always got the feeling they were either dead or didn't speak.' She pulls the sleeve of her sweater over her left hand, fiddles with the cuff.

'Lydia told you that?'

She shrugs. 'I don't know why I think that. She always changed the subject when they came up.'

I reach for a notepad and click my pen. 'You know where they live?'

'I couldn't tell you the exact address. I think it was close to Ballyfermot.'

'Their names?'

'I'm sorry. I don't know.'

I remember being in my early twenties – life all about what you were doing, what you're about to do. Who you are seeing, sleeping with, where your work was going. We didn't speak about family often. There's a part of you at twenty that wants to make life on your own terms – you're cutting the ties physically and mentally, so it's not all that surprising that Neve wasn't told much about Lydia's family.

'Has she taken off before?'

'There was one time, months ago, when she didn't come home for a weekend. But nothing like this.'

'Is there a reason she wouldn't want to be in touch with you?'

It takes her a moment to hear the implication in my question, then she places a hand on her chest and says, 'No. We get on well. It's not that she doesn't want to return to the flat.'

'Has she any enemies? People she was having trouble with?'

16

She shakes her head. 'I don't know of anyone.'

I click the top of my pen, put my notes to the side.

I smile at her. 'Try not to worry too much. Often when people disappear, it's simply a matter that they left of their own free will. And sometimes they don't want to be found. That could be the case here with Lydia. But we'll run some searches, try to get in touch with her family. Do you have a mobile we can reach you on?'

She grips the underside of the chair, shuffles closer. 'Please!' She gives the notepad a desperate glance. 'She's tall, like me, brown hair, grey eyes that on some days might be mistaken for blue. Pale skin, like really pale. This tooth—,' she pulls down her bottom lip and points to her lower right incisor. 'This tooth isn't real. She fell from a trampoline when she was eight, knocked it clear out with her knee. Scarred herself just above the kneecap. She still has the scar.'

And she goes on like that. How she met Lydia at the bar a year ago. Lydia was looking for a new place. Neve a new tenant. How bright Lydia was but that she'd never got to finish school. I heard about how when Lydia was ten, she won some kind of scholarship or bursary for some high-end private school. She left the school – not because she found it difficult, Neve insists, but because she was bored. A decision she regretted, so in the last year, she'd studied for her school finals. Studying part-time around her shifts at the bar, so that she could apply for teacher training.

And I know where Neve's going with all this. She's telling me Lydia Callin had plans. She's telling me that Lydia was in control of her life. Moving forward. That she'd invested too much time in her future to walk away.

17

Finally, she pauses, locks her eyes onto mine. 'Please. I've waited all this time. I know something's not right.' She grasps a handful of her shirt. 'I can feel it in my gut.'

It's not really our gig, missing persons. Or mispers of this kind. We have Dolan's case on the boil because it's of national interest. Unfair as that sounds. I know the public wouldn't like it were they to look closely at what it takes to graduate from local plod investigating to the Bureau's multi-system case management.

But I know the feeling Neve describes. That feeling of unease that pulls in the gut like a servant's bell demanding attention. Every detective knows that feeling.

I turn to a fresh page in my notebook. Click the top of the pen again. 'How about money problems or romantic relationships? Is there anyone new in her life? Boyfriends? Girlfriends? That kind of thing.'

A quick shake of her head. 'No money problems. I mean, she isn't rolling in it, but she's always been able to put down for rent.'

I wait for her to answer the relationship question but she doesn't. I think about asking her again, then decide that if I'm going to look into this case and Neve Jameson hasn't given me information on her friend's love life, something as Lydia's flatmate she would know about, then she'll not be giving the true version now. An interview isn't always about harvesting information; sometimes it's about the gaps. What people don't tell you. What they avoid telling you. These are the strings you use to set out your tripwire when you next have the chats. When I ask her this question again, I want to have someone else's version of events up my sleeve.

Picking up the phone, I dial DI Paul Collins who answers with a polite, 'Yes, Chief'. I can imagine the flush of colour making its way from his jaw to his hairline, the tuck of his chin as he draws it in above the collar of his shirt. Paul, in many ways, is the pan in the river, shaking dirt free from anything that looks to be of worth. He deals with the public – he reaches out and they reach in; there's rarely a moment when he's not murmuring down the phone, dealing with online queries or with the press.

I tell him to contact Kilmainham station and see where they are on Lydia Callin.

When I hang up, I catch a dark look on Neve's face.

'Everything okay?' I ask.

She swallows down something.

'We'll definitely look at this closely. Don't worry,' I say when she frowns.

She looks at her hands, pushes her tongue against the inside of her cheek; a pout on her mouth. She reaches into her bag and produces a folded sheet of paper then flattens it on the desk. She tells me it's a picture of herself and Lydia. They are arm in arm, their heads tipped towards one another, the smooth green flats of Phoenix Park stretched out behind them.

'This was taken over the summer,' she says.

I take the picture and place it to the side. 'Thank you,' I say, then close my notebook and push back from the desk, stand, signalling that it's time for her to go. But she doesn't move.

'Teddy Dolan,' she says. 'She knew him.'

I sit back down, study her face for a few seconds then ask carefully: 'Why didn't you mention this sooner?'

'Because it's not all about him,' she says. 'Why should it be?'

I push a hand through my hair, massage the ache at the base

19

of my skull. The petulant tone in her voice makes me think she's lying. That she clapped eyes on Teddy Dolan's picture on my wall and pulled out his name, like a rabbit out of a hat, so that the Bureau would take on her friend's case. But desperate and all as Neve Jameson is for us to look into Lydia Callin's disappearance, we're more desperate for a lead on Teddy Dolan.

'The wrong information at the start of an investigation can really hinder a case further on down the line,' I say, letting the warning sound clear in my voice. 'If what you're saying is not true, it won't help your friend.'

'She knew him,' she says. 'She told me not to tell anyone.'

'They were together?'

'Together. Shagging. Whatever,' she says, and I think, perhaps unfairly, how old she sounds. 'He was using her.'

'Using?'

'She thought he was going to leave his wife for her.' Her mouth twists.

It was no secret that Dolan had a severe case of the wandering eye. We'd interviewed all the women we knew about, but this one slipped through the net somehow. Besides, it might not be the truth – God knows we've not been lucky with the fucking truth on the Dolan case.

'Is that so?' I ask. 'How long did they know each other?'

And Neve gives a half-smile of satisfaction. She figures she's got my attention now. And she figures right.

The moment Neve Jameson leaves my office, I run a search on her name. She comes up clean. Opening a browser on the internet, I click through her social media which is set to public, but she's not a regular or big poster. The odd competition shared. A stream of birthday wishes last month. I scroll through her friend list, make a copy and print it out. Finding Lydia Callin among the names, I highlight it. Lydia's page gives me nothing. Not even a friend list. Not a single photograph. She joined in 2008. The rest is set to private. I try a few other social media platforms and the same: all accounts locked.

I pick up the phone, call out to the floor.

'Chief,' Detective Steve Garvin answers.

'I need you to run some background on a Neve Jameson and a Lydia Callin. I'm forwarding you their details now.'

'Sure, is this in relation to the Dolan case?' he replies.

'Possibly.'

The sound of tapping comes down the line. 'I've got a Lydia Callin here. Born April second 1991. Address: Cherry Tree Close. Ballyfermot. You want a search warrant for that address?'

'That and her flat on South Circular Road.'

The tapping on the keyboard gathers momentum. Detective Garvin, Steve, stays on the tech side of our investigations and has the complexion to show for it. He and Emer Kelly transcribe for the rest of us the ones and zeros of the digital world. The computer footprint side of crime has never been something to blow the coals for me – evidence, psychology, faces are what keep me hungry. Computers. They're not a fair playground. There was a time, not too long ago, it seems to me, when paper, hand-written statements, reports and in-your-hand evidence were all we had to deal with in crime but now the shape-shifting digital world takes precedence. Less paper to deal with but, in its place, we have the spectre of the faceless criminal. Or teams of them

21

working silently against us. Invisible. And our tech team, led by Steve, with what looks to me like some kind of witchcraft, coaxes them forth. When it comes down to it, eventually, it all plays out in real life: the foe manifesting from the digital ether, flesh and blood. Because there is always flesh and blood behind it.

I hear the crack of a can opening. Steve, like he's warming up for a race, prepping with some sugary concoction for what will hopefully take us on to the next square of this investigation. Spreading the picture of the two women out on the desk, I study the gentle point of Lydia Callin's chin. Shoulder length hair, smooth skin, her eyes glinting like pale stone from beneath dark lashes. She's wearing a deep maroon scarf over a white T-shirt. A fashion accessory, rather than something to guard against the cold. The weather is good in the picture. Phoenix Park is an oasis of green spread out behind her and Neve. The trees are full. Even though Neve shares the same space, I have to make myself look at her; Lydia draws the eye. Not a beauty, but magnetic. Of the pair, she's the only one looking directly into the camera. Neve's gaze is on her friend's face, a soft smile of what looks like pride or admiration curves around her mouth.

Steve is giving me details on Lydia's family but I'm only half-hearing him. I lift the picture from the desk, peer down into it. The reflection of cloud and blue sky is mirrored on the sunglasses perched on Lydia's fringe, and just about visible, her earrings, long strands of silver that rest on the fabric of her scarf. And it dawns on me why I recognize her name.

I pause, Steve's voice drifting further away.

'Chief? Should we phone her dad first? Oh, there's just her dad—'

'Hang on, Steve. I'll call you back,' I murmur and hang up.

Reaching down, I open the bottom drawer of my desk. The red gloss of The Murder Box looks up at me. I take it out. Careful. Pushing notes, files and my keyboard aside, I place it on my desk. The overhead light glows gold on the red lid. I open it, remove the envelope of evidence contained within and turn the contents out on the desk, locating the hair strand and the bus ticket. And the silver earring. Taking up the picture of Lydia and Neve, I look from image to reality. The earring in the picture is identical to the one in the box. A match. Happy birthday to me.

CHAPTER 3

The team are huddled around the case board like half-starved children, ready to fill their bellies on what they hope will be the scraps of a lead in the Dolan case. Steve and I have taken photographs of the murder-mystery box contents and as we pin them up, there's plenty of 'I don't believe it' and 'would you look at that'. I can hardly believe it myself, and there's a good part of me thinking this is some far-fetched wind-up that'll end up going viral online and taking my career with it. The chance that the earring is not Lydia's at all, that this is some strange coincidence is there. But generally, I'm not one for believing in coincidence, especially when it comes to potential murder investigations.

The box itself is on fast track to the labs. As soon as I realised what we could be dealing with, I phoned our lead scene-of-crime officer, Keith Hickey. Eager as the rest of the team to get a look at The Murder Box, he was here within twenty minutes. When he arrived to test the contents for blood, we crowded around him as if he were a magician about to perform a trick. Of course,

Keith being Keith, nothing short of basking in our attention, straightened his white coat, lifted a hand and waved out at us as if we'd only turned up for him. Then he hooked a paper mask to his face, laid out his tools like a surgeon, donned his gloves and peered down at the earring.

'Now what do we have here?' he murmured.

On a good day, I work along with Keith grand, even though he's got more confidence than a twenty-year-old lad hitting the dance floor after ten pints. On those days, I can tune out the banter, as he calls it, and appreciate the fact that he's the best crime-scene investigator Dublin has, hands down.

'Just relax now, this can't be rushed,' he said, despite the fact he was doing nothing more than a simple Kastle–Meyer test on the post of the earring. I had to bite down on my tongue to prevent myself from telling him to get a fucking wriggle on.

A swab of the earring and a series of drops from different bottles later, then the test was complete. The room fell silent as we watched the cotton tip in Keith's gloved hand turn pink.

'That's blood, alright,' he said, holding up the result for us to see before taking a narrow tube from his kit and sliding the cotton swab inside. 'Well, isn't that a dark little box of tricks,' he said to me. 'You'll be wanting to send a few SOCOs to the gaff, then?'

I hesitated, unsure what path to go tramping down first. If the game was to be believed, then we'd a potential crime scene at the nightclub. A crime scene that was already a month old. There were no reports on our system and I'd have assumed the club owners would have called it in if they'd come across a body. But you never fucking know.

25

'Yes. Go out to their flat,' I said. 'And we may want you for the club later though.'

'No bother, I'll get going with this now, get it seen to sharpish.' He sealed the earring in a bag and labelled the contents. 'A little birdie told me it's your birthday.'

'Yes.'

'Well, happy birthday to you. How many candles is it then so?' His small eyes flashed at me over his mask.

'Enough,' I said. 'Keep me posted with how you get on.'

And he raised his hand to his forehead and gave me a mock salute. 'I will indeed.'

Baz leans in to get a better look at the picture of the slide. The label on the case says myocardium. 'That's heart, isn't it?' he asks.

'Heart muscle,' I answer.

He takes a step back, looks over the case board. 'Any hits between their phones. Between Lydia and Teddy?'

'Nope,' says Steve.

Steve has already taken over from me on the murder-mystery game's website. His perverse wonder at what the box could mean, something to behold. I don't think I could've handed him a better project. I'm just hoping whoever's put this box together has underestimated our tech's ability, although I'm mindful of not underestimating theirs. They've gotten this far. I know Baz is thinking that Neve Jameson pushed a connection with Dolan because she wanted us to take on her friend's case, but if the contents of this box come back relating to Lydia Callin, then considering the breadth of planning that's gone into putting it together, I won't be crossing Dolan's name off the list any time soon.

'Let's get ourselves ready for when those results come in. Baz and I are going out to the Callin house now. Helen, liaise with Keith to take a team to the flat on South Circular Road. Full search of Lydia's room.'

'Anything in particular we're looking for?' she asks.

'Any connection to Dolan. Signs that she wasn't planning on leaving, seize any electronic devices. Whether any of the neighbours have CCTV, dashcams.'

She makes notes, nods. 'I'll go to the nightclub after too, have a look at the bus route suggested in the murder-mystery box. Most of them have cameras now.' She stands, gathers up her bag and coat.

Detective Inspector Ryan Twoomey watches her go, then looks to me askance. 'I could head out to Dolan's place, ask the wife if she knew the victim?'

Ryan's a good midfielder but wants to be a striker. His eye never lifts from the next rung on the ladder. He's consistent, but won't push himself beyond what's asked of him. He's a move-it-along kind of bloke, not one to look too closely. In some ways, a good thing in a detective; in other ways, it can make you sloppy. Investigations are often solved on the details.

I shake my head. 'No, go out to the bar where she worked, The Hanamaran on Reuben Street near Earls Court. Take a uniform with you. Verify why she left there. Was there friction between her and any of the staff? Any relationships that we should know about and, crucially, when was the last time she saw or spoke to any of them?'

He nods, removes his suit jacket from the back of his chair, shoves his mobile into his back pocket. 'Yes, Ma'am,' he says.

Baz waits beside me. When they leave, he says, 'Lookit. I've to pop out for an hour or two so don't think I can head out to the Dolan house with you. Could you take Jack or Paul on this one?'

'Very funny,' I say. There's not a chance in hell that Baz would miss out on a lead like this. Taking out my phone, I double-check Lydia Callin's family's home address.

When Baz doesn't move, I look up from the screen. 'You're serious?' And I notice that he's dressed smarter than usual. His suit pressed into sharp creases down his arms and legs. His tie neat at his throat.

'Something's come up and I have to deal with it now,' he says.

I wait for more but when it doesn't come I look over his shoulder towards Jack. 'You alright to come out to the Callins'?'

'Sure,' Jack says.

I look back towards Baz. 'Don't worry about it,' I say to him and mean it. No one could ever accuse Baz of being slack when it comes to a case. 'I'll update you later.'

'Thanks,' he says, a ghost of a smile, then he retreats to his office.

The Callin family home is situated in a wide rectangle of terraced houses named Cherry Tree Close. The houses, two-up two-downs, are varying shades of grey with the occasional red brick breaking up the colour scheme. In the middle of the close, is the council's version of recreational amenities in the form of a green space. The grass is worn down in patches, a large puddle on one side, a blaze of sunshine captured on the surface. Not a cherry tree in sight.

We're parked near the Callin house. Jack is taking up too much space beside me, his coat falling over the handbrake, his thick hand clasping the fabric of the seat. He's looking out the passenger window. Nerves coming off him like steam from piss. His eyes are fixed on the black carcass of a burned-out car that's wedged at the opening of an alley on the other side of the green. There's a swing set between it and us and a young fella is standing on one of the seats, holding the bar above, knees pumping the swing over and back. From the tip of his head, it's clear he's not lifted his eyes from us since I pulled up.

'Number eighteen,' I say. Joe Callin, Lydia's dad, is her only living relative. Helen's summary of the family's background was grim. Two brothers, one dead of an overdose seven years ago; six weeks later, the other dead after a motorbike accident. Mother also deceased. Mr Callin is not a stranger to opening the door to a guard bearing bad news.

I push out of the car. A quick look over at your man on the swing. He's stopped, now balanced on the seat and peering over at us.

Clancy huffs out of the passenger side. 'We'll have no bloody wheels by the time we get out again.'

'Should perhaps throw a few coins this direction next time you're signing off the budget,' I reply. I click the lock and walk towards the house. Stepping over a discarded toy car, I make my way up the short path that leads to the Callin door.

Jack catches up, pulling his collar around his throat and

breathing with the tightness of someone worried they'll catch something.

'When was the last time you did one of these?' I ask.

He sniffs. 'I'm not above dealing with the public,' he says, scanning the flat-faced houses around us. 'Just be careful around the Dolan case. You say anything about that and it'll be in the papers first thing.' He means our commissioner doesn't want her nephew associated with a young woman's disappearance. It's good to be reminded that the law can be choosy about who they go after.

The doorbell triggers a series of barks from inside.

'Alright. Alright,' comes a male voice. The barking stops and we see the shadow of a man approach on the other side of the glass pane.

'Who is it?'

'Mr Callin?'

'Yes.'

'It's the Gardaí. I'm Detective Frankie Sheehan and I'm with Jack Clancy. We wanted to ask you a few questions about your daughter?'

The door opens a fraction and he holds out a hand for my badge. I hand it over, he traces an index finger over the bottom.

'Come in,' he says and reaches down to give the collar of a golden retriever a tug backwards. 'Don't mind him. Bark's worse than his bite.'

We step inside the hallway. Joe Callin is not a tall man. A stomach as proud and round as a mother-to-be's strains against the pale cream of his shirt. He's ruddy-faced and clean shaven, a few wisps of hair combed into obedience over his skull.

'Is Lydia okay?' He pushes a pair of tinted glasses back up his nose.

'Let's go in, have a seat,' I say.

We follow Mr Callin down a short hallway. The house is warm, homely. Plenty of framed pictures on the wall. Baby photos, school photos, wedding. A picture of a young man standing next to a motorbike, helmet tucked beneath his arm, a possessive hand on the seat. Lydia poses in her school uniform in one. Her smile is of a wideness gifted only to the youth, the two rows of her small teeth pressed together. I can almost hear the word cheese.

The dog circles behind us.

Jack asks: 'What's the dog's name?'

'Charlie. Supposed to be a guide dog to help me get around, you know,' he points to his eyes. 'Useless, would walk me into a brick wall in the pursuit of a pat on the head. But we get by,' he says, ruffling Charlie's ears.

He leads us into the kitchen where, up along the doorframe, there's a series of lines drawn in pencil, a scrawl beside each one. I know that if I looked closer, I'd find Lydia's and her brothers' names there, aged four or maybe six, their height recorded proudly. My dad used to do the same thing for my brother Justin and me. Every Christmas, we'd press our backs to the wall, chins tipped up as far as they'd go and my dad would pluck the pencil from his ear and declare us growing like weeds. The image gets me full in the throat, drives home why we're here.

'Make yourselves comfortable,' Mr Callin says. He points to a round table pushed up against the inside wall, then lifts the kettle from its stand. 'Tea?'

'That'd be lovely,' I say, just as Jack declines.

The washing machine trembles to a spin beneath the worktop.

Joe laughs. 'One of youse is eager to go.' He gives up on the tea, faces us and folding his arms over the top of his stomach, he leans against the sink. Charlie, sensing a change in mood, settles under the table. 'So what's this about?'

It's a little jab of a question but I know what it's taken to ask it. No one wants to be on the other side of the answer to that one. Joe Callin especially. I can see him bracing himself for the answer: his shoulders come up, his chin draws in.

'Mr Callin,' I say. 'One of your daughter's friends contacted us this morning, her flatmate, Neve Jameson?' I give a pause here for him to acknowledge the name but it doesn't register on his face. 'She says she's not seen Lydia for nearly a month. We were hoping you could tell us where she might be.'

His arms tighten atop his stomach. 'I haven't seen her. She came round for a few hours, must be – what date are we now?'

'It's the ninth of September.'

'Would be . . . God now, it'd be over a month ago,' and a tiny flash of pain moves across his face. 'It was a Sunday. I did a roast. We had dinner together, watched the TV. God, is it that long ago?'

'Have you talked since then, on the phone, text?'

'I don't text, just find with being a bit poor-sighted I can't get on with it. And if we need or want to talk, she'd call round or phone on the landline. I think she might've phoned that week. I've always been one for company over chatter myself. Lydia has a bit of that too.' The washing machine kicks up a gear and he reaches back, holds a ceramic tea caddy in place to stop it skipping across the counter. 'Is Lydia okay?'

'We are concerned about her,' I admit. 'Is there anywhere she might go, if she wanted to escape or needed some time on her own?'

A shake of his head. 'She always comes here. It's only us since her brothers passed. Have you tried her work?'

'We had her down as working at The Hanamaran pub up until August the second?'

'Yeah. She was planning on leaving, but she got on well with the staff. She told me they'd sometimes get a takeaway together after a shift. She could be with one of them.'

'That's good to know. We can check that out. Do you know if there was a reason for her leaving her job?'

'She got herself a position in one of the colleges for teaching. When she called round, she needed a few bob to see her over which I was always happy to give. She doesn't ask for much, never has. Do you want me to try her phone? She might answer to me?'

'Maybe in a moment. When she visited last, how did she seem? Happy, depressed?'

He frowns, thinking. 'She seemed grand. As I said she wouldn't be one for burning your ears off but there was nothing on her mind. She often tells me if things are worrying her. If anything, she was excited about starting teacher training, her grant was in place, she had it all organized.'

'It sounds like you two are close?'

'We are. They say that about fathers and daughters. When she was born, I wasn't much sure what to do with her. After two boys, I guess I just panicked about stupid stuff, like I wouldn't get what she was into or know what to do with her hair.' He shakes his head, 'But she was the easiest child. Full of warmth and kindness. A smile that'd turn a day around.' The colour in his face deepens. I can see the muscles in his throat working, trying to batten down emotion. He gives a quick, sniffling inhale, then asks: 'Should I try her phone now?'

Jack gives a nod. 'That'd be good, Mr Callin.'

Using the worktop as a guide, he shuffles out of the room.

A few moments later, we hear his voice coming through the thin walls. 'Lydia, love, it's your dad. Just wanting to know you're alright.'

Understanding the loss Lydia has experienced in her life, it's not all that surprising that she didn't share that past with her flatmate. People are weird about death. I've no doubt that were we to ask any of the Callins' neighbours about what kind of people they were, they'd lead with the tragedy first. No judgement on that – it's the kind of story that puts a groove so deep in the landscape of a person's life, how would you not mention it? Reading between the lines about who Lydia was seeing and what shape her social life was in, her career plans, I can see why she'd hold that part of herself back, if only to feel a little lightness for a while.

Jack gets up while we wait, takes his time looking around the kitchen, leans towards the photos on the windowsill. Charlie remains under the table, his shaggy tail thumping beats out on the linoleum floor.

'No answer,' Joe Callin says quietly when he returns. 'But you're able to look at her phone and stuff. I saw them do that on *Silent Witness* one night, where they tracked this person's phone? Youse do that?'

'We're looking into it,' I say. I give Jack a quick glance before

I go in on the question around Lydia's love life. 'Mr Callin, is there anyone new in Lydia's life that you know of? A love interest or even a new friend?'

'Please call me Joe. I don't know, to tell you the honest truth. I don't remember her mentioning anyone.' He rubs his jaw between thumb and forefinger. 'Then, she wouldn't be telling me about that part of her life. When she was still living here, there'd be a few young fellas she'd go to the pictures with, but I wouldn't be kept abreast about who exactly she'd be going with. After everything with her mammy and then her brothers, for a few years, I wasn't exactly on the ball. Then, when I did get my act together, she seemed to be handling that part of her life grand, so I was inclined not to interfere.'

With each passing second, I see him sink lower into himself. 'Do youse think something bad has happened to her?' he asks.

And I feel a physical pain in my chest for him. How unfair life has been to Joe Callin.

'We have reason to believe so, yes,' I answer.

He licks his lips, hooks his hands on the counter for support. 'Like what?'

'All we know presently is that Lydia hasn't been seen by anyone for a month and the last time she was seen was on or before a night out. We've recovered some items we believe were taken from Lydia that night, an earring, a strand of her hair.'

Joe looks from me to Jack. 'Taken by who?'

'We don't know.'

'Well, what? Has she been killed by someone, then?'

'For the moment, we're still gathering information but we are worried about her.'

He stills. Face pale. His mouth opens then he shuts it again.

'Is there someone we can call for you? A neighbour?' I ask.

Jack gets up, suggests Joe sits, puts a hand gently under the man's arm.

Joe allows himself to be guided to a chair. 'No. No. I'll be grand. When will you get the phone results?' he asks, meaning locating Lydia's phone. If only it were as easy as that. Lydia's phone is not active and therefore untraceable.

'We should know more about all this in a day or so and we'll be in touch as soon as we do. But until we know more, it's important that any details stay between us and don't get into the press,' I say.

He nods. 'Thank you, Detective.'

Jack rests his hand briefly on Joe's shoulder. 'Would it be okay if we had a look at Lydia's bedroom?'

'Yes, yes,' Joe replies, his voice hollow. He lowers his hand and Charlie pushes his nose into his palm. 'It's upstairs, the first on the left.'

'When she visited last, did she stay in it?' I ask.

'No. She left a few hours after dinner.'

'Thank you, Joe.'

We leave him in the kitchen. There's a small, stingy rectangular window at the top of the stairs, a Child of Prague statue sits on the sill, her palms turned out, head tipped to the side in piety, her back to the world. The hall has a cloying rose scent. As we hit the top step, there's a hiss above us and a mist of air freshener descends from a dispenser fixed high on the wall. Clancy mutters a swear and swats his hands in front of his face. The sides of the short hallway that leads to the upstairs rooms is clear of clutter apart from a single sideboard bearing a framed photograph of Lydia. There are no decorative vases or potted plants. The weave of the carpet still has that mown look that happens after vigorous vacuuming and I've a feeling Joe doesn't spend much time up here.

Jack pauses on the threshold of Lydia's room to put on a pair of gloves, I do likewise. We open the door and look inside. There's always a moment before stepping into a victim's room where I feel a prickle of discomfort, not just because it's not our property, not our space, the smells are wrong, the air different, but because I know what I'm trailing in with me – like I'm dragging across a dark veil that will divide this place into before and after.

The room is sparsely furnished. A wardrobe in the corner, a narrow dresser and a single bed dressed in a plain peach duvet and pillow set. On the cream walls a series of light blue marks where previously posters or pictures were fixed. Behind net curtains, the top window is open a fraction. Above the bed, two shelves, a few books. I look closer to see what they might tell us about Lydia Callin. Fantasy novels. There's a desk beneath the window. Notebooks stacked up alongside a stationery holder. I turn over the pages of one. Scraps of ideas, notes on characters intermingled with what appear to be sketches of a skyline, the same one over and again, a swing set and a row of houses against different skies, different seasons; the view from beyond the window.

Jack peruses the dresser. There's not much left behind by Lydia. A half-burned incense stick in a glazed clay holder. He picks up a hairbrush, turns it over, then holds it towards me. 'Might be a good idea to seize this. Get a DNA profile from the hair possibly.'

I nod. He opens a few of the drawers, turns a hand through them. Then goes to the wardrobe. A couple of hoodies and a pair of jeans. I get down on my knees, remove my torch and sweep it under the bed. No hidden boxes, not even a stray pair of shoes. I slide my hand beneath the mattress, run it up the side of the bed but come away with nothing.

I straighten, look over the small bedroom. I picture Lydia, younger, on the bed, headphones over her ears, her head bobbing to music, one hand holding open a textbook, the other moving swiftly across her notes. On her dresser a stick of incense smoulders and a silver string of smoke curls upwards dispersing the scent of jasmine into the warmth of the room. The door is ajar and her mother's voice rises over the sound of her music. Lydia pushes the headphones back and closes her work. Downstairs, her brothers are arguing over who has the bigger plate of dinner. She joins them at the table, pausing briefly before sitting to drop a kiss onto her dad's rough cheek . . .

Jack makes the call to our crime-scene team, alerts them to the few items we've seized from Lydia's room. The brush and her notebooks. Below us, I hear Joe's murmurs as he croons words of comfort into Charlie's ear and I feel the desperate emptiness that has already opened up in this house. Even as we wait for confirmation that it's heart tissue on the histology slide contained in The Murder Box, I know that Lydia Callin is dead.

CHAPTER 4

When we get back to the office, Baz greets me at the door. A weak midday light glows along the windows, casts shadows across the top of the room, hinting at shorter days to come. The floor is quiet, most of the team still out hunting through the morning's tasks.

Baz hands me what we've got on Lydia's mobile. 'Lydia Callin's phone hasn't hit a single mast since the night she went missing. The last one at eight-thirty pm on the Saturday night.'

He looks bloody knackered. Like two sleepless nights have passed since I saw him just a couple of hours ago. 'The last location was near the nightclub you suggested. The Score nightclub. I know it's a long shot but we ran the same for Dolan's phone, over the week before and just after he went missing. Nothing there. Paul has finished going through Dolan's phone records; not one call to Lydia's phone.'

I turn through the reports. One of the numbers on Lydia's report is picked out in yellow marker. 'What's the highlighted number?' I ask, putting my finger on the list.

'That's her dad's landline.'

One month ago, a twelve-minute call on the 8th of August. Two days before she was last seen. 'That's in line with what her dad told us. Have Paul go through Dolan's records again. Look for a mobile number that's coming up repeatedly. They might have been using another phone.'

'If Neve never actually saw them together,' Baz says, 'could it be that Lydia was lying about the affair or, I don't know, created some fantasy or a practical joke?'

I hand him back the paper. 'I didn't get from her dad that Lydia would be one to do that. But we should talk to Monica Dolan again.'

Baz nods in agreement. 'There's questions to be answered for sure.'

I pour a strong coffee and hand it to him. 'You get that thing sorted?'

'Thanks,' he says, taking a hasty gulp. 'Thing?'

'You said something came up?'

'Yeah. Sorry. All done now.'

'You sure you're up to seeing Monica Dolan? You look tired. I can head out there by myself, fill you in later.'

'I'm fine.'

'Alright. What have we got from the histology slide in the box?'

'It's undergoing rapid analysis. We're still waiting on a DNA profile but Pathology have confirmed it's human cardiac tissue,' he says, voice grim.

'Jesus,' I murmur.

He pushes up his sleeve, glances at his watch. 'She anticipates

40

she'll have a DNA sequence before the end of the day or first thing tomorrow.'

'That's something at least,' I say. Not altogether thrilled with the news, but it pulls a little more of this case out of the shadows. I look towards the board, where the images of The Murder Box are displayed. It had to have taken months to plan. Murder is all too easy for some to commit, but to cut into a body, remove the heart to display on a glass slide and write that victim into a game calls for someone with a strong stomach and a cold hand.

'There was a hairbrush in her bedroom. We might be able to get a comparison from that if nothing comes up in the flat,' I say.

'Not looking good for Lydia Callin, is it?' he asks.

I look over the case board again. 'No.'

Jack walks over with a fresh coffee and a handful of biscuits. 'You'll need to brief your team, Frankie, on keeping this tight. They're already buzzing about this box and we don't want to put out information that might benefit our perp.'

'They know how we work, Jack,' I reply.

'Right so, keep me informed of matters. The commissioner is on the phone daily for any updates on Dolan.'

'I'm glad she has the time,' I say.

He throws me a quick scowl. 'Just get cracking on it and let me handle Hegarty.' He rubs crumbs from his fingers, gives a final look out over the Bureau floor, making sure all heads are down, then says, 'Right, I'm off. See youse at the pub later?'

'The pub?' I ask. A sharp look passes from Baz to Jack. 'Is this for my birthday gig later?' I take up my bag and hook it over my shoulder.

'What?' they say in unison.

41

'Birthday drinks at the pub?'

I enjoy the slow widening of eyes.

'I didn't hear anything about that?' Baz says. He turns to Jack. 'Did you?'

'You two would never survive interrogation; snap like biscuits within seconds. Ryan hit me up to spot him a fiver for "another fucking birthday kitty".' I offer up a smile. 'Don't worry, I'll be there – that is, unless we strike lucky with this case, then that'll be all the celebration I need.'

'We'll be seeing you at the pub, then so,' Jack says, shoving the remains of a biscuit into his mouth.

'Thanks for the vote of confidence. You ready?' I say to Baz.

The Dolan house is quiet out front. No paps, no cup-of-tea-holding neighbours, no kids eating chips on the benches across the road, ready to snap a quick shot of the celebrity's distraught wife. It's the kind of street where you feel watched. High up on the lampposts that line the pavements, cameras. Mantel Road. Booterstown. Not a bad place to live. The Dolan house is big. The old-school moneyed version where you can tell from the height of the windows that the ceilings are high and the drapery lavish. We get out of the car, the roar of the Irish Sea behind us – not that the Dolans appear interested in taking in the view. They've kept the evergreens that border the inside of the property's walls, thick and tall.

Baz tidies his jacket over his shirt. Adjusts his tie. 'Feel like if I stand here long enough, money will just fall into my pocket.' He inhales deeply. 'You can smell it.'

I look down the street. 'I know what you mean.'

42

But there you are, death isn't fussy about what kind of house you live in and oftentimes, neither is murder. And although we've no hard evidence that Teddy Dolan is dead, I've yet to see a body return alive when parts of it have started to come through the post. Either whoever abducted Teddy Dolan is stalling for time or, if the dark feeling I have about Lydia Callin and The Murder Box, is anything to go by, Dolan's not coming back.

I called Monica on the way here; I was surprised she was so easy on the phone. Yes, she says, no problem to stop by. There was a tightness in her voice, as if she was holding back anger, like my mother used to do when we were kids and had muckied our good shoes, but there were neighbours out and she couldn't shake the living daylights out of us in front of them.

Monica's voice comes crackling out through the intercom when I push the buzzer. 'Detectives,' she says, and I notice the tiny fish-eye lens positioned above the speaker. 'Come in.'

Baz fiddles with his tie again. Then the gate pulls back, retreating along the wall and we step through.

Teddy Dolan grew up on the meaner streets of the city. His dad was a scaffolder with a demanding gambling habit; his mother, Donna Hegarty's sister, a stay-at-home mum who, over the course of Dolan's childhood, gradually succumbed to alcoholism. She'd had aspirations of becoming a singer, dragged Dolan around the pubs in the evenings where she'd sing covers and he'd drink red lemonade and sate his hunger with handfuls of cheese and onion crisps. As Dolan grew, his mother's alcohol problem did too, until eventually, it was Teddy singing to the roomful of punters.

At seventeen, he was spotted by a media scout. Soon after

came his first album – a collection of old-school covers. He got on the right talk shows where his gift of the gab eased open the celebrity door. Even though he'd already burst on the media scene, already had a wad of cash under his belt when they met, Monica made him sign a pre-nup. I feel the humiliation on his behalf. Financial equals don't necessarily mean class equals. Monica had no need to dirty her hands on the rungs of the social ladder. She was born onto it. Part of Dolan's schtick was his came-from-nothing background, but there was more than a whiff of the reckless about him. And it trailed after him like a shadow.

Even me – when the case first came in, my thoughts were that he'd be found in a hotel somewhere, sleeping through a day-long binge or, worst case, OD'd in some random's house. Then Monica told us about his aspirations. How he'd been pitching to production companies for the last year for something a little more serious. That he'd found the rejection and pigeon-holing difficult. Then she back-pedalled quickly. 'No,' she said, catching my reaction. 'He found it difficult,' she stressed, 'but he wasn't depressed about it. He was energized. Determined. Teddy hasn't killed himself. He's been abducted.' She sounded so sure. Then the finger arrived, and I was more sure too.

We follow Monica into her home. She's wearing what my sister-in-law, Tanya, would refer to as loungewear chic: a white satin blouse with a chunky-knit cardigan across her shoulders over a pair of pale yoga pants. She moves with a confidence that makes you think she's not one for putting a foot wrong, an elegant stiffness to her upper back as if she were balancing books on her head.

The house is as luxurious as you'd expect. Wood panelling along the hallway. A stairway leads off to the left. And in front of us a short, wide hallway opens out into an open-plan kitchen and dining room. We strip off our coats and hang them on a coat rack next to the door.

Within sixteen hours of her husband going missing, Monica was on every channel calling for his safe return. She launched into a critique on the Gardaí, about how she'd had to endure those initial hours in agonizing frustration because she wasn't taken seriously, twisting the metaphorical knife in Hegarty's gut. And it blew up. From that moment, Teddy Dolan's face was all that could be seen on the nation's news. And the commissioner's voice, Donna Hegarty's, was the only thing I could hear down the phone.

Now, Monica guides us into her spacious living room to a white leather suite softened with mink-coloured chenille cushions. She sits, choosing an armchair at the head of the room, tidying the ends of her hair over her shoulders and settling her sparrow hands quietly in her lap.

'Please sit down,' she says.

Baz and I sit, both of us sinking low into the creaking leather. Baz crosses his legs, then thinks better of it, pulls himself straighter.

'Has there been news?' she asks.

'We have a possible lead,' I say, storing up the connection to Lydia for later. I don't like to miss an opportunity to go over a potential witness's story and I don't want the idea of her husband and Lydia Callin clouding her thoughts. 'We wanted to get a few things clear around when Teddy was last seen. Some of the questions we've been through before.'

Her foot begins to wag. 'Okay.'

Baz opens his notebook. 'Where were you on the evening Teddy disappeared?'

She tilts her head, fixes me with a look of contempt. She wasn't expecting we'd go back to scratch, but thing is, I'm not interested in the PR version of her husband and that's all she keeps dishing out. We are not the press. We want all the dirty details. We know about the women. We know that despite what Monica tells the press, there were many nights that her husband didn't return to the nest. Point of fact, everyone knows it, but either his wife is so used to glossing over her husband's indiscretions that she's come to believe her own white-picket-fenced version or she's hiding something. A woman like Monica Dolan does not strike me as someone who wouldn't know who her husband was shagging on the side and when. And if that someone is now a murder victim, if that someone is Lydia Callin, we need to rule out Monica's involvement.

'I was at home. He was at the art exhibition on Cope Street.' She shrugs, searching for the next step in the narrative. 'He went out for a cigarette. We talked on the phone. That was the last I heard from him.' She finishes with a small lift to her chin.

I wait for more. But she waits right back. I know to move carefully with family members. Best to peel back the layers of their stories slowly. When something falls out from between the folds, you don't want to miss it. But more than that, it's about easing them in; both suspects and witnesses are equal in that regard. You get them comfortable in the water, then turn up the temperature slowly. If they're lucky, they won't even feel it when the surface begins to bubble. But now I see Monica turn

46

her wrist, a furtive glimpse at the face of her delicate watch. It's not boredom but frustration. She's not one for pussyfooting. She wants to say more, but it's clear she's little faith that we'd know what to do with it.

'And he went out to the exhibition alone?' I ask.

'Yes. He went directly from work.'

'Did you talk about who was there?'

'No, but I got the feeling he was desperate to come home, to get away.'

Baz shuffles forward on the sofa, bumps up against me. 'Sorry,' he says, then turns with a smile to Monica. 'He was at the TV studios before?'

'Recording the show, yes.'

'What time does he normally finish?' he asks.

'Four, four-thirty.'

All consistent with what she's told us before.

'And after that?' Baz asks.

'Like I said, he went to the exhibition.'

'The exhibition didn't open until eight.'

'I assume he went for something to eat.'

'Do you know where?'

'No.'

'When you spoke to him, how did he sound?'

'He was fine. A little tired – as I said, like he wanted to come home.'

'He didn't seem concerned or anxious about anything?'

'No.'

'Had he been drinking?'

She levels Baz with a glare. 'He was grand. Why don't

you have any suspects yet? I've answered all these questions before.'

'We're trying to build a picture of his last movements,' Baz says.

'And I've given them. I don't know where he went.' Her voice catches over the last word but she composes herself. 'It's been nearly five weeks,' she says quietly. There's a flash of pain in her eyes, like a spark cast out from a flint. Her hand comes up, she touches a fingertip to the diamond stud in her ear.

I say: 'I know it's been hard, Monica. We're doing all we can to bring him home, I promise.'

'I know.' She blows out a breath. Blinks tears away. Straightens.

'Was Teddy into gaming?' I ask.

She frowns at the change in direction. 'Like gambling?'

'No, board games? Or online gaming sites?'

'No. In the time I've known him, he's not so much as played a card game. His dad had a gambling problem, so he stayed away from that kind of thing. Why?'

'We've been sent some information, around a mystery game. It's likely nothing to do with Teddy but we wanted to cross it off our list,' I say. 'He hadn't mentioned anything like that to you?'

'No. I don't think so.' Her answer leaves us with a few possibilities. One: she's lying and has some kind of perverse involvement in the box herself. Two: the affairs are not the only part of Dolan's life she doesn't know about. Three: Teddy Dolan has no involvement with the box at all, nor was there ever an affair between Teddy and Lydia, which would mean we've been sent wheeling around the merry-go-round by Neve Jameson, just so as she could get us to take her friend's disappearance seriously. I can barely bring myself to think about the last one.

'Monica,' I say, 'we're trying to establish if there could've been someone with Teddy on the evening he disappeared.'

She looks down at her hands. 'I suppose you mean another woman?'

'Yes.'

'No. As I've said before, he went alone.'

'Had he been seeing someone else?'

'No.'

'Everything was happy in your marriage?'

'Teddy sometimes strayed but . . .' she shrugs her right shoulder, 'they were nothing. He knows it. I know it.' She flicks a glance over my shoulder towards the window. 'They were minor distractions that mean nothing to our marriage. We both understand that.'

I wait to see if she'll add more. But she stares through the silence as if it were a competition. I don't buy open relationships. Too many downsides. For one, where's the fire in an affair if you're not getting away with anything? Isn't that the point? At best, you're shagging one person only, at worst you're shagging two and at least one of them is planning revenge.

Removing the picture of Lydia Callin from inside my jacket, I hold it out to her 'Do you know this woman?'

She takes it, looks down at the picture without inclining her head so that I can make out the varying shades of lavender eyeshadow dusted across her eyelids. She puts the picture down on the glass coffee table between us and doesn't look at it again.

'I've never seen her before.'

'This is Lydia Callin. A twenty-two-year-old woman who was last seen early August. Shortly after your husband went missing. We've reason to believe Teddy might have been seeing her. Romantically,' I add.

She digests this information slowly. On her lap, she's pressing her thumbnail against the knuckle of her index finger over and again.

'I don't know who that is.' She reaches towards the table where there's a gold tissue dispenser. She snatches one free, folds it over a finger then dabs at the corner of her eyes.

'Monica,' I say, lowering my voice and lacing it with compassion. 'I know these questions are uncomfortable, but we have to ask them – that way, we can get a good idea of how Teddy was, how your marriage was. Sometimes in an investigation it's more about eliminating possibilities than searching for new information and you're helping us with that.'

'He didn't leave me,' she says. A rose-pink blooms in her cheeks. 'There's no reason for him to leave. I know you think I can't know that. That the little missus can't know the half of what her husband is capable of doing. But *I* do.'

50

CHAPTER 5

'What do you think?' Baz asks when we get outside.

I pull up my hood against the drizzle. 'I believe her.'

'Yeah, she's either a talented liar or we've just given her another reason to not sleep at night. She seem a bit too put together to you?' he asks.

'What do you mean?'

'Nice hair and, like, made up.'

'I'd say Monica Dolan doesn't even realize she's putting on make-up for the day, just another way to place one foot after the other.' Ducking against the rain, I make for the car. 'Odd wording, don't you think? About her knowing what her husband is capable of.'

'I caught that too. Though I did think she meant more in relation to herself – you know, hurting her emotionally, fucking around.' We get to the car, Baz opens the passenger door, waits for me to get to the driver's side. 'There has to be another phone somewhere if he was in touch with Lydia,' he says, looking back at the Dolan gate. 'We should get a search warrant for the house.'

'Agreed. Although, I'm not holding out much hope on finding another phone. I think if there is one, it's likely with him.'

We get into the car. Baz clips his seatbelt closed. 'All this time, I've been feeling bad for Teddy,' he says suddenly. 'That his body has been dumped somewhere and we'll never find it and then after the amputated finger, imagining the places where he's been held. Now, I'm thinking that he's killed his girlfriend and done a runner.'

I shift in my seat to face him. 'You think that's what's happened?'

'Don't you?'

'Wouldn't be the first time. Is it worth the price of a finger though?'

'Up against a life sentence, I'd say so,' he replies.

'Why send it at all though? If he has killed her and already run? I'd say he's succeeded in getting away. Why would he re-ignite the fire by lopping off a digit and sending it to his wife?'

He shrugs. 'It's just a feeling I have.'

'That's helpful.'

Schoolchildren are emptying out of a bus up the street and into the arms of waiting mothers and fathers. I start up the car.

I'm feeling a little uneasy that we're not on the same page on this one. Generally, that wouldn't bother me on a case – Baz and I are often over and back, challenging one another, ensuring we've turned over all those stones. What's concerning is that it's not just the unlikeliest theory of what's happened with Teddy Dolan and Lydia Callin but it's the easiest. And if the contents of The Murder Box are any indication of how this is to go, the easiest theory will not cut it.

It's almost four-thirty and the conference room at the Bureau is filling fast. A tall bloke in a trying-too-hard suit casts himself out as a newbie and approaches. Too much confidence. That I enjoy knocking the shiny corners off new blokes in suits is not the reason I don't look up. I'm reading through the notes we've had through from our pathologist, Dr James. The tissue from the slide in The Murder Box has been confirmed as taken from the heart muscle of a human victim. Unsophisticated approach, she'd said, meaning that whatever methodology normally used to mount a fragment of tissue on a slide was not implemented. She adds a note detailing the type of equipment that might be employed to prepare such a slide, the use of paraffin as a protective base. A machine called a microtome to slice the tissue sample. Were these omissions by our killer born of ignorance or a lack of opportunity?

'Detective Sheehan, hi, I'm so happy to be here. I just got brought over today from traffic, of all things. I'm Detective Smith Mullins,' I glance up in time to catch Newbie's smile. 'Fascinating case. I was looking over what we have on Dolan the night he went missing and I thought we could—'

His use of the word 'we' is about as comfortable as a finger in the ribs every time he says it.

'Mullins?'

'Yes, Ma'am.'

'We're going to need coffee. There's a pot out on the case-room floor. And,' I point to the end of the room, 'you'll find the milk jug in the sink at the back.'

'Oh,' he says, smiles again, 'no bother at all.' He heads off.

Baz approaches. 'Enjoy that?'

'Don't know what you're talking about.'

'Clancy will burst a vein if he catches you playing with his new recruits.'

'He shouldn't leave his toys lying around, then.' I close the report. 'No scene at the nightclub. Helen says everything at Lydia's flat is how Neve reported to us. Brand new laptop on her dressing table, all set for beginning her teaching training. The college said they haven't heard from her. We're just waiting on the DNA match now but I think we can assume murder.'

He scans the room. Watches as staff stop to collect copies of the report, before choosing where to sit. 'What we need is the body.'

'Or the crime scene. We don't find that, everything else gets much more difficult, including locating a body.' Including locating the killer.

The items from The Murder Box are wrapped in clear bags and positioned in the middle of the table. Steve is at the bottom of the table, putting final touches to a powerpoint presentation on the case.

Looking over the arrangement of photographs on the table, I seek out Lydia's image then Teddy Dolan's. Drag them both forward. 'I still can't fully believe this is real,' I say. 'That someone's plotted this out. A murder-mystery game with a real victim. Why?'

'Any thoughts on a criminal profile yet?' Baz asks, and I sense the question is more so he can check a list against Teddy.

I sigh. 'There might be anger behind it, a person who believes they've been slighted in some way. Their brilliance unrecognized. We could be looking at someone in, from their point of view, a middle-of-the-road job. They'd need time to put together so they don't have a heavy work-load, probably no children, and either have a secret location or room to work in or if they're single, live alone where they could spend time indulging this project. It's bold. Arrogant, right? The idea that you know people will play along. Possibly a narcissist or a sociopath.' I pick up the image of the histology slide. 'Or it could be none of that. No question, the box is a labour of love. Whoever put it together took their time sourcing the materials, all generic, mass-market, the case-board handcrafted, the histology slide lab-grade. Not one fingerprint retrieved from any of the items.'

And I imagine our perpetrator measuring out the right amount of heart muscle to cut. Slicing thinly. He holds the translucent flap of tissue to the light, takes up the bottle of saline and rinses it clean. Using tweezers, he lays it on a glass slide. He's sweating, glad that the hairnet captures the beads of moisture forming on his forehead. He knows better than most what it would mean if he left any trace of himself here on this fine piece of glass. A light dusting of his own skin cells could be the end of all his plans. And he has big plans. Plans that people will have to pay attention to. He'll be known. Finally. The anticipation! To see this done. Finished. It's almost too much to think about. He focuses on keeping his hand steady. The slide is done. A smile edges across his face and it feels like it's breaking across his entire body.

'Steve knows a games designer who specializes in games psychology and theory. He's set up a meeting for us for later today. Camille Forbes,' I say to Baz. 'You heard of her?'

He shakes his head. 'I'm not big on the games front.'

'If Teddy's case is connected,' I go on, 'we have to assume the killer knew about the affair. If he's not connected, then short of anyone else new in Lydia's life, it could be that she was chosen at random. Wrong place. Wrong time. Camille Forbes might help us narrow this down.'

'Chief?' Steve calls out.

We head over and he directs me to his screen. He opens up the website provided to us by the murder box. 'I was just taking some screenshots of the site for the presentation and noticed this. What does it look like to you?'

At the top of the page there is a digitized series of numbers.

'Subscribers?' Baz says.

I stare down at the numbers and the realization of what I'm seeing crashes through me. 'I don't think so, unless they're disappearing by the second.'

'It's a clock?' Baz asks, leaning in.

Steve glances back at me. 'If these are hours and minutes, we're looking at an end date of,' he opens another window, brings up a calendar, 'the fourteenth of September.'

'That's five days away,' I say.

Ryan, catching the tail end of the conversation, wedges in between us, dumping a stack of files and notebooks on the table beside Steve. He leans over, pushing Baz out of the way. 'Fucking dark,' he says. 'What'll happen then?'

Baz gives the back of his head a hard glare. 'Well, it's not going to be a medal for the winner, is it?'

Straightening, Ryan tugs the front of his trousers up, passing thumbs around his belt. 'Relax, will ye.'

'Fuck off,' Baz replies.

'Steve?' I prompt.

'The introductory letter hinted that there could be more

victims. Reading it, knowing what we do now, its tone seems menacing,' he says.

'Victims? Taken from anyone playing along?'

'Possibly. Looking through the site, we've got a total of eighty-five subscribers,' he says.

'Any names?'

'Not yet.'

Baz pushes a hand through his hair. 'Eighty-five? They couldn't all be involved in this?'

Steve shakes his head. 'We don't know yet. Likely they're unaware of what the game means.'

Across the room, Mullins finally reappears, a full coffee pot in one hand and a plate of biscuits in the other, the milk jug held between his forearm and chest. The staff follow him to the end of the room, eager for coffee. Some of them take their seats, wait expectantly for the briefing to start, some stand or lean along the walls of the room, balancing cups and notebooks on windowsills.

'What time's Hegarty here?' Baz asks me.

'Soon,' I reply, feeling queasy about the thought of suggesting a connection between the Dolan case and The Murder Box. A glance around the full room tells me the effect the box has had on the team. The animated chatter in the corners, the lingering glances at our table of evidence. The atmosphere could be likened to an audience at a cinema waiting for the start of a movie.

'Coffee?' Baz asks.

'Yes, please.'

He gives my arm a squeeze of reassurance. 'It'll be okay.'

The mouths of the press were already watering when Teddy went missing, recognizing a story that had legs enough to run the front pages for weeks. Hegarty hemmed and hawed over whether to reveal the family relationship during the initial press conference, but eventually decided she'd best get out ahead of it. And that's what she did.

Before the press briefing began, I watched as, primped to the nines, hair and make-up pristine, she disappeared to the toilets for a 'comfort break'. When she returned, ten minutes later, the press were already seated and checking their watches. She stood up to the lectern and I saw that the usual measured layer of light pink lipstick was absent, her face pale and the usual neat sweep of her hair was flat as the top of a portobello mushroom. Say what you like about Hegarty but she knows how to perform for a camera.

Baz had murmured in my ear. 'The Gardaí today, the Emmys tomorrow.'

'You'd better believe it,' I returned.

Bringing Lydia Callin and this mystery game into the picture will tip sympathies in the wrong direction for both Dolan and Hegarty. The public, like Baz has, will have him pegged as the guy who killed his lover then disappeared because it all got a bit complicated. And I've no doubt that Hegarty is trowelling through Lydia's past faster than we are but for different reasons. Some hack is going to have themselves a few breaking stories that involve anything dodgy in our victim's past if this news breaks. One of the reasons, I've already requested we keep this case tight. The other being that until we know who is behind this murder box, I don't want to give our perp any head starts.

I'd hoped we'd escape Hegarty's gaze for another couple of days until we could either establish a firm link between the cases or discount the connection altogether, but that was wishful thinking. After leaving us this afternoon, it's apparent that Jack, a little too eager to show Hegarty we'd a possible lead on the Dolan case, trotted straight up to her and told her all about Lydia; proud as a cat with a bird in its mouth.

Steve gets up, wipes the back of his hand across his forehead. 'Okay, we're all set here,' he says.

Jack Clancy, as he has a talent for doing, materializes at the door. He's freshened up and even from where I'm standing, I catch the faint tang of his aftershave. He scoops a palm over the side of his head and presses obedience into his hair then walks towards me, the tips of his black shoes catching the glare of the fluorescent lights above.

'We right?' he says, frowning around the room. Under the notion that we're waiting for him.

'We'd best wait for Hegarty to show,' I say.

There's a rumble of conversation outside the door and I know she's arrived.

'Okay, let's get started,' I say, loudly. 'Some of you've been working the Dolan case since we took it on almost five weeks ago. We've had a report of a possible connection between Teddy Dolan and a missing woman. For the purposes of those new to the case, there are summaries in the packs you've been supplied.'

Hegarty stays at the back of the room as I speak. She holds a saucer and cup, a biscuit between her thumb and forefinger.

The details light up on the screen and I move to the side. 'Dolan is thirty-six. Five foot seven. Dark hair, cut short. Clean shaven. White. He was last seen on the second of August at approximately ten-thirty, outside a gallery on Cope Street.

59

He was wearing a black shirt, black trousers and a pair of—' I look down at my notes. 'Lavair trainers in white. CCTV available in the area has so far given us nothing, but we are reviewing it again in light of recent revelations involving this other case which we will get to shortly. We've no witnesses who report seeing him leave. Cell site analysis gives us Cope Street as his last known location.

'Dolan is married to Monica Dolan, née Cary. They live in Booterstown. Have no children. Mrs Dolan tells us they have a happy marriage, but we know of at least two affairs and there could have been more.'

I move the briefing along. 'On the thirtieth of August, an amputated finger was delivered to the Dolan house. The finger was tested and confirmed as belonging to Teddy Dolan. Our pathologist believed, because there appeared to be a good amount of blood at the amputation site, that Dolan was alive when the finger was removed. There's been no ransom note and no demands from whoever is holding him. We went to work again on CCTV around the house, interviewed the neighbours, put out notices to the public on all platforms. We received upwards of two thousand calls, but again, no solid leads.'

I take a drink of coffee, give them a moment to switch from we've nothing to we must have something because we're all here.

The screen changes to an image of The Murder Box. 'Yesterday, a package, a box was delivered to the Bureau.' I nod down at the conference table where the contents of the box are laid out. 'Detective Garvin will take you through the details we've discovered so far.'

60

Hegarty moves up the room, stands over Ryan's shoulder. He, without looking up, senses her presence and shifts in his seat so that she can look down on The Murder Box herself.

Steve reaches for his notebook, stands. 'I'm Detective Steve Garvin,' he says to the room. He scratches a finger along his jaw, finds his place. 'The box we received claimed to be a subscription murder-mystery game. For those not familiar with the set-up, this is where you sign up and a fictional murder mystery will be delivered to you to solve. Many contain fictionalized witness statements, last movements, documents or clues the player can put together to make a case and get started on their own investigation. So, for clarity, these types of games are normally centred around an invented murder mystery. They do not involve real-life murder.

'This box contained the story of a missing twenty-two-year-old, female. And that woman is Lydia Callin of South Circular Road, Dublin. Reported missing on the fourteenth of August by her flatmate, Neve Jameson, who this morning presented at the Bureau.' He clicks through the details of The Murder Box. 'As you can see, the box we received tells us that its victim was last seen on August the tenth by her flatmate. We are given a PE report, certain items of evidence: a bus ticket, a strand of hair, an earring that we're told was removed from the victim's right ear prior to the PE. And a histology slide labelled as heart tissue.'

Mullins raises a hand.

'Questions at the end, please,' I say.

Mullins' hand lowers, he makes a note.

Steve finds his place again and continues. 'As I said, the histology slide was labelled heart tissue. Myocardium. The earring found in the box appeared to match a pair belonging to Lydia Callin.' He pauses, looks out at the room. 'We have conducted tests on the earring and can confirm the presence of human blood. We've also had confirmation that the tissue labelled myocardium in the box is, in fact, human tissue, but it will be tomorrow before we get a DNA profile from it, if one is retrievable at all.'

A wave of murmurs swells through the room. Some of the team lean forward on their forearms, wanting to draw in, get closer, not miss a thing. Cases like this don't happen often, if at all. Cases that we know will morph into true-crime folklore by the time they've run their course.

'Chief?' Steve says.

I step forward again. 'Neve Jameson told us that Teddy Dolan and our potential victim, Lydia Callin, were having an affair. So far, we've been unable to verify this, but seeing as we have been investigating Dolan's case and the box has been sent to the Bureau, it seems to me that there is quite likely some connection between both cases. As I said, not fully established, but something to keep in mind as we proceed. Lydia's father, Joe Callin, last spoke to his daughter on the eighth of August and has not seen or heard from her since. Lydia is not working currently but was expected to begin a teaching-training course this week. None of her ex-colleagues nor the offices at her course have heard from her. We've seized a laptop from Lydia's bedroom on South Circular Road and a couple of personal items from her room at the Callin home including a hair sample in order to compare DNA profiles with the heart tissue in the box.

'Lydia Callin was last seen entering a newsagent along the south quay of the Liffey on the tenth of August. The newsagent was able to confirm a purchase of cigarettes and a tooth-cleaning product. Again, this is in line with information given to us in The Murder Box.'

I pause, wait for the room to look up from their notes. 'With the evidence that we have secured so far, paired with the fact that no one has seen or heard from Lydia Callin in a month, we have launched a murder investigation. Joe Callin lost his wife and two sons over the last decade. Lydia was all he had left. We need suspects. We need a crime scene. We need to locate her remains. We need to find the person who put this game together and bring them to justice.'

Steve flicks to the final slide on the screen and the landing page for the game's website appears.

He highlights the top right corner of the page. 'The game's website displays a countdown clock. We're not sure what this means yet but given the nature of the game presented, it's not too wild an assumption that if we fail to locate our perp within the time remaining on this site, there will be more murders. Victims chosen from among the subscribers, perhaps, or at random.'

'Questions?' I look at Mullins, but he's quiet. His gaze goes from the gleaming red box that's displayed on the screen to the contents of the game in front of him.

There's silence. The couple of inspectors by the window have moved forward to examine the box in the flesh.

'Next move from us—' I begin and Mullins' hand goes up. 'Yes?'

'Do we know why she might have been targeted as the victim in this . . .' he searches for the right word, 'game?'

'Not yet,' I say. 'It is what we aim to find out.' I continue. 'I want full cell site analysis of Lydia Callin's phone. As much as we can glean from her internet activity. DI Paul Collins will assign roles. We'll need door-to-door out from Lydia Callin's doorstep on South Circular Road to the bus stop. Talk to any staff that worked with her at The Hanamaran pub. It's also worth chatting to some of Dolan's colleagues again, see if we can place him with Lydia anywhere. CCTV is vital. I want at least three of you on that.' I look to Paul and he nods his agreement. 'From her flat, her home, nearby libraries, internet cafés, tablets, phones, computers – that's priority. Liaise with Detective Steve Garvin and Emer Kelly if you need more information on that. I want background checks on her flatmate, Neve Jameson, their history, any longstanding grudges, the usual. Bank details, all transactions over the past three months. There is the chance with this that one case might help us with the other, which is why I'm asking you to push so hard.'

Hegarty, sensing a close to the meeting, makes the first exit. I already know there's a warning coming.

Slowly, people get up from their seats to look at the table. Some confer over the details. Some already know their roles, have read up and are eager to get to their individual tasks. 'Remember that the packs you've received do not leave this building,' I say. 'Mullins, when CCTV comes in, you're on traffic. I want ANPR on all cars and vehicles from around Score nightclub.'

He's about to object, not expecting to be back on traffic when he's finally got his foot in the door at the Bureau.

'You've experience in that area, don't you?' I ask before he has a chance.

He looks to Jack who inspects his tie, staying out of this one. 'Yes, but—'

'Good. That's it. Let's get to it.'

CHAPTER 6

I ease out of the underground car park and join the city traffic. The sky is darkening. The streetlights already warming up for the night. Baz sits quietly beside me, his body angled away, his thumb flicking over his phone.

I creep the car forward. 'You thinking about the case?'

He looks quickly towards me in a way that suggests he's almost forgotten I'm there. 'What?' he says. Then wiping a hand over his face, 'Yes, sorry. This specialist, Forbes, what are we getting from her?'

I move down a gear, stop at a red light. 'I'm hoping for some background about the type of person who'd be able to put The Murder Box together. If there are aspects of the game that echo other games she's familiar with, it might help us build a profile of our perp.'

'It's strange to me, if the cases are connected, that there'd be no mention of Dolan in the box. Surely that would be the perfect lead-in, if attention is what this guy wants.'

'We don't know that it's a guy, or that it's only one person.

66

Perhaps you're right and Dolan is behind it. That he's disappeared so that he could put this in motion.'

'But you doubt that?'

'A finger's worth of doubt is all,' I say, thinking that if someone had the stomach to cut off their own finger to maintain interest in their own missing person's case, then they might also be capable of much more. Pulling away from the lights, I turn left over the Liffey. 'There're numerous cases where people fake their own death and not always because they want to disappear but because they want to experience the legacy it might leave behind. In the early eighties, the British painter Robert Lenkiewicz, wanting to promote an upcoming exhibition on death, faked his own. He said, "I could not know what it was like to be dead but I could discover what it was like to be thought dead".'

'I knew you'd come round to my way of thinking,' he says, throwing me a smile. 'I have this niggling feeling . . . Bear with me,' he adds when I frown. 'That Dolan's finger only turned up when the press started running with the theory that he'd disappeared voluntarily, that there'd been sightings of him as far as the Caribbean. A body part in the post would have sufficed in putting that theory to bed,' he says.

'But the same motivation could apply to his abductor, no? Looking at Dolan's profile, he shows no inclination for more attention than what he was already getting. His marital indiscretions hit the gossip columns, but if what his wife tells us is true, he was looking to get away from the showbiz persona and into something a bit more serious.'

Baz pushes back in the seat, lets his head fall back and sighs. 'Think this case is going to haunt us for a long while.'

'I hope that's not the sigh of someone giving up.'

He closes his eyes. 'No, just some days it feels like what's the point. We solve one and another pops up in its place.'

'Maybe you should have come to Joe Callin's this morning. An hour watching that man trying to grapple with the fact that he's most likely lost his daughter would remind you what the point is,' I say.

'I didn't mean it like that.'

I throw a quick glance in his direction. There's a tension on his face, his eyes pinned on the road ahead, the muscles over his jaw clench and unclench.

'Is everything okay?' I ask. I indicate, then move out a lane. 'You seem like you've something on your mind?'

'I'm fine,' he says. 'I've a few personal things to sort out, that's all.'

'Alright. If there's anything I can do—'

'This morning, I just thought if I wasn't needed, I could clear this one thing up, that's all.'

'Okay, are you sure?'

He gives a dry laugh. 'What is this? I dip out for a couple of hours and you think I've lost my drive?'

'No,' I say, surprised at the defensive tone. 'Of course not. I'm asking as a friend.'

I keep my eyes on the road, sensing he wants to say more but whatever it is, he shoves it back down again.

We fall into a tense silence. Those friends I have outside of work, I don't talk to about what I've seen that day, the grisly cases I'm knee deep in. There's no way to traverse those worlds. Once you sink below that line of knowing, knowing what's beyond the next-door neighbour's smile, or a deserted warehouse on the south side, flat 4c above the local gym or that big fancy house owned by that young friendly couple where he always seemed nice and she never went out – once you know, it separates you. I have my dad, a retired garda who understands the shorthand for 'this case has me beat', my sister-in-law Tanya, a defence lawyer, who even at seven months pregnant craves an opportunity to talk over a case. And I have Baz. He knows every move. He's there with every failure and every success. And I know he didn't mean he's tired of the job, but even the suggestion that he might give up makes me feel uneasy.

Flicking down the indicator, I turn onto Dame Street. I might've put too much on the idea that if we can unspool this game quickly, we'll not only find Teddy Dolan but have Lydia Callin's killer behind bars before the end of the week. But to be handed so much evidence and freely is, quite literally, a gift. We've gone from no leads to finally having a strategy, not to mention a team of rejuvenated detectives who want to bring home the big win.

Baz is still quiet beside me. He's either sulking or his thoughts are on the same path as mine, planning next moves.

'Gemma's doing a dinner this weekend,' he says.

Or maybe not. Baz and Gemma recently got back together. In the half year or so they've known each other, they've been on and off more often than a kitchen tap. The common fault line appears to lie in Baz's working hours which are, like every detective's, not always compatible with romantic relationships.

'Nothing big,' he says, 'but we thought we'd invite a few of the team. It would be nice for her to finally meet everyone.'

'You have the address?'

'It'll be at my gaff. Hers is only a bedsit. You wouldn't think it from the bloody rent she's paying. It's extortion. Fucking rent prices as well as house prices are daylight robbery.'

'I meant Camille Forbes' address,' I say. 'Think it should be around here somewhere.'

He fishes a scrap of paper out of his suit pocket, looks at it, then points through the screen. 'That gated joint up there. Christ, that's gone in there well. Was that always here?'

'No idea,' I say, pulling up along the kerbside. 'There's a restaurant on the ground floor. We're to meet her there.'

Reaching into the back seat, I drag my bag onto my lap.

Camille Forbes, game designer, or psychologist or digital-ethics scholar, I couldn't quite take in her title from Steve when he said it to me. But he assured me, if anyone could give us a sense of The Murder Box, this was our woman. Thirty-five years old, French-Canadian–Irish, author of two books on game design and philosophy, podcast host, lecturer at DIT, city colleges and consultant to some of the biggest gaming companies in the world.

To understand the mind is to understand the crime. This is what I want to know. I don't want to feel about in the dark to get a sense of who we're dealing with or what might happen once that clock runs down. If there's any way to pre-empt what might be coming, then I want to know. Profiling helps with this and Camille Forbes is going to give that to us. I hope.

The restaurant is Moroccan-themed, dark and cavern-like, lit up with dozens of votive candles set in along the clay-coloured walls. Baz presses his hand to his stomach as soon as we step inside, and I know he's moments off ordering food we won't have the time to eat. Camille Forbes is waiting at the bar. She's wearing a red polo-neck sweater over a black pencil skirt that tapers in below her knees. Her hair is long, dark as treacle, large eyes are rounded with black eyeliner.

'Frankie?' she asks.

'Miss Forbes,' I shake her outstretched hand and a jingle of fine gold bangles chime at her wrist. 'This is my partner, Detective Harwood.'

'Baz,' Baz says with a smile.

'Lovely to meet you both. Apologies I couldn't come to you but I'm shattered and just couldn't face the trek across the city.'

'Thank you for giving up your time so readily,' I say.

She waves that away. 'Oh please, when Steve mentioned he'd a murder-mystery game he thought I should look at it, I cleared my evening. Before he called, I'd not spoken to him for years.' She looks over our shoulders out at the street. 'He's not here?'

'He couldn't make it,' I say. 'But sends his best.'

'Sounds like you're all busy,' she says. 'Coffee?'

'That'd be great.'

A man behind the bar, sets down the wine glass he's cleaning. Nods a smile at Camille, then scoops a tray from beneath the counter.

'Come through. Cormac here has reserved my usual spot,' she says.

She leads us through to the back of the restaurant, to a round table nestled in a corner. It's too early for dinner and the place is empty, but the scent from the kitchen sets my mouth to water. I let Camille sit first, then sit facing the exit and kitchen door.

Baz slides in across from me, all traces of our previous conversation gone from his face.

'So you've studied profiling?' Camille asks me.

'Behavioural analysis mostly,' I say.

'Well, I hope I can be of use to you.' She gets straight to it. 'May I see this mystery game?'

Removing a tablet from my bag, I open The Murder Box folder. 'This was delivered to the Bureau yesterday.' I hand it over, not wanting to prompt, not wanting to taint a first impression.

The corner of her mouth lifts in a half-smile as she studies the screen. 'Beautiful set-up,' she says, the tip of her finger gliding over and back on the screen through the images. 'I'm now regretting not making the journey to you this evening. I'd like to see the actual box.'

'It's currently being processed but whatever you can tell us now will be helpful. I've a feeling we'll be calling on your help again,' I say.

She focuses on the screen. Occasionally, she pauses, brings the tablet towards her face, expands something, squints down, then moves on to the next image. I see the moment it dawns on her that the victim in the game is real. The report from Abigail James, stating that the cardiac tissue found inside The Murder Box was not a simple play-piece but real human flesh. Her entire body stills, her eyes widen. Then, beneath the thin woollen fabric of her polo-neck, the muscles of her throat move. She swallows. Her tongue touches her top lip, and she lifts her gaze from the tablet to meet mine.

'It's real,' she says. Not a question.

'Yes.'

She looks down at the tablet again, flicks back through the images. 'There's a countdown?'

'We think so. We have our theories about what it could mean for the game. Another victim, maybe.'

She's nodding. 'Yes, the game could reset which would give you another victim. It could mean nothing or it could mean a cost for the players who don't solve the mystery in the given time.'

She studies the image for a few seconds more, then places the tablet down gently, as if it were a bomb about to go off.

'We wondered what you thought might be—' Baz says.

'The next move?'

'Let's start with the type of person who would put something like this together,' I say.

'You don't know?'

'We have our thoughts.'

She hooks a lock of dark hair behind her ear. 'Firstly, it looks incomplete,' she says. 'There are elements to come, I imagine.'

'We believe so. On the website, you enter your progress; if you're on the right track, another stage is illuminated.'

She's nodding. 'Of course. What I meant was—' she stops, thinks about how to dumb things down for us non-gamers. 'There's an obvious goal. As a player, your job is to solve the crime, right, as with a traditional murder-mystery game, but the layout for this one suggests that we are given our victim—'

'Lydia Callin,' I say.

'A proposed manner of death—'

'Murder.'

'A possible location where the murder took place,' she pauses. 'But no suspects. Clues to the suspects but nothing solid to go with. How did this come to you?'

'It was delivered to the Bureau.'

'To you?'

'Yes.'

'Hmm,' she says.

'What?'

'I'm thinking anyone involved at this stage will be both player and potential suspect. There are certain boundaries within the gaming world – this is one of them. You cast your imagination out, fill your sheet,' she picks up the tablet again and expands on the small, lined notebook that came with the game. 'Anyone is game.'

'*Anyone* playing could be a suspect?'

'Or if the game was sent to you. It could mean you are.'

A quick glance at Baz. 'I think we can cross my name off the list. How about who put this together. The creator. Can we count them among the players?' I ask, thinking of the list of suspects we're about to unveil from the website.

'It could be they see themselves as a gamesmaster of sorts rather than an active participant but with how they've planned this out, I believe they'll have been longing to sit down at the table for this one. Will want to be involved in all the turns. For that reason, I'd assume that once you have your list of players, your killer will be among them.' She chews down on her lip. 'The victim's flatmate? Do we know if she is a player?'

'We're looking into it. She says she stayed home the evening Lydia went missing. We've had a team out at the shared flat all afternoon, they've not returned anything that suggests she's part of this. More than that, she reported her friend missing,' I say, thinking about which stack of cards Teddy Dolan's name sits on: suspect or victim. I point to the tablet. 'There are eighty-five subscribers in total. Are you saying that all of them are suspects?'

She sighs, takes up her coffee. 'In the game? Yes. In the real world, jumping ahead here of the creator, it's hard to know, but I'd say it's a possibility,' she smiles. 'Sorry, I know that doesn't make your job any easier.'

'We're not in the business of easy,' Baz says.

'Thanks for bringing me on board. It's definitely not the run-of-the-mill murder mystery.' She sips on her coffee. Baz looks up from his notebook, waiting for more. 'I guess you've a choice to make. Do you play? Hope for more information when you input your findings. Progress into the game and win. Whatever that might mean. Or do you remove the element of the game altogether, approach it as you would a standard murder investigation? You've been to the suggested location? Of the crime scene?'

'We've had feedback, yes. No crime scene. No reports. We're looking through CCTV now for any sightings of the suspected victim.'

'How did you know to test the slide?'

'The earring. It matched one similar to a pair belonging to the victim, Lydia Callin.'

'Hah,' she says. 'But there was no evidence of a murder scene at the club. So there are elements of abstraction.' She smiles. 'Fun.' Then adds, 'If you're not dead, I suppose. Parts of the game truly represent what's happened. Others are an abstraction, they are a symbol of what happened. The game's creator needed

75

a likely crime scene to frame their narrative, so they created one. Other elements are true pieces. Like the earring. Others could be red herrings. This is a murder mystery after all. Unfortunately for you, only time will tell which is which. I wonder what the other boxes contained,' she says.

'We thought there could be more,' I say.

'Undoubtedly. If there are eighty-five players, it would make sense to think that all of them have a murder box. Although,' she skims back down over the content on the tablet, 'they couldn't all have been furnished with an earring, for example. They must be different to that extent at least. It's possible they've all had slides, of course – plenty of meat in heart muscle. I'd assume they'll contain photographs of these pieces of evidence or reports, perhaps. They really saved the best for you,' she says.

They wanted to be noticed. Wanted to compete with top brass.

Baz taps his notebook. 'You think Frankie could be a target here? In that it was addressed to her?'

A purse of lips then, 'It doesn't seem to me like that would be a coincidence. It could be that the creator simply wanted the Bureau investigating. You deal with high profile cases, right?'

'Yes,' I say.

She nods. 'That would make sense,' she pauses, puts down the tablet again. She takes a slow drink of her coffee, eyebrows drawing together. 'The creator wants more than one element of reality at play here. More than, sadly, Lydia Callin as victim—'

'We've yet to find a body,' I remind her. 'We can't confirm yet that Lydia Callin has been murdered. We just know that the game is connected to a real missing person case.'

She nods her understanding. 'I think you can, with some

certainty, say she's been murdered even if procedure demands you keep that door open.' She leans away, her expression regretful. 'There is a type of gaming called augmented reality gaming. You have the real world – the world we inhabit – and the game is projected on to that. It interacts with your environment.'

Baz scratches his head with the end of the pen. He frowns. 'Like virtual reality?'

'No. With virtual reality you play out the game in a virtual world. Here,' she touches the corner of the tablet, 'the elements of the game are moving into the real world. Hence, your real murder victim.' She straightens. 'The game has called upon its subscribers to act as sleuths but the creator wants that real world addition.' She meets my eyes. 'That's you. The real detective.'

She finishes her coffee. 'They don't want to win against just any old player. They want to win against you. My sense is that there will come a trade-off point where you'll be forced to engage. I hope you can avoid that, but it will depend on how well the game's creator has planned this out.' She frowns, her eyes darkening. 'But a warning. Games that ask for physical participation from the players or that can be directly affected by players may alter the stakes. Like say, in a boardgame if you were to use a weapon card, you might have to tear it up afterwards and that narrows your options or broadens them dependent on your success. My point is, your move could have a physical and permanent cost in the game itself.'

'You're saying that what we feed back into this system could translate into more victims?' Baz asks.

'A wrong move in any game has consequences. For anyone playing. Who knows what that could mean here?'

'And if we don't play?'

She scrolls through the pictures. 'I think it might be rather too late for that, don't you? They're expecting your investigation, I would think. It's why you got the box to begin with. This way, they get to control what you know, what you don't know. Move your case from the streets into their realm. If the creator and killer are one and the same, then they'll not be expecting interaction from the off. They'll understand there's a pattern to how you investigate, will have even factored this into the game itself. Some of these elements, like the crime scene, for example are only there to lead you further into play, like passing through a curtain, say.'

'Like the post-mortem?'

'Maybe. Obviously, your victim didn't undergo an autopsy at Whitehall, like it states here. These are clues to lead you to the truth. In the creator's mind, you're already playing. It's only a matter of time before you begin to engage. I'd take advantage of that. The only thing they won't have predicted is that you might be prepared to forfeit normal procedure and interact with the game from the start. You've probably already got this covered, but for the sake of saying it, it's clear this person has some knowledge of procedure. Perhaps a background in law enforcement or at least a fascination with it.'

'We can push our normal procedure to an extent. But we can't throw it out the window,' I reply. 'As much as I want to at times.'

'Of course not,' she smiles. 'But I think you'll need to get creative with this one. If I were in your shoes, I'd be thinking of ways to get in there. Get among the players. Bring them out, flesh and blood.'

I experience a shiver at her words. Words that I've spoken in my own mind. I swallow, meet Baz's eyes.

Camille Forbes takes a sleek leather purse from her bag, removes a tenner and leaves it on the table. 'Welcome to the magic circle, detectives.'

CHAPTER 7

Shouldering my way through the pub, I find my team already well on it around the bar. Enda, the bartender, catches my eye, scoops a wine glass from above his head and turns to the fridges behind him. He lifts a chilled bottle of sauvignon blanc over the rows of punters in my direction and I give a nod. He smiles. Ignores the heads turning, trying to catch his eye and pours my drink. I go to the end of the bar and he puts it down in front of me. When I reach for my bag, he shakes his head, points to my colleagues.

'On the house, Detective. Happy birthday,' he says.

'Bad news does travel fast,' I smile at him. 'Thanks.'

I spot Jack standing by the empty fireplace. His elbow pitched up on a stone mantelpiece, head down, Ryan talking into his ear. I don't need to see Jack's eyes to tell he's well oiled. The signs are there in the pose of his hands, crossed at his chest and the purse of his mouth, the earnest way he's listening to Ryan, bobbing his head in agreement every so often. I take a mouthful of wine and head over.

Helen extricates herself from a group of people; some I recognize – Emer standing stiffly sipping water through a straw, a bloke from archives, I think, next to her looking like he's at his first outing to a pub.

'Happy birthday,' Helen says, her voice alarmingly close to a squeal. 'Oh, you can't drink that. We got you a cocktail,' she removes the glass of wine from my hand, stopping it mid-journey to my mouth. It sloshes down the front of my trousers but she doesn't notice. She turns to a high table and lifts a tall glass of the sort used for ice-cream sundaes and presents it to me, hand under the base as if it were a trophy. It's pink and yellow and sprouting two green umbrellas and a cherry pierced with a cocktail stick.

'Thanks,' I say, take it and immediately look to where I can put it down.

Helen waits. Watches.

Realizing she's waiting for me to taste it, I lift the straw, push the umbrellas aside and take a sip. It tastes like cough mixture and settles in a skin over my teeth.

Helen's nodding at me with some enthusiasm. 'Divine, isn't it?'

'Hey,' Baz's voice comes from behind me.

I shuffle to the side to make room. 'Nice,' he says. 'Can I try?' he asks, and I hand him the glass with relief.

'Wait!' Helen puts out a hand. 'That's not for you.'

But Baz has already inhaled half the cocktail either to save me from drinking it or to prevent Helen feeling hurt when I dump it into the nearest plant. All the same, Helen groans, then shoots me a conspiratorial glare. 'They really do take everything, don't they?'

81

'What is that?' Baz asks, smacking his lips. He takes another gulp, frowns, then, 'Fruit salads. Remember those sweets? It tastes like liquidized fruit salads.'

'Should I get you another?' Helen asks me, throwing daggers at Baz.

'Thanks, but I think I'll stick with the wine for now.'

A woman squeezes in next to Baz.

He smiles down at her and all of us pause to look. There's an intimacy in the smile that says girlfriend. Even Emer has pushed her dark fringe out of her eyes and moved closer for a better look. Helen coughs and Baz straightens.

'Everyone, this is Gemma,' he announces. She blushes.

'I hope you don't mind,' she says to me. 'I know it's staff drinks, but we so rarely get to spend any time together socially,' she says. She moves slightly ahead of Baz and her hand goes back as she speaks, her knuckles touching against his chest as if she was putting a hand out in the dark to check he was still there. With her other hand she produces a clumsily wrapped small box. 'Happy birthday!' she says, then feigns a wince. 'Sorry about the wrapping.'

'Thank you, but you didn't need to,' I say, as she pushes it into my hand. The scent of rose floats up through the wrapping.

'It's a candle,' she says.

'That's very thoughtful of you,' I say, looking around for somewhere to put it, then squeezing it into my bag. 'Can I get you a drink?'

'I shouldn't, I'm driving.'

'Water?'

'No really,' she says.

'It's okay, babe,' Baz says.

Babe.

She flushes up at him. 'Okay, well, a coffee, a cappuccino would be great.'

Turning away, I join the back of the two-deep queue, thinking how much Enda, who only has one other member of staff helping him this evening, is going to love an order for a cappuccino.

I ask for another wine, a gin and tonic for Helen and mumble cappuccino. Enda squints, cups his hand around the back of his ear. 'What was da?'

'Cappuccino, please.'

He gives me a look that could burn through a stone wall, but I shrug back at him. Then with a shake of his head, he turns to the coffee machine.

I carry the drink back to Gemma and she takes it with both hands. 'It's unreal,' she says to Helen, her eyes wide. 'A bit exciting though, right? How are youse going to handle it?'

Helen takes a long drink of her cocktail. 'I guess like any other case.'

Gemma wrinkles her nose at that. 'Where's the fun in that?' she glances up at Baz, looking for agreement.

His hand moves up and down on her arm. 'It's early days,' he replies, and I see the warning look he gives her to keep quiet, but she misses it.

'There can't have been many cases like this before,' she says. 'To get a case delivered like a board game?'

'I hadn't realized case briefing had moved to the bar,' I say.

Helen looks away, rattles the ice in her drink.

Gemma looks from me to Baz. 'Oh,' she says. 'Sorry, I was just—'

83

'It's fine,' Baz says. 'Only a bit of banter.'

Gemma's cheeks redden but she rests a hand on my arm. 'I was only saying that the case is different, right, from the usual. We didn't discuss details,' she says with a smile.

'Different how?' I ask.

'Just, you know, the mode. Or what do you call it, babe?' She clicks her fingers next to her ear trying to bring the term forward.

'The MO,' he says, and has the grace to look embarrassed.

'That's it.' She lifts the cappuccino to her mouth. 'Sorry, I hope I haven't breached any rules or something or seemed insensitive.'

'Don't worry about it,' Baz says.

'It's fine,' I say and look for a change of subject. 'What do you do, Gemma?'

'I'm a surveyor. I'm with a consultancy firm in town. Mostly commercial assessments. Not as adrenalin-inducing as your work but it has its moments.'

'Gemma's just been shortlisted for an award on innovative transport solutions,' Baz says.

I raise my eyebrows at her. 'Incredible. Congratulations.'

She blushes again, looks down at the milky foam in her drink. 'Oh, my role was not conceptual – more to create a report on where might be the easiest locations to develop. Identifying and selecting routes that are already utilized by commuters who cycle, run or walk to work and suggesting ways to clear them of traffic.'

'Saving the planet,' I say, impressed.

'I wouldn't go that far, but it's kind of you to say so,' she replies, her blue gaze as open and soft as a child's.

'Excuse me,' I say. Leaving the heat of the pub, I head out into the back garden. Around the edges of the garden is built-in seating, but the lack of outdoor heating means it's empty. I stand near a round table at the door and remove my cigarettes from my pocket.

The night air is cool with a freshness that promises frosty mornings to come.

The door opens and Baz steps out beside me. 'Nice to get out for a few drinks,' he says, a touch awkwardly. I hand him the pack of cigarettes and he shakes one free, clasps it between his teeth while I dig out the lighter.

He lights it. 'Been thinking about what Camille Forbes said.'

I inhale, then blow out a cloud of smoke. 'What's that?'

'We should get out ahead of this. Get straight in there.'

'As soon as Steve gets some names from that site, we will. Cross-check them with Dolan or Lydia and see where we are.'

'I've looked at a few of these sites, these subscription games and this one feels more like the traditional murder-mystery game that Camille mentioned. Like a boardgame. In that usually when you subscribe for one of these games, you'd expect to be solving it by yourself but if what Camille says is accurate about the potential that all those subscribed are suspects then they are effectively playing against each other, right? It could mean that they know each other.'

'What eighty-five players?' I ask.

He shrugs. 'I'm told,' he smiles, 'that online people can congregate, become friends without ever having to meet in person. It wouldn't be that wild that they all could be involved in the box's creation in some way but for the sake of the game not be sure who is behind what. Like you would if you sat down at a murder-mystery dinner.'

'Everything's possible right now.' I agree.

'Eighty-five other players,' he points his cigarette at me, 'have had a decent head start and they haven't cracked it yet. I'm not liking the thought of what will happen if we can't solve this in time.'

I tip my head back, stare up at the dark sky. 'Eighty-five amateurs,' I say. 'They don't have our resources.'

'That we know of,' he says. 'And just to make sure that doesn't limit our choices too much—'

'God forbid,' I say.

'Our convo about Dolan earlier, you know about him cutting off the digit,' he makes a scissor action over his little finger, 'I saw a documentary once about a surgeon who was on an expedition in Antarctica, removed his own appendix.'

'Educational,' I say, enjoying the cool breeze on my face.

'It was actually.'

'Dolan's no surgeon.'

'Kill your girlfriend, go on the run, find out that everyone assumes you've been abducted and decide to egg that on,' he says.

I sigh. 'We need to narrow this down. My feeling is that we should focus on Lydia Callin. If there's something there connected to Dolan, we'll find it. I'm not so sure I see him behind the game but if he's had a hand in his girlfriend's death, the game doesn't change a thing.'

He puts his cigarette out. Shoves his hands in his jacket pocket, slides a glance at me, 'Listen, sorry about Gemma bringing up the case in there. She's nervous.'

It's a side effect of the job that over time, as a detective, you become more careful when talking to those outside of your work, especially if you're used to working murder. After a few years, you find yourself assessing strangers. People's actions and behaviours take on a different meaning. You learn to measure your responses. And while, after a time, the feet might go up when having the chats with new friends, it's only once mental checks have been made. The problem is that Gemma doesn't think like this, how easily she could let slip something about the case to the wrong person, blowing it open to media, giving our killer what they want and all that we know. I've seen year-long investigations dissolve like sugar cubes in hot water after the wrong detail fell into the wrong ear.

But I say, 'Don't worry about it.' Then, 'It's going better this time?'

When Baz was with Gemma before, it didn't take long for the reality of detective work to hit. And when he had to leave her alone on a mini-break, the P45 on their relationship came through the post special delivery. I don't blame her. In this way only, the job takes no prisoners. It's rare that anything outside of the work survives.

'I think so,' he says, tugging the zip of his coat higher, even though it's as high as it can go. 'Yeah, sure.'

'Don't gush all at once.'

'It's grand.' He raises his eyebrows. 'It's great. She's hot, she's clever, kind and she does get the job,' he turns around and adds quickly, before I can say anything, 'she wasn't prepared last time, that's all. She understands that there's a side of things that will always be a challenge. The only problem is,' he gives me a rueful smile, 'and I know I'm saying this after her talking about The Murder Box, so don't jump all over me about it but—' he pauses, figuring out how to phrase it. 'It's not that I can't talk about work,' he lowers his head, gives me a meaningful look from under his eyebrows, 'and I'm referring to the shit that keeps you blinking into the darkness at night. It's that I don't want to. I mean, I do want to, I want to fucking dissect the bloody horror sometimes, the outrageousness of it, but it almost feels like I'd be taking something from her by doing that. From anyone, really. Here, love, there's a slice of darkness with your evening tea. You know?'

'I know.'

Not ready to return to the noise and heat of the pub, I lean back against the edge of the garden table.

'You having a good birthday?' he asks, tilting a half-smile in my direction. Knowing that as much as I enjoy a night out occasionally, there's nowhere I'd rather be than knee-deep in my case notes.

But I answer. 'Yeah, sure. Nice to get away from the office for a bit.'

He laughs, reaches out and rubs a hand in sympathy along my arm. 'There. There. It'll be over soon.'

I give him his laugh. 'If Dolan's not our perp, then this is a huge job. The Murder Box. That wasn't thrown together. As Forbes says, it's long-term planning. Months, perhaps longer.'

He jogs his shoulders against the cold. 'Eighty-five unknown suspects and Dolan. This is what I hate about this job. You wait an entire month for a suspect then you get eighty-six all at once and you're not one millimetre further ahead than you were at the beginning.'

I laugh.

There are some cases that come in and you know they'll sink into the past and settle there. Victims' faces will occasionally rise to the surface, but a few times in a detective's career, you get a case that you know, even from the minute it lands on the desk, that it will follow you for the rest of your life.

'You're right though. We need to get under the hood of this quickly,' I say.

'How we going to play it?' Baz asks.

I straighten up. The temperature has dropped and my breath stains the night air white. 'I'm not sure.'

We head inside and I wait for the cake that I know is coming. Blow out candles and watch Jack get tanked, every now and then slapping Ryan on the shoulder, looking at him with the eye of someone who's either about to kiss them or sing at them. The latter is what happens and a few bars of *On Raglan Road* rise out of his mouth, the notes charged by pure emotion, the kind only felt by the drunk; his face going scarlet with the exertion and the veins at his temple and neck standing up like the twisted roots of a tree rising from the ground.

I slip away; the alcohol sucking what adrenalin there's left in my body and exhaustion laying itself like a mattress across my back.

When I get to my flat on Grafton Street, the sound of Clancy's voice is still turning in my head. Dropping my keys on the bookshelf just inside the door, I remove my coat then kick off my shoes. There's the musty smell of rotting food and I lift the lid off the bin, remembering I threw a half-eaten takeaway in there yesterday. Holding my breath, I remove the bag, knot it tightly, then grab my keys and head down to the bins on the ground floor. Back in the flat, the smell lingers and I remove the gift, the candle, from Gemma and Baz from my handbag. I light it, then set it in the middle of the counter beside a bottle of wine that Justin and my sister-in-law Tanya, left at my door. I peel off my coat, throw it over a chair. Then I go to the window, pull it down a fraction and draw the curtains on the muted lights and chilled streets of Dublin. It's not that late – ten-thirty – and I imagine the night is still going on in the pub. But I'm glad to be home. I reach for the bottle and head for the sofa.

I sit down, uncork the wine and pour a glass. The evening throbs against my ears. I see again the small exchange between Gemma and Baz. The lift of her hand up and back, the light touch of knuckles to his chest. And later, when she made him laugh and he squeezed her forearm gently. Something twists in my stomach.

I put down the wine. Stretch out my neck. Try to shake the feeling that there's a goodbye coming, but not able to anticipate from where. And I'm wearing a school uniform again, growing up. My skirt too long, the sleeves of my blouse ballooning out from under my sweater. Dropping me off at secondary school, my mother has a look in her eye, a sadness around the corners of her mouth. She pauses a fraction too long. Like she's searching for something that's no longer there, and I feel a tremble of fear.

I tell myself it's all good, let my eyes sweep over the familiar safety of my flat. On the end of the curtain pole, a slip of plastic is trapped beneath the bauble of wood that keeps the curtain rings in place. I've a clear memory of pulling the protective plastic away on the first day of moving in. It didn't come away cleanly, the strip remained. But my arms were getting heavy, the sharp Irish sunlight through the pane causing a sting in my eyes and a sweat down my back. I hopped down from the chair I'd been standing on, telling myself I'd have plenty of time to pluck it free later. That was over fifteen years ago. I think about removing it now but can't muster the desire to get up from the sofa. My eyes drift closed and I sink back into sleep.

'Frankie! Are you in?'

Christ's sake. I sit up, rub my eyes.

'Frankie! It's Cedric.'

New neighbour.

I get up. Open the door. 'Hi Cedric.'

He's the type who's built himself into looking good but is too aware of it, which is one of the many off-putting things about him. Even though it's late, wraparound sunglasses sit in his dark hair, which he has brushed down into a fringe to hide a receding hairline. His smile is generous, but there's a tightness to it that makes his blue eyes appear too fixed like he's attempting to pin me to the spot just by looking and grinning. He's in thigh-length shorts, flip-flops and a navy workout shirt. Every time I see him, he's dressed similarly, as if he's always prepared should a triathlon spring up.

'I thought I heard you come in,' he looks over my shoulder into the flat. I know it's not about checking if I'm alone, or busy but just because he's one of those people. Needs to know. Needs to feel included. Involved. 'This arrived today for you,' he twinkles.

He holds out a letter. 'Think it's a maintenance bill. I got one similar and yours landed in my post box. He looks beyond me to the birthday card on the breakfast bar. 'It's your birthday?' He doesn't wait for a reply. 'You should have said.'

'I'm having a quiet one. Thanks for bringing this over.' I take the letter from him, put my hand on the door to close it.

'If you're alone, we could have a drink?'

'I've work. Sorry.'

Suddenly, he frowns. 'You okay?'

'Great. It's been a long day.' Raising the letter, I say: 'Thanks for this,' and close the door before he has time to ask any more questions.

Throwing the letter on the counter, I return to the living area, take up the wine, bring it to the kitchen and chuck it down the sink. The day has me beaten, but tomorrow holds promise for the Lydia Callin and possibly the Dolan case. Leads and a plan for The Murder Box. Steve has a long night ahead of him at the Bureau but he's sure he can uncover most of the eighty-five or so IP addresses from the site. He'll have a base for us to begin with come the morning.

I tidy my laptop into my bag, ready for tomorrow. Opening the washing machine, I pull out a load of damp clothes and hang them across the clothes horse near the radiator. Then I head for bed.

I open my bedroom door then stop in the doorway. Something is wrong. The smell. It hits me full in the face, like an assault. I reach around and turn on the light. It feels as though every muscle in my body tenses as I take in what I'm seeing. Bile singes the back of my mouth, my heart punches against my ears.

Over my bed. Blood. Red and savage, on the far wall. Over the bedclothes, the shape of a body but no body as if some bloodied being had laid themselves down for a while before disappearing leaving only a scarlet silhouette on the sheets. My chest burns and I snatch a lungful of air then immediately regret it. The stench claws at my nose – the thick, sickly scent of blood and something else: urine.

There's blood spatter across the walls, a burst of droplets on the headboard. Nausea stirs in my stomach and I can feel the colour in my face, leeching away, drawing down, my limbs growing heavy. I take three steps into the room towards the window, wanting to let air in then stop myself. This is a crime scene. A murder scene. No. The smell is not right. It smells different. What is that? Animal? Make my mind work. Detach myself so that I can see through the eyes of my work. The curtains are closed. My book is still on my bedside locker where I left it two nights ago, the cover now speckled with blood. Nothing has been moved. I don't think. Stepping a little to the side, I push open the door to the en-suite. The towel I used to dry after my morning shower is folded neatly over the radiator. No blood stains streaking the sink. No fingermarks on the mirror. Again, everything in its place.

Wiping sweat from my forehead, I edge out of the bedroom and out of the flat.

CHAPTER 8

The forensics team are here within half an hour. Baz arrives shortly after, beer on his breath and fear on his face.

'What do you mean they're all over the city?' He stares at Keith as if he might grab his shoulders and shake answers out of him.

'Detective Harwood,' Keith says loudly, a blustering rage builds on his cheeks, a warning for Baz to move back. He's in full bunny suit. I'm on the sofa clutching a mug of coffee and hoping this is just some nightmare that will pass over, come the morning. 'It's not my fault youse lot don't dally with the grubbier crimes in the city.'

Baz pulls his chin in defensively. 'What's that supposed to mean?' He towers over Keith, won't even bend his neck to look down at our lead crime-scene officer.

Keith doesn't flinch, even though I know that with little effort Baz could flatten him with a slap if he took a mind to. I should stop them, but who am I to get in the way of them knocking some sense into one another.

'Cut it out,' I hear myself saying. 'What other scenes, Keith?'

A scene-of-crime officer comes out of my room. 'The same, boss, pig's blood.'

'That explains the stench, then,' I mutter.

'As I was trying to tell your partner here,' Keith says with a dismissive wave of his hand towards Baz. 'We've had similar callouts, three to be precise, over the last few weeks. Someone's got a very warped sense of humour. Bleedin' messers with too much time on their hands.'

Baz points towards the open door of my bedroom where a team of SOCOs are methodically going through my possessions. Peeling prints from walls, sifting through drawers, picking up books, objects, photographing, checking latches. 'How did this person even get in here?'

Keith shrugs. 'You're the detective.'

I stand and hold up my hands between them. Keith has lines that he'll cross and lines he won't. His work he shields like a school kid trying to protect his exam paper from a cheating neighbour. He marks up his test sheet and his only. He might give an opinion on ours, if he's asked nicely, but he doesn't like to be wrong and he won't be forced into giving thoughts on something that's not his turf. 'Relax. We're having someone check the locks.'

Keith turns to me. 'In fairness, they're hardly advanced. If someone was prepared, then they could pick it easily enough.'

'My neighbour,' I clear my throat. 'Cedric. He might have seen someone.'

'Let's ask then, shall we?' Baz says.

And I smell the farmyard stink of the blood again. I put down the coffee, stand and tug the legs of my trousers straight. 'I'll talk to him. I look at the door. It's a B&E. Technically.'

'Or a threat,' Baz says.

'Hardly,' I say, but knowing it's true. You don't need a wealth of experience to understand it's not a run of the mill break-in. There's nothing missing to start. Whoever it was, was only interested in one room and then their intent was clearly to terrify. I cast my mind back. I've enemies enough. It might not be a stretch to imagine that every person I've helped put away might have more than a little grievance with me but then I think of the other scenes Keith mentions.

'Any insight into the other scenes? What type of people or houses were hit?'

'Domestic residences all. Elderly gentleman, I remember him. He was shaken up quite a bit by it. A young woman, think she was a trainee nurse. You'll have to dig out the case files for the other one.'

'Any of the victims work in law enforcement?' I ask.

'Not one.'

I nod. 'Can probably rule out a vendetta against the gardaí then.'

'Doesn't make it any less vicious,' Baz says. And I know he's looking out for me but I feel an irrational stab of annoyance at him. He continues, 'This is serious, Frankie. Someone was in here. In your home. Knew your routine—'

'I don't have a routine. As you well know,' I answer. 'And yes, I'm aware that this is my home. I'm aware that someone has been in here.'

Pushing a hand through his hair, he blows out a mouthful of

air. 'Sorry. I know, I know.' He turns away, goes to the kitchen and pours himself a glass of water.

I watch the SOCOs traipse by with armfuls of my bedsheets, a lampshade, brown paper bags with God-knows-what in them. Keith is hovering inside the door, telling his team to get cracking, make sure everything's on camera so they can replay it back at Forensics. Replay my room, line it up like tracing paper over their other cases.

'Did you put this here?' Baz calls out from the kitchen.

I go to his side. Stuck to the fridge door, a red card. 'The Murder Box', it says, in tiny black letters on the front.

Keith comes up behind me. 'Huh,' he says. 'We found those at the other scenes too.'

Baz turns to him, outraged. 'You do know what case we've been working on?'

'As I said, it's not my job to be piecing evidence together,' Keith's small round face flames. He knows he's fucked up. 'You read the reports, the information is there for you. I'm not the detective here.' He shuffles a little, uncertain. 'Besides, it was Harcourt Street that was looking after these cases.'

Baz lets out a long sigh. 'Give me strength.'

Police departments not talking to one another is the rule rather than the exception. Keith's right. Why would this be flagged up to the Bureau? Our murder box has only just come through. We've kept the details of the investigation tight. There's no reason a few cases of morbid vandalism would be flagged to us and no one outside our team would understand the relevance of the red card.

'What else can you remember about the locations of these other scenes?' I ask.

'They were pretty spread out. One down in Donnybrook – one of my colleagues took that one. Another in Kimmage and one in the Maryland area.'

There's always a chance in an investigation like this, where we've possibly got an organized killer set on their path, that eventually they'll turn on the detective pursuing them, but this feels different. Camille Forbes could be right: whether I want it or not, in this killer's mind, I'm a player in this game.

'We'll need to check whether any victims of those other scenes received a box.' I look to Baz, 'Steve's in the office still. Maybe get him to pull the files?'

He nods, pleased to have a task. Removing his phone, he moves to the window and pushes the curtains open to look out on Grafton Street while he talks.

I walk out into the hall, go straight up to Cedric's door. There's not a peep from him. It occurs to me that he can hear the floor squeak as I cross the threshold of my flat but can't hear half of Dublin's crime scene team trundling in and out of my home. I rap on the door. No answer. Rolling out my shoulders, I try to stem my anger. I know it's not his fault. He's not expected to watch over my property while I'm out. I've been telling him with my eyes to back the fuck off since he moved here. But he hasn't. He's poked his nose in at every opportunity. Taken my bloody post into his flat to babysit. He can fucking answer now. I beat against the door again.

'Cedric! It's Frankie. Open up.'

Nothing. Then, 'I'm busy at the moment, Frankie.'

'Open this door. Now!'

There's a sound of shuffling, then footsteps approaching before the latch on the door goes. He opens it a fraction. 'Sorry, Frankie. I really am busy.'

'I need to speak with you.'

'Now's not a good time.'

I reach into my pocket for my badge. 'Make it a good time.'

He stares at the badge, sighs, then opens the door fully.

I step inside and feel an immediate strangeness. His flat is arranged like mine. Sofa positioned in the same place. Coffee table. Same coloured cushions on the sofa, same soft greys on the walls. I've seen this flat before. I viewed it years ago when I first came to look at the building. All the flats were painted beaming white, a blank canvas, furniture not included.

'Tea?' he asks.

I stare at him. 'No.'

He shrugs. 'Hope you don't mind if I do. It helps calm me down.'

'You do realize what's going on next door?'

'I saw some commotion,' he nods at the door. 'Through the look-hole thing.' He shakes his head, the dark glasses buried in his hair catch a beam of light from the ceiling. 'What is it called?' he frowns. 'Peephole sounds . . . dirty.' He acts out a shiver.

'You saw some commotion?'

'Guards. Those forensic people. I don't want to get involved in whatever it is. I don't know anything. You know me, Frankie, I keep myself to myself.'

Like shite, he does. 'Where were you today? This evening.'

He pours boiling water into a mug, then takes up the paper

99

label of the tea bag, swirls it a few times before looping the string around the inside of the mug handle. He adds a drop of cold water from the tap, then cupping long fingers around the mug, takes a sip. He sighs. 'I was working. I was here. I'm writing a book,' he points to the only piece of furniture that fails to match my own: a thin-legged table, propped up against the window and on it, one of those easy-carry laptops. Beside the computer a notebook and a tin that holds a handful of pens and next to that, a pair of heavy-duty headphones. 'They're noise-cancelling,' he says, chinning the air towards the headphones. 'I don't hear a thing when they're on.' He approaches, mug still in hand, but reaches out with the other, looking down into my face with concern. 'Sorry. You're not hurt, are you?'

'No.'

He relaxes, as if that makes it okay.

I hear Baz calling for me and I close the door. 'Have you left your flat at all today?'

He gives out a short laugh. 'What?'

'I have a few questions.'

'We're neighbours, Frankie. There's no reason to be so formal. I'll help. Any way I can. I just get nervous around . . . drama. It gives me anxiety, even when it has nothing to do with me. I know that probably makes me somewhat . . .' again, looking for the right word, 'cowardly, I guess, but I like to wear life lightly. Can you understand that?'

'No.'

He smiles. 'Of course not.'

'It's my flat. Someone broke into my home. Took the time, at a leisurely and considered pace to spatter pig's blood over my

100

bedroom walls, soaked my bed with it, turned my flat into what looks like a murder scene. So, if it's okay with you, I think I'll take that seriously.'

His eyes are darkening the skin around his lips and nose paling. He makes a retching sound, heaves a little into his fist, then suddenly cups his palm over his mouth. A sharp glance that could be pleading, then he runs to the bathroom, tea sloshing over his hand.

After a moment, once the sounds have settled down, I tap gently on the bathroom door. 'Cedric?'

'Could you make me another peppermint tea, please? My stomach is a little dodgy.'

Jesus. I go to the kitchen. Kettle in the same spot. The kettle is the same charcoal colour as mine. And, hang on, I lean closer, also the same make as mine. Tightness in my chest. Not sure who to trust but if Cedric knows anything then we need to know too. I flick the kettle on, fingers tapping on the counter, comparing similarities. Fruit bowl in the centre of the breakfast bar. Same. Except his is full. Plums, oranges, grapes, bananas, fresh and gleaming under the overhead lights. TV in same position, radio next to cooker. I open the fridge. Stacked full. Some white fish sitting in a bowl of marinade, covered in cling film.

I go to the bedroom, open the door, bed against the inside wall, white sheets, same pale grey walls, dark blackout curtains. A row of trainers arranged neatly under the window. Wooden shelves on the wall facing the end of the bed. Same. Except mine hold a collection of novels that I reread when I can't sleep. Comfort. His hold a potted plant, some kind of ivy, foliage spilling over the edge. A candle. A selection of manuals on sleep, self-help books and triathlons.

Another cough barks out from the bathroom and the flush goes. I hurry back to the kitchen, open the drawer where I expect to find cutlery but there are towels instead. Finally, I locate a spoon in the second drawer. Then the tea bags. I open the cupboard next to the fridge, cereal boxes, muesli and a large tub of protein powder. The synthetic chocolate smell sticks in my throat. I find an array of teas next to the cooker and locate the box of peppermint tea. By the time Cedric exits the toilet, the tea is made, the menthol scent steaming from the cup.

'Oh, thanks,' he says. 'I'm sorry about that.' He takes the cup gratefully. 'I have a condition – hyperesthesia; it makes me very sensitive to . . . description.'

'Description?'

He presses his fingertips to his mouth. 'You were describing the inside of your room. I can't think about that,' he says firmly, closes his eyes and appears to swallow away any thoughts about the shitshow that is my flat next door.

'How did you know where to position your furniture?'

'I'm sorry?' He looks around the room, follows my gaze to the kettle, then flushes, taps his head. 'I tried to imagine the space differently, but once I'd seen yours, I couldn't. I've seen it – the first time, remember? When I'd just moved in. You hadn't called round so I brought you—'

'The honey cake.'

He beams. 'Yeah, a family recipe.' He nods, then when he sees I'm less than interested in the honey cake, he says: 'It just seems like that's where everything should go. You had questions?'

'Did you go out today?'

'I got up, had a shake, went for a run. Eight miles out to the coast and along the sea front and back. It rained. Grabbed an espresso from the coffee shop down the street on the way back. Came up here, had a shower. Ate a banana, then sat down at my computer to write and haven't moved much since.' A finger goes up. 'Nope, sorry, I tell a lie. I made an omelette for lunch, had fish for dinner and marinaded another fillet for tomorrow then returned to the desk. Didn't hear or see anything.'

'Right.'

'I really can't with those headphones on.'

The adrenalin, or whatever it was that drove me to Cedric's door, has seeped out of my blood. The need for answers. To charge someone. To get someone for the invasion of my privacy.

'How did they get in?' I murmur more to myself, but he answers.

'Wait until another tenant enters, catch the door, wait in the foyer until they go up, then follow and pick the lock. Or had you anyone do any work there recently? Heating, fitting a cupboard?'

'No,' I say. Either someone managed to pick the locks – unlikely – or, I swallow, they have a key.

There is a firm knock on the door followed by Baz's voice: 'Mr Cole? Gardaí. Can you open up please?'

CHAPTER 9

I look around the hotel room. If the reason for being here wasn't so hideous, it wouldn't have been a bad place to spend the night. Wide bed. Sleek, polished furniture. A two-seater and table at the end of the room on which there's a small, round glass bowl containing three fat roses. Cream and tipped with pink. I'm going to have to ignore this charge on my credit card. I thought about staying in my own flat last night, if only for the sake of not letting whoever did this win, but I couldn't bear it. The shock of the invasion. The tramping of Crime Scene in and out of the door, the debris of forensics, black dust on the handles, little square stickers left behind on the bed, on the floor, the mirror. The violation loomed in the air, all the warmth of my home let out. But we're a day down in this game, and if our killer had in mind that a roaring scene of violence would make me stumble, they're wrong. I shove the last of my clothes into my bag, disconnect my charger and phone from the bedside socket and head for the Bureau.

Four crime scenes. Identical. Almost. Differences only due

to the shape of the bedrooms. All signed off with The Murder Box calling card. Forensics say the blood spatter matches that of a knife attack but other than that they gave us little we already know. There are no prints, not a trace of evidence. No victims. Or dead ones, I should say. The residents of these locations are victims, of course. All of them will be traumatized by what has happened. One, a man in his eighties, a widower, living alone in a quiet cul-de-sac in Donnybrook hasn't returned to his house. The for-sale sign went up in days after the break-in and he's now living in a retirement home along the Waterford coastline. Steve has been in touch with all of the break-in victims and said that none of them had received a murder box. And again, it prompted me to think about Camille Forbes and her list of checks for a murder-mystery game. Some *elements are true pieces. Others could be red herrings.*

By the time I get onto the office floor, all the scenes are pinned on the case board, alongside photos of The Murder Box contents. Teddy Dolan's picture remains at the centre, Lydia Callin's sombre grey gaze peering out next to him. A large map of Dublin is beneath it all, yellow markers where Teddy Dolan and Lydia Callin were last seen.

Cedric was none too happy when Baz directed Keith's team into his flat. Nor did he appreciate the mouth swab which left him running for the bathroom again. But his day checked out. We tracked his progress on the laptop that evening, verified where he'd grabbed his coffee after his run, but more than that it quickly became clear that there was no way Cedric had the stomach to do what was done in my flat.

'What've we got, Steve?' I ask.

He collects a set of index cards from his desk. 'We're making good progress. I've had a good look over the site, managed to trace quite a few of the IP addresses that have subscribed. I'm thinking there's a vetting filter of sorts. I contacted the network providers, but they won't release names or addresses until we've a warrant.

'Get on that.'

'Already in hand, Chief. And we should have some names from the site within the hour. Don't worry, we'll take this game apart.'

'I know they said they didn't receive a murder box but run the names of the break-in victims against whatever you find.'

'Yes, I'd already a mind to,' he says. 'I'm sorry about your gaff, Chief.'

'Thanks,' I reply. 'I was thinking about something Camille said about various elements of the game being red herrings.'

'You're thinking that's what these crime scenes are?'

'As we've not been able to establish a reason for them then it could be a diversion to get us to spend time, resources where we don't need to, to set us back.'

He holds up a finger. 'They could also be clues. After what happened last night, Mullins had the idea that if this is part of the game, it might be worth setting each of the locations of the break-ins on a map. See what it says, if anything. The other three crime scenes mentioned by Keith. Donnybrook,' he pushes a red pin into the map. 'Maryland,' he moves his hand northwest, locates the address. 'Kimmage and, of course, yours, Grafton Street.' He stands back, folds his arms, surveys the map. 'Interesting, don't you think?'

'You could draw a circle through them.'

'That's what I thought.'

'So the scenes are not random?'

'Doesn't look like it to me. They're all south of the Liffey. Whoever did this must've been watching those homes or at least studied the routines of the owners.' He pauses, chews on his bottom lip.

'What is it?'

'I don't know, just there's something of a board-game layout to it, don't you think?'

I look up at the pins on the map. Then over at the case board provided by The Murder Box. The fog shifts briefly, and I can make out a silhouette of who this person is. The arrogance. The utter commitment. I can feel the fizz of their excitement run down my arms. The catch in my chest at the sheer breadth of what they're daring. They set the ball bouncing into the darkness and look. Look! At all these people running after it.

'I've had Mullins dig a bit deeper on a geoprofile of the offender, what we know of them based on the locations of where they hit, and I reckon we're looking for someone in an address or affiliated with somewhere around here.' He turns his finger around the middle of the circle.

'That's good work. Well done,' I say.

Baz is at my side, phone in hand and huffing and puffing with some new frustration. 'First, Keith phoned just before you came in. Obviously, the guilt has got to him for missing the relevance of the card as he's got clean-up under way already. And we've just finished with your landlord, Larry Gallagher.'

I take a moment to tell Steve to let me know as soon as he has our list of suspects, then lead Baz out of earshot.

'Well?'

'Said he was broken into a month back,' he tells me. 'Computer snatched and a box of tools stolen. The computer was found dumped in a bin, next street over from his house. He didn't realize that the spare keys to your building were also missing until we contacted him.'

I take a deep breath. 'Fucking eejit.'

'My thoughts exactly. He was all "what harm", until I suggested that any one of his tenants could submit a claim for the trauma, and it would be best he get in touch with his insurance company to make sure he's covered. Practically shat himself then.'

'Good.'

'Breakthrough of sorts, I suppose. He did get a couple of officers out at the time. They took statements. Our suspect, if it is the same person, was perhaps a little less careful at your landlord's joint than he was at yours. The officers called out got a nice print from inside the back window of the Gallagher place. Clear as the wrinkles on Jack Clancy's forehead.'

'It almost makes having my bedroom thrashed with pig's blood worth it.' There's a scuffle on the far side of the office floor and I look over to see Paul push back quickly from his desk, his left hand stopping his coffee cup from rolling to the floor, the other desperately rescuing papers from the desk in front of him. He plucks a handful of tissues from a box beside his computer and begins feverishly dabbing at his keyboard. I turn back to Baz, 'Have we run the print through the database?'

'Yes. No hits.'

'Well, that would be asking too much. But at least we have it.'

'Chief?' Paul calls from across the room. I glance over, nod to let him know I've heard him.

'I don't even know where my landlord lives,' I say to Baz, wanting to know exactly how far this perp had travelled to gain access to my flat.

'Kilbarrack,' Baz answers, watching the expression on my face carefully.

I turn away, look at the case board. 'That's north of the Liffey, outside what we'd hoped was our area of interest,' I say, drawing a circle in the air over the pins Steve has just placed in the map.

'From the look of the report on the other break-ins, they were all one storey or ground floor. Yours wouldn't have been so straight forward. I can see why they'd put in the extra leg work for the keys.' He peers at the map on the caseboard and is about to say something when Paul comes up beside us.

'Sorry, Chief. We got something—'

I hold up a hand. 'Just a minute, Paul.'

Baz taps the map, gives me a hopeful look. I'm thinking he's seen another angle to open this case up but instead he goes for a shot at making me feel better. 'Your landlord's could be just another break-in, the keys taken in the heat of the moment by your run-of-the-mill burglar,' he says.

'Unlikely,' I say. 'Whoever wanted to mess up my flat needed the keys, entry to the building and that was that,' I say. 'The other break-ins, have we asked any of victims if they knew of or had met Lydia Callin?'

'Chief?' Paul says again, a finger going up.

109

Baz says: 'Yes, none of them have heard of her.'

'Chief!' Paul shouts and immediately his face flames. 'Sorry, Chief. Sorry,' he says, redness building in his cheeks. 'Dolan's phone hit a mast about two hours ago.'

'What? Where?' I rush to his desk.

He shuffles after me, then bends over his desk, reaches for a handful of damp coffee-stained tissues and dumps them into a wire bin next to his chair. 'Near Clonskeagh,' he says.

He hits a key on the computer and once again, I'm looking at a map of Dublin and its suburbs. Clonskeagh is only a pin-prick on the map, a mix of industrial developments and residential property, easy to get to the city, plenty of greenery about.

'What's the range?'

'Five miles.'

The rest of the team have their heads down, already scouring the traffic cams and alerting any units we have in the area. At the next station, Steve has our Facebook page open and is typing out a reminder for the public that Teddy Dolan is still missing and to call this number should they see him.

Dolan's phone has likely been found or nicked, sold on to some poor fool who we'll drag into custody, only to release him a few hours later, when some red-top will pay to print his sorry tale about the time he was questioned about celebrity Teddy Dolan's murder and he was staring down the line at twenty-five years, all for making a fucking phone call. But discounting the tentative link between Lydia Callin's murder and Dolan's disappearance, this is the first bubble of hope we've had on the Dolan investigation in almost two weeks and I'm going to hold it down until it pops.

110

I look to Helen. 'Who're Dolan's contacts there? Do we know of any?'

'No friends or relatives in the area on our list,' she says.

For the first time this morning, I feel the steadiness return to my hands. 'Baz, get a couple of firearms issued, tog up—' Then to Paul, 'Broaden the analysis for all routes out of Dublin South and West, might be late coming in, but at the very least, it'll give us a direction to follow.' A breath. 'Go back, the week before he went missing, see if his phone has been in that area previously. Get Mullins to go through his contacts again, and Lydia Callin's too, for the Clonskeagh area.' I throw in, 'Hotels, hostels, where they could have met up. Helen, put out an alert to local stations to send a unit out. They might just get there before us. Put a stop and search on the main route heading back towards the city.' If there's a chance we can secure Dolan, not only to have him back in one piece but to have a living witness to all of this, then it's worth rattling coins out of our budget. 'Thanks, Paul.' I pause then add quietly, 'Make sure to feed back to the officers running stop and search that we could be looking for Dolan's remains in a vehicle.'

Collecting my vest from the back of my office door, I shrug it on, then hurry towards the lift.

'Frankie,' Baz calls from behind me. He's not moved. Tapping his phone against his thigh he says, 'I was going to pop out for a couple of hours, maybe Ryan or someone could take this one.'

'This is the first decent lead we've had on Dolan.' I study his face, unsure why he's wanting to step aside for the second time in two days. 'Is everything okay?'

He looks towards Ryan's desk then back, keeping his eyes

111

down as if he's working on re-ordering something in his mind. A quick glance at the screen on his mobile, then he shakes his head, pockets the phone. 'Yeah, no. Actually, it's fine,' he says. 'Gemma had wanted to meet, is all. Let's go.' He grabs his coat. 'My vest is in the car,' he says and sweeps ahead of me out the door.

When I get to the car, he already has the engine running. The moment I close the door, he speeds up the ramp and out on to the Dublin streets, hitting the sirens as he goes.

I get Paul on the radio. 'You get that stop and search up?'

'Dundrum patrol is out and not available. I'm still trying Donnybrook.'

Probably eating sandwiches somewhere with a nice view. 'Patch me through to Dundrum.'

'Yes, Ma'am.'

Baz is quiet, eyes on the road ahead.

'Firearms?'

'Sorry. A bit too eager to leave. I've a taser,' he says, flicking a glance towards the back seat.

'I guess if the other guy has a taser too, we'll be alright then so.'

'Don't knock 'em, till you've had one of those prongs lodged in your thigh,' he says.

I point to the right. 'Head out via Milltown. If Donnybrook gets going, they can come down the other side and hopefully we might be able to get a signal on the phone.'

'Dundrum station,' a female voice says in my ear.

'This is Detective Chief Superintendent Frankie Sheehan, I need a unit to head to Clonskeagh immediately, please.'

There's the sound of distant laughter and I hear her mutter 'Would you fuck off' to someone, followed by more laughter.

'Hello?' I ask.

A throat clear, 'Sorry, Ma'am, our patrol car is out presently. I can patch you through to the next station?'

'Where are they?'

'Sorry, who?'

'Where is the patrol car?'

'Um, let me see.' We hit a series of road humps and I brace myself against the roof. 'They were called out, ah, near Clonskeagh. Oh,' a note of surprise. 'Human remains.'

'I need that address,' I say, pulling a map out of the glove compartment and finding Clonskeagh.

'Yes, yes. Of course, Ma'am. Right, got it here. It's along the river.'

I find the river on the map. 'The Dodder?'

'That's it. Near the old paper mills.'

I hang up, look to Baz. 'I know it,' he says, indicating to overtake a lorry, his foot squeezing down on the accelerator.

The sun is attempting to break through an overcast sky and occasionally a beam of yellow warmth slides over the windscreen before a turn of the road takes us into shade again. Looking out at the morning traffic, I think on what it could mean to have Dolan's phone activate where human remains were just located. Some killers can't help themselves. They return to the body so they can relive their crime. Others go back to make sure they haven't been found out. There is the chance the remains we'll find here are unrelated to our case but the likelihood is we're about to find Teddy Dolan's body. I'm ashamed of the brief flash

113

of relief I feel. After all Teddy Dolan must have suffered this is not the end we want. And just as I think that, Lydia Callin's face pushes into my mind because there's a chance that it's her we'll find here. There's a chance that, even as the clock ticks down on the murder box game, we'll soon be able to verify Lydia Callin's murder.

CHAPTER 10

The mills no longer exist. Flattened some time after they closed in 2005; the gap in the street filled in with grey boarding. We pull up and get out.

Clonskeagh. The site of the old mills is flanked by the road on one side. The road is wide and busy, it gives me some hope that we might be able to find witnesses to whoever dumped the body. From the map, I know that the river Dodder cuts a narrow path on the far side of the site. There are a few houses nearby and across the road, a large commercial building is partially hidden by a row of trees.

The forensics van is here already. A SOCO stands at the back of the van. She heaves a clear bag of what looks like rubbish into the open doors.

'Come on,' I say to Baz. I find my ID and get out of the car.

'DCS Frankie Sheehan from the Bureau for Serious Crime,' I say when I approach the scene-of-crime officer.

She straightens away from the van, loosens the zip on her suit, glances at my ID. 'Ashra Campbell. Technical Bureau,' she answers in a soft Scottish accent. As we draw near, another SOCO appears at her side. 'This is my colleague Kate Boyne.'

'What've you got?'

'Two suitcases. A torso and arms in one, head and legs in the other. The coroner has just left, we're about to take the remains in.'

'Male or female?' I ask.

'Looks to be female. Found by a group of teens this morning. White as ghosts the three of them were by the time we showed up.'

'Where are they now?'

'At the station, I'd expect.' She zips her suit back up, hands us each a suit and a pair of foot covers, gestures that we should follow her. 'We got everything we could from the inner cordon, save the suitcases themselves, but you can never be too cautious.'

I thread my legs into the bunny suit, slip the covers over my shoes. Baz does the same, then donning gloves, we follow Ashra Campbell around the side of the site and through a gap in the boarding.

The area is a concrete wasteland, an empty footprint of where the mills once stood, the outline of the buildings picked out in pale lines on the ground. The trees and bushes along the banks of the river are flush with leaf still, a spring green, even though we're heading into autumn. The River Dodder is brown and low, too shallow to carry something as weighty as the suitcases downriver.

'The cases were backed up on the weir there,' Ashra says. 'There was a fair bit of debris caught behind them. The kids

116

were drinking there,' she points to the bank next to the weir. The area is marked off by a strip of blue and white tape that beats in the light breeze. The weir itself stretches at an angle across the water and is only a couple of feet deep. A little way off, near the bank, a couple of gardaí are talking beneath the canopy of wiry young ash trees. 'They didn't see the cases at first,' Ashra goes on, 'but then they decided to go paddling or some other nonsense. Anyways, somehow the cases got dislodged and curiosity killed the cats,' she gives a little chuckle at her own joke, then coughs to clear it. 'Sorry, need a bit of humour in these jobs, as I'm sure you know. They opened one, saw what was inside and called it in immediately. They won't be wiping that from their minds for a while, that's for sure.'

'Cause of death?'

'You'll have to wait for the PE for that. It looks like they've been in the water for weeks. Hard to say whether they were thrown in here or further up the river, but I'm inclined to say here. The sergeant there said that after the hot spell the river's been low for most of the summer and it's not quite recovered.'

'Detectives,' one of the guards shouts as he approaches. 'Sergeant John Crilly,' he puts out a hand to Baz.

'Detective Harwood,' Baz says, holding up his gloved hands, 'and this is—'

'Not the way the day started, eh?' John says finishing Baz's sentence with a wink and bestowing me a quick glance, 'How ya?' at me, then back to Baz: 'They're over here,' he waves us on. 'This is Malachy,' he gestures to his comrade. 'Would youse mind signing in?'

Malachy passes a clipboard to me and I sign us in.

'You have any missing person cases over the last few weeks, Sergeant Crilly?' I ask.

He hooks his thumbs on the edges of his white suit. 'We're in convo with Donnybrook but nothing stands out. Nothing active on the books. Probably someone got mixed up with the wrong crowd. We've got the three young fellas down at the station. We were just saying, weren't we Mal, that they know more than they're letting on.' He keeps his attention on Baz as he speaks like I'm barely there. I'm feeling a glow of warmth around the idea of writing up my report later, where every error he's made in the infancy of this discovery will be highlighted and then some. And I know there'll be errors because I can practically smell the laziness coming off this eejit.

'Doubtful,' I say.

He gives me a withering look. 'It's a known fact that killers return to the scene of the crime.'

'Thank you,' I say. 'Although they're less inclined to phone in their own crime.' I turn to Ashra Campbell. 'Have you alerted the pathologist's office?'

'They're expecting us within the hour.'

Crilly looks from me to Ashra with some confusion.

'Right, erm, this way,' Crilly says.

The suitcases are lying on a square of blue plastic by the edge of the river. Black in colour, but algae has grown green over the sides, so that you can make out how far the water reached over the fabric. A tangle of weeds are caught around the wheels of one. They are closed over but through the open zip, I can make out a sliver of grey skin.

'Talk about what's in the box,' Baz says into my ear.

118

I hunker down to get a closer look. Crilly makes a retching sound and steps back.

'You okay, Sergeant?' I ask.

He coughs into his hand. 'I'm fine.'

I get closer still. 'You've taken photographs already?' I ask Ashra.

'Pictures and video.'

Baz already has his phone out and is snapping pictures to send straight back to the Bureau. The suitcases are identical; cheap, plastic wheels, a plastic logo stuck to the front. Taking a quick breath, I open the nearest. The smell of death, rotting flesh and the earthy, damp stench of river water floats up and soaks the air. Crilly coughs again but holds his ground. The first suitcase contains head and legs. Only the jaw of the face is visible; the rest, or what's left of it, is covered with matted dark hair.

'No teeth,' I say to Baz. 'From what I can make out.'

'Young woman, looks like,' he replies.

I blow out a mouthful of air. 'Hard to say, there's a lot of decomp. Lydia Callin had an implant, lower incisor on the right. Don't know if the pathologist will be able to find evidence of that. We need this escalated,' I say to Ashra. 'An ID of the body and cause of death as soon as possible.'

'Now, hang on,' Crilly says, objecting to me giving the order.

I stand. Face him. 'Have you a problem with the remains being examined, Sergeant?'

His chin draws in, producing more chins above his collar. 'Of course not, but—'

Moving around to the other case, I bend and open it. Torso and arms in late-stage decomposition. I lean over the case,

119

try to see through the loose, sagging flesh over the ribcage. Baz follows.

'The sternum looks intact,' Baz says, his face scrunched up. 'Thought it might be broken up, you know, for the heart.'

'They could've gone up and through the diaphragm,' I make a swooping motion with my hand to indicate my meaning.

Ashra steps forward, her assistant with her. 'You think you know who this is?'

'Possibly. Let Dr James know to contact me once she is ready to start the exam, would you?'

'Is there something in particular you want her to look for?'

I look down at the remains, think of the histology slide that came with The Murder Box and the sliver of tissue that was trapped on the glass. 'The heart,' I say.

We move away. I peel the gloves from my hands, wipe sweat from my palms and battle hope from both sides that we've found Lydia Callin's body and we haven't. Using the plastic sheet to protect the suitcases, Ashra and Kate go about getting the remains up and into their van. And I let Sergeant Crilly know that he may put his feet up and hang around until we can get a couple of officers out to man the site. He takes to that as well as I expect.

'Well, hold on there a minute. This is my case,' he says and again looks to Baz, a mix of incredulity and annoyance on his face.

I take the clipboard from Malachy, sign us out. 'We'll be taking it from here.'

'I'll be talking to your superior,' he threatens, the skin over his jaw turning an unhealthy mottle of purple and pink.

'I am my superior, Sergeant.'

By the time we leave, the unit from Donnybrook has arrived. The pair exit the car slowly, donning their hats and straightening stab vests. They saunter on down the path towards us like time was never an issue for either the living or the dead. The first to approach is older, not so much grey as white around the temples, that drowned-out paleness around his eyes and into his top lip that tells me retirement is sniffing distance away. His partner, also male, stops beside him, tucks his hands in through the armholes of his stab vest, as if to warm them, then looks up at the older guard and waits for him to speak.

'Garda Mooney and this is Garda Williams. We were out on traffic.'

'You're on door-to-door,' I say, glossing over the introduction and pointing to the nearby residences. 'I want all names and numbers of the residents and what they've seen over the last month. Anyone coming and going. Construction workers, whatever.'

He looks out over the houses, sniffs in a breath. 'We know who the vic is?'

'Not yet. You need anything, you discover anything, you contact me here.' I hand him my card.

'What are you thinking?' Baz says, getting into the driver's seat.

'Lydia Callin,' I say.

'Any sign of Dolan's phone in those bags?'

'Not that I could see, but I sorely doubt it'd be sending out a signal if it were.' The reason for Teddy Dolan's phone putting blips on our radar is becoming clear. 'Whoever dumped those suitcases in that river didn't want us to miss out on the discovery of this body which again makes me think that this is Lydia Callin.'

'Or they want us to think Teddy Dolan is behind it.' He pauses. 'Or he *is* behind it? Nothing more from Paul?'

I check my phone. 'No.'

He starts the engine. We watch Ashra and Kate ease their evidence into the back of their van.

'Perhaps it is Dolan. Been missing for the right amount of time. Now his phone is pinging on masts just as it's likely Lydia Callin's body is found,' I say.

On the other side of the street, the driveways are empty. Residents still at work. On the outside wall of one of the street-side houses, a huge billboard: *The Gathering 2013. Be Part of It.* A stab at boosting the country's economy by calling Irish abroad home. A couple of teenagers kick a ball between them as they make their way down the pavement, sports bags hooked over their shoulders, legs muddied from their game.

'If this is not down to Dolan, do you think our perp could be a resident here? Watching from one of the houses?' I ask.

'Could be. Lives here, works in the city.'

'If we think of the geoprofile, this would be right along the bottom of our zone.'

Baz glances at his mirrors, eases the car out onto the road. 'How accurate is that though?'

'Not sure in this case, but we can say with some confidence that our perp has a vehicle. When we look at the locations of the break-ins, bring in Lydia's home address, we have a hotspot region near the centre where the killer is likely to live, work or frequent. Hard to know how useful it is here until we get some new information. Some of the theories are notional, reliant on certain assumptions that a criminal will only travel so far to commit a crime. Distance-decay factor. If these,' I nod out the window towards the mills, 'are Lydia Callin's remains and related to The Murder Box, we're looking at a series of offences all contained roughly within a region of south Dublin that's approximately two miles radius.'

'Just a hundred thousand or so suspects, then so,' he says, grimly.

'No. Eighty-five. And I'd say we'll have that number whittled down very soon.'

CHAPTER 11

I sip coffee, keep my eyes on the scene below me, for once grateful I've missed lunch. Abigail James, with the help of her assistant works over the body on the chrome table in front of them. The DNA results from the fragment of heart muscle and the hair samples we retrieved from the brush in Lydia's room came through an hour ago. There is no doubt that the histology slide contained in The Murder Box displays cardiac tissue belonging to Lydia Callin. And once the postmortem is done, we'll be able to confirm that these are her remains.

Two new threads have appeared on the murder game website. One asks about the skills needed to put together the histology slide, which then spawned a discussion on whether the heart tissue was symbolic – was there a spurned lover involved? And another, suggesting that the earrings could have been a gift from the killer. Helen has already run searches for the earrings. They were mass produced and sold at every affordable accessory store a few years ago. The heart? We can't say with certainty that it's not symbolic. But looking at how the game is set up, I don't think that's what we're dealing with. Vengeful ex-partner? Possibly. But the heart cut up like this, I think it's as cold as, it made a good fit for the game. A nice slice of shock-factor for us to unveil once the penny began to drop on what the box really contained.

'We been in touch with Joe Callin yet?' Jack Clancy is leaning up against the far wall, choosing to watch the post-mortem examination via a TV monitor.

Baz, not the greatest fan of an autopsy, has returned to the Bureau.

'No,' I say to Jack. 'I wanted to wait until we were sure.'

He sighs, sags a little. 'Never fucking stops, does it?' Echoing Baz's sentiments yesterday.

I trained myself long ago not to look up and out too far. With murder, you can always rely on the hands to come round again. For us, that means more cases but for the family of the victim, only one case matters and that's my focus now: Lydia Callin and justice for her father.

'Who the fuck takes a young woman like that, dices her up to be chucked away in a river?' The colour rises in his face as he speaks. 'Like a bloody sweet wrapper.' He loosens the tie at his throat.

'The teeth were removed,' I say, nodding down towards the body. 'Neve Jameson mentioned that Lydia had a false tooth. She'd knocked her own out on her knee as a kid. If that is Lydia Callin, then whoever killed her could've known that. Didn't want her identified.'

'Unusual in the grander scheme of crime, but not so much for cases like this, where an identification could lead us straight to a perp,' he replies. And he's right. There's a reason we come at cases victim-first. You know all you can about the last movements of your victim, it's not long before you bump up against a suspect.

I go on: 'Dolan's phone lights up in Clonskeagh at the same time a group of teenagers are discovering Dolan's girlfriend's remains.' I take the time to throw him a meaningful look. 'If the aim was to lead us to her remains, or flag it to the Bureau, then why remove the teeth? On the one hand we have the killer dangling the carrot, but at the same time attempting to hide the identity of the victim.'

Clancy blows out a mouthful of air. 'Or Dolan himself fucked up. Turned his phone on without thinking. Went back for a gander – wouldn't be the first killer who returned to gloat over their victims, waving a flag at us as he goes.' He moves closer to the screen as he speaks, eyes fixed on the proceedings below. 'You know what my mammy used to say to me when I was little? Hard to believe now but I was a worrier. I could conjure up all sorts of monsters and darkness happening, night or day. And if it wasn't monsters, it was danger. Everywhere I saw it. Life was a waiting catastrophe.

'She'd say, "Common things happen commonly, Jack. Don't be worrying about what might never happen, what's fanciful or unlikely." Probably why I headed for the force in the end. I needed to see the worst in a way. And you know what I saw? The worst, sure, but mostly, it's just bad fuckers doing bad things. Not fanciful. Just human greed, jealousy or fucking weakness. If Teddy Dolan's phone came on in Clonskeagh, a man who's been missing for over a month, and now his lover's body has turned up there, then I'd say it's Teddy Dolan who's put her there.'

He reaches out and angles the monitor a little.

Abigail is slowly reporting her findings: 'Left external auditory canal is absent. Due to decomposition, it's impossible to say whether the tissue was removed ante- or post-mortem, but the edges of the wound are clean and uniform, suggesting that the ear was cut off rather than torn.

'Despite the degradation of the tissue, there's significant bruising visible in the skin over the left maxilla and a notable depression at the left infraorbital region. Radiological examination reveals a moderate fracture of the orbital floor on the left and under histological examination there is some early osteoblast activity around the fracture site, suggesting that it was ante-mortem and possibly a couple of days old at the time of death. All teeth have been removed. Not possible to say whether ante- or post-mortem; however, lack of effusion in the gums suggests post.'

Clancy removes a notebook from his breast pocket. He opens it, takes a pen from his pocket and makes a couple of marks on the page in front of him.

I press the intercom. 'Have the fingerprints been preserved?'

Abigail glances up at me then moves down the table to where her assistant supports the torso as she assesses the hands. 'No tissue,' she glances at her assistant who turns over the opposite palm.

Jack massages the back of his neck. 'Perhaps Dolan saw those boys heading towards the paper mills, knew what they'd find and thought he could somehow walk back to his old life. Frame the kids who found her.'

'It doesn't explain the box though, Jack.'

'You don't know what little schemes a fella like Dolan might be into.'

'But why?'

'For the disturbed mind the question might as well be, why not? This. This'd be a grand alibi all the same. How could he have done this and be strung up somewhere by a lunatic?'

'Not sure arresting Dolan for his own abduction and a young woman's murder is quite the feather in the cap our dear commissioner was hoping for.'

He breathes out a sigh of longing. Gets a faraway look in his eyes then snaps out of it. 'I guess Hegarty's not the worst. At least she does her job. Used to be one years ago, thought his job was best run from the nineteenth hole at the K club.'

'What I'd give for Donna Hegarty to develop a sudden passion for golf.'

He laughs, then his face becomes serious as Abigail begins to cut through the ribs. She doesn't waste time in beginning to look for the heart, and after a few seconds, she looks up and shakes her head.

'No heart,' she says. Her assistant holds out a steel bowl and she lifts a mass from the chest cavity. 'The left lung, both upper and lower lobes, have been cut away from the bronchial tree, the diaphragm shows some evidence of disruption.' She continues to search, removes a mass of tissue and places it gently in another steel bowl. She turns it over, assesses its integrity.

'What was the time frame you were looking at, detectives?' she asks.

I lean on the intercom button. 'She went missing on the tenth of August.'

'That could be about right,' she says. 'But I can't be conclusive. Especially with it cut up like this. If the conditions had been different, temperatures lower, then perhaps we'd be able to give you an exact date – but we've had some pretty mild weather over the last month and you said that the cases were found partially submerged, right? Hot, damp and outdoors: the perfect environment for decomposition.'

Clancy removes his notebook again. I watch as he moves down the short list he's written out. I recognize the results of the post-mortem from The Murder Box. He draws a line under the date.

Steve almost drags me to his desk when I return to the Bureau. 'I managed to get the numbers of the IP addresses listed on the site. I tried calling the first three, no answer. Finally got through to Louise Johnson, nurse, part-time, lives in Cork with her ten-year-old son. I told her I was from customer services and wanted to see how they were finding being part of The Murder Box. She hadn't the foggiest what I was on about. I asked her if her son could've subscribed and she said not a chance, that their internet is locked unless she's present. I wasn't sure whether we could trust that fully, knowing that as a boy, if I really wanted something, I'd find a way to get it, so I tried another subscriber. Woman, sixties this time, no clue what I was on about either. And again with the next. We could go through the entire list to make sure, but I'm pretty confident none of the people I contacted are part of The Murder Box, nor had they heard of it before I called them.'

'Have we any names?'

'I was getting to that. I thought maybe someone had just

taken a bunch of IP addresses and fed them into the system, to make the game appear more popular than it is, encourage more subscribers or whatever. I'd a look at when they got their membership, when they logged on, if ever. And turns out, all these IP addresses do log in, but at the same time. Like they're one big entity.'

'What's that mean?'

'I'd think it's a kind of cloaking system. Or our perp hoped it would be. The addressees that log on simultaneously only count seventy-nine subscribers.'

'Seventy-nine?'

'Yes. Five players have logged on randomly. At all hours. And your address.'

Is it going to be this easy? Although saying that, discounting me, having five persons of interest is a fucking eureka moment that should carve its way into bloody history after starting out with eighty-five, but even if we get a suspect out of that, we still need to link them to Lydia Callin's disappearance, and if the postmortem examination is anything to go by, murder.

Steve tears a page from the notebook on his desk. 'Five players,' he says with a smile and hands me the sheet. 'And here are their names and addresses.'

We add the five players to the case board. Ashley Noone, twenty, Harrison Lloyd, twenty-two, James Mayfield, twenty, Pippa Dunne, twenty-two, Derek Cohen, twenty-one. Mullins stares up at their faces, his hands stuck on his hips.

'They're so young,' he says. Part of me envies his naivety.

'Home addresses a bit further afield, but they're all second-year students at Trinity, bar one – Pippa Dunne, who's third year,' Steve says.

'All at the same uni?'

'Yes.'

'Isn't that cosy?'

He grins. 'I thought so. I couldn't find much interaction between them beyond the murder box site.'

'Interesting.'

'The question is, do we bring them in?' he asks.

I know why he's hesitant. Besides accessing the site, we've nothing that could lead us to an arrest. These people, these players, may well be as innocent as I am and have subscribed to this murder-mystery game in good faith. We bring them in now, with nothing else but the game connecting them to Lydia Callin, it's likely we'll be releasing them twenty-four hours down the line with nothing new to show for our efforts.

'How're their individual online profiles looking?' I ask.

'Couple of them heavily into social media but nothing standing out. We're going through them now to see if we can match up any posts with dates relevant to the investigation. Where they might have been photographed out or checked into clubs.'

'Any links to Lydia Callin yet?'

'Nothing coming up so far.'

'It does suggest they think the game is fictional. I'd imagine if they thought they were looking at the possibility of a real murder, they would put out a call online for more information. Mention her name?'

'You'd imagine so. The forum on the game's site has a few threads but for the most part the conversations centre around various methods of procedure, like how'd you go tracing the manufacture of the earring, where it was bought, her clothing, that kind of thing.'

And I know it's a long shot before I ask it but ask anyway. 'Any discussion on Teddy Dolan?'

He shakes his head. 'Nothing. And none of them seem keen to share any thoughts on a suspect in the game.'

'How about the usernames they're using on the site?'

'Apart from one, they've not been used anywhere else online as far as we've been able to deduce. Emer is still running searches. This one,' he points to Harrison Lloyd who you can tell, even from the head shot, is a tall, sporty-looking guy, straight from the pages of a modelling catalogue. Sallow-skinned with light brown hair, artificially enhanced with a few strategic highlights. He's wide-shouldered, well-built but with a childlike cherry-blossom pink across his cheeks. 'He used or uses the name Tabiya. Chess-related term meaning strategy, but can't find it on any of the other common gaming threads online.' He moves along to Pippa Dunne, 'Engineering. She used a series of numbers and letters for her username. No pattern that I could make out. Elsewhere online she uses her real name. There's a possibility that they only know each other through their online personas but seeing as they're all attending the same university . . .'

'We'll find that out soon enough,' I say.

'All are living off-campus. Might make it easier for us to carry out some surveillance if we need to, before making a move.'

I lean on the table, look down at the students. Sigh. 'We take in one, the rest could scarper or match their stories. We take them all in, we're on the clock and we've nothing to charge them with.'

Mullins, who is working at the next desk, stops flicking through traffic cams and pulls his chair towards us. 'But they're connected to the game,' he says.

'Well, so am I. Doesn't mean I've got Teddy Dolan stuffed under my floorboards or that I murdered Lydia Callin. If we time this wrong, we'll have a big old mess on our hands. Having a good idea that our killer is close to or among this group but not being able to charge anyone because we rushed in too soon would be a disaster.' I level Mullins with a look. 'That, we don't want.'

He nods quickly and retreats back to his station.

'If you look here,' Steve says, taking a step back and pointing up at a screenshot of the members' forum. 'There's a green bar beneath each of the names.'

'What's that?' I ask.

'A progression bar, I'd say, a marker of how far they've got in the game,' he answers. 'If we were thinking of questioning any of them, these two might be a good place to start.' He rests a fingertip first on Derek Cohen's image, then on Harrison Llyod's. They look like they're furthest along.'

'Or, when the time is right, we go for each end of the scale. Best and worst: Derek Cohen and Ashley Noone.'

He nods in agreement.

I straighten. 'Where's Baz, anyway? He should be here for this.'

Steve folds his notes in half, runs finger and thumb along the crease. 'He said he had to go home for a bit,' he says awkwardly.

I frown, again feeling a jab of worry for my partner. It's only been a day or so but he's not one to back out once an investigation gets going and I don't think there'd be a member of my team that would leave a case like this even if I ordered them home. 'He say why?'

'No. A call came through and he said he'd be back as soon as he could.'

I look at my watch, then begin gathering up the pictures on the table. 'Okay. Mullins, we need to brief the team on this. Can you set this up on the case board and have the rest of the team gather?'

'We're not waiting for Detective Harwood?' Mullins asks.

'Unless you're able to let this killer know to hold off for a bit while we wait for our colleague to get here, then no.'

'Yes, Ma'am,' he says and heads out the door.

'Steve, I know you're already on this but for the sake of making sure, can you pull up everything you have on the players. Background on the courses they're studying too. Entry requirements and how they got there. School results, scholarships. Any sports they play. Gaming clubs or societies. Money. Are they working through studies to pay bills? Flatmates, housemates. We might have someone logging in on their behalf. Times active on the site – do they match with when they're on social media?' I pause, teeth over my lip. 'Can you get Ryan and Helen to put the feelers out for resources? If we can't narrow this down, we'll have to bring all our persons of interest in at the same time. Monitor that website closely for what other questions are being asked by the players, it might give us some insight into what they know.'

My phone rings just as Steve says, 'Yes, Chief.'

Turning away, I answer it. 'Sheehan,' I say into the receiver then see that it's an internal call. 'What is it, Paul?'

'Dolan's mobile has activated again,' he says.

'Christ,' I mutter. I switch the call to my mobile, grab my coat and head for the door. 'Where?'

'Henry Street.'

'Get Baz Harwood now. Tell him to meet me at the top of Henry Street in ten minutes,' I say. 'Paul stay on that signal, let Steve know and feed back how many street cameras we have in the area.'

'Yeah.' Paul says. 'There're two uniforms alerted already. I spoke to one officer on the street, no eyes on him yet.'

'How specific is the location?'

'There're two masts, one at either end of the street, the mobile is hitting both.'

'CCTV?'

'We're in luck, we have an earth cam on the East side.'

Henry Street is busy even on its quietest day. Even with someone as well-known as Dolan, it will be difficult to find him. 'Circulate Dolan's image to as many of the stores on Henry Street as you can. Get Mullins on CCTV; his background on traffic might be useful here.'

If it is indeed Dolan with the phone, the first question that comes to mind is why hasn't he contacted us? Turned up at a hospital? But I know that's the dream. That if Dolan was in fact trotting down Henry Street, it would make this task not easy but at least possible. Between events last night, the other crime scenes and Dolan's mobile popping up like a jack-in-the-box, I've the distinct feeling we're being played. The punches are coming in fast and from all the sides and I don't want to wait around for a direct hit. I look at my watch. Six-fifteen pm.

Closing time for the shops. Enough light still in the sky and a bright, dry day means that Henry Street will be jammed. I can only imagine the throngs of people milling down that shopping highway. It does happen that the pendulum of luck swings in our direction during a case but as a rule, I'm not one to rely on it. Still, I find myself sending a quick request to the skies that somehow we find this phone, even as I acknowledge that whoever has it could sidle on right by us and we'd be none the wiser.

Baz finds me at the corner of Moore and Henry Street. He's halfway through a cigarette which he pushes out on the top of a bin as he greets me.

'Dolan again?' he asks. He looks out over the bustle, stuffs his hands in his pockets. There's an edginess about him, something of a frantic gleam in his eyes. Shoulders high, as if shielding from the cold even though the evening is mild enough.

'The phone's somewhere down there,' I say, holding a palm out towards Henry Street. 'Where've you been?'

'I had something to take care of,' he says. 'Let's get going.' He makes off down the street.

I keep pace. 'You get the update on our players?'

'I had a quick look on the way here,' he replies, turning sideways to move past a young couple. 'Paul sent a report and photos to my phone.'

'Our focus is on Dolan, but we should keep a lookout for any of those individuals.'

'Got it.'

Down the way, on the left, above the crowds of shoppers and tourists, I can make out the distinctive yellow lettering of Arnotts department store. A busker croons out the opening bars to the Beautiful South's 'You Keep It All In' and the lyrics lodge in my head as we push through the crowds. Flower and fruit sellers line the top of the street, children pull on parents' arms to return to a favourite shop. Another group of pedestrians have paused to take pictures of a performance artist; he's dressed in an oversized coat, a black fedora low over his eyes and around his chest a harness supports a selfie stick, the phone at the end angled towards his face. Under his collection tin, #KeepLooking is written on a piece of white card; a nod to our new world of narcissism.

I scan the crowds, push down the feeling of hopelessness. Dolan's a needle in a haystack. We continue down the street. A kid presses closer to her mother rubs an ice cream along the side of my coat. A charity worker in a red vest smiles, clipboard in hand, asks for a moment of my time. I step over the wheel of a pushchair. Then ahead, there's movement, a skirmish. The crowd parts briefly and someone is running. A glance at Baz and we're off, up the street. Baz, beside me, is already on the phone, calling for a unit to seal off the top of the street. But before we can clap eyes on our runner, a hand on my arm pulls me to a stop.

A guard in uniform. 'Shoplifter. Not our guy.' The radio at his shoulder clicks, a scratch of static. He tucks his chin towards it. 'Young male, dressed in a blue Nike hoodie. He's headed down the back of the Jervis Shopping Centre.' The radio beeps and another voice: 'Alerting security now. Over.'

I look down the street, knowing that whoever it was is already ricocheting through the warren of alleyways that criss-cross the city.

The guard's hand drops away. 'Sorry, Ma'am.'

'Any sign of Dolan?' I ask, trying to catch my breath.

He shakes his head.

'Keep looking,' I say.

'Yes, Ma'am,' he turns away.

I lift the hair from the back of my neck and allow the light breeze to cool my skin. We've reached the end of the street. 'You want to split up?' I say to Baz.

'Think that might be quickest,' he says. 'What height is he again?

'Five seven.'

He lets out a sigh. 'Doesn't make it easy here.'

'It doesn't,' I say, the futility of our search registering. 'Let's do one more pass. We may have to wait until whoever this is moves out of the area. Track the phone as it hits other masts. At some point, they'll get on public transport where it'll pick up the Wi-Fi, or into a car where we'll be able to narrow things down a bit.'

'Okay.' He keeps watch as he says, 'I'll go up that side of the street, you this side?'

'Yes.'

We move in unison on either side of the street. Shopping bags bump against my knees, a giant helium Peppa Pig swims into vision, then bobs away. Removing my phone from my pocket, I reconnect with Paul. Tell him no eyes on Dolan yet. He says the phone is still in use, in the vicinity.

'Internet connection. Signal's pretty consistent,' he says.

I stop, glance over the front of the buildings that line the street. 'In one of the shops, you think?'

In the centre of the street, a man in a green baseball cap passes; his nose stuck in his phone, thumb swiping across the screen. In his left hand, he grips an Arnotts bag. Right height, right build.

'Hang on, Paul,' I say. I signal to Baz. He sees him too. He almost climbs across the people in his way.

The man bumps up against a group of teen girls.

There's a collective: 'Hey!' Then one of them follows that up with: 'Watch where you're fucking going.'

The man holds up a hand, mouths sorry and the girls move on. For a second, he shows us his face. Nose too narrow, too long, eyes too deep. It's not Dolan.

Across the street, Baz blows out a breath of frustration. We return to our paths.

'I'm back,' I say into my phone.

Paul continues: 'We can't narrow it down. Not one of the shops, just the city council's free Wi-Fi.'

A little way off, above the din, the buskers, the shoppers and the far-off sirens, there's an escalation of raised voices, then a piercing scream that stiffens the muscles across my shoulders. A quick look at Baz and we're running towards the sound. People move in a thick wave in the opposite direction. Some have stopped, necks craned, to gawk – to catch sight of whatever is causing the commotion.

A man's voice shouts: 'Get back.'

I don't have to check that Baz is with me. I know he'll be moving towards whatever it is, just like I am. Both of us sure that when we get there, we'll find what we're looking for. We break through an opening in the crowds. People push back. Some turn to run. Others reach for their phones. Set them to record.

CHAPTER 12

It must be frightening for the kid we find in the centre of the wide space. She can't be more than thirteen, skinny but in an athletic way. Her hair in a high bun. Tracksuit, white bottoms with a navy stripe down the side, a zip-up sports top. A stud glints in her left nostril, thick gold hoops in her ears. She looks like she's poised to run but she holds her entire body still, only the whites of her eyes move as she follows our approach. Her right arm is up, the rest of her body angled away. Next to her, is the performance artist we passed earlier. He hasn't moved. Still as statue, the selfie stick protruding out from his body but the girl's hand clasps the phone at the end of the stick. For a moment, I don't understand the scene in front of me. The girl has clearly seen an opportunity to snatch the phone but I don't understand why she hasn't run away with it.

As we get closer, the girl lifts a finger away from the mobile and the tiny movement triggers a low growl from the figure next to her.

'Don't move,' he says.

The girl stiffens.

Edging nearer, I feel the pinch of Baz's fingers on my elbow, a warning not to get too close. I can't quite get my mind to believe what I'm seeing. *Who* I'm seeing. He's taller than he should be, standing on something, maybe a box or a crate obscured by the lengths of the coat he's wearing. His face is hidden beneath the shade of his hat but his hand is just visible beyond the long sleeves of his coat. I count four fingers. Teddy Dolan.

'He says there's a bomb,' the girl says. A whisper. A plea. 'He says if I move it could go off.'

I signal to Baz to stay back, keep my eyes locked on the girl's and creep closer.

'Frankie,' Baz cautions.

'Hey,' I say to the girl, flattening the shake from my voice. 'What's your name?'

Her eyes strain in my direction. 'Orla,' she gets out.

'Hello, Orla. I'm Frankie. I'm a guard. A detective, actually,' I keep the smile welded to my face.

'My arm is beginning to hurt,' she says.

'We've help coming. Try not to move until I see what's what, okay?'

'Okay.'

'Teddy?'

His breathing is laboured, a snorting inhalation and exhalation. Beneath the hat, his face is red, his eyes wild and bloodshot. 'It's around my chest.'

'Alright. Hold on. We'll get you out of this.'

I get down on my knees, fish around the inside of my coat for my torch, take a look. Teddy's standing on a plastic milk

141

crate. The white card beneath the collection tin mocks me. #KeepLooking. I pass the beam over and back, look for wires, trips, tricks but can't see any.

I shuffle back, get up slowly, so as not to disorientate either Dolan or the kid.

She's crying. She squeezes her eyes shut briefly, the skin beneath swollen, turning pink.

'Frankie,' Baz says from behind me.

'Not long now, Orla. Okay?'

'I don't think I can hold on,' she says, her voice distorted with tears.

'You can. Only a little while and we'll have you out of here.'

She begins to shake her head. The fingers around the phone twitch. I reach into the air, ready to catch or prevent the phone from dislodging then stop myself. No. If I grasp it, I could well be as stuck as she is, unable to move in case it triggers the device.

'Orla, look at me.' Blowing air through twisted lips, she shuts her eyes. Shuts me out. 'Orla! Listen to me.'

She drags in a lungful of air, nostrils flaring.

'Look at me. Orla?'

Slowly, her eyes open. Glacier blue. I want to pull her into a hug, tell her it's going to be fine.

'Can you hold your breath with me. Okay? Can you do that? Just this one thing, right?'

She meets my gaze, draws in a breath. I breathe in with her. Hold and count for three, let air out through pursed lips. She follows. I repeat the exercise. She copies. Over and again, until her tears stop and there is quiet in her eyes.

'Keep doing that,' I say. 'Just think about the next breath.

That's all you have to do. Only the next breath. Nothing else.'
She nods through a slow exhalation. 'I'm just going to talk to
Teddy now, but I'm right here.'

'Teddy?' His eyes turn to me. 'I can't see any triggers. What
do you know about the device?'

'They gave me instructions. Said if I didn't do this, they'd
harm Monica. They'd already got this thing on me. They told
me where to go and that they'd have control. If I didn't do it,
they'd . . .' he looks to Orla and trails off.

'What were your instructions?'

'Stand here and wait.'

Beside me, Orla continues to draw in long breaths.

'Wait for what?'

He blinks sweat out of his eyes. 'You.'

The bloody scene in my flat flashes in my mind. 'Me specif-
ically?'

'The guards.'

His eyes close briefly. He swallows, licks dryness from his
lips. 'If I move, if anything moves, it goes off.' He winces at the
phone. 'They're watching.'

'Who are they?'

'I don't know. I never see them.'

'We're going to get you out of this. Just hold on,' I say.

He lets out a cautious, shaky laugh. 'Don't have much choice.'

I return to Baz.

'Bomb squad a minute out,' he says, keeping his voice to a
low murmur. He looks back over my shoulder. Wipes a hand
over his brow and I see the shake in his fingers. 'Should we be
so close? We should wait until ATO get here. What if it goes off?'

Orla's focused on some point on the ground, her lips pursed as she draws breath in and then blows it out.

'I'm afraid if we leave, she'll run. It could set the device off.'

I look back up the street; some of the crowds have dispersed but not enough. A couple of gardaí are trying to push them back, but all the way down the street, shoppers and staff are still exiting stores. My eyes catch on the pink Peppa Pig balloon a little way off. 'We need to clear the area. Evacuate the entire street.'

As I speak, Orla's feet shuffle just enough to tell me she's weighing up her chances.

'Don't move,' Teddy shouts.

The desperate terror filling his voice sends a low tremble of panic down the street as people grasp what's here. You can feel the moment comprehension dawns. Suddenly, there's no need for the gardaí to nudge rubberneckers back. People begin to run and the gardaí call for them to keep calm. Baz watches the retreating crowds.

'You okay for this?' I ask.

He takes a moment to turn and answer. 'Yeah, yeah.' He glances quickly at his watch then out over the street. No sign of the bomb squad yet.

'You sure?' I ask.

He glances at me again then back at Teddy and Orla. 'Yeah. Just, you know, it's a bomb.'

'We should probably make sure the shops are empty,' I say to him. 'If there's emergency exits at the back, use them. Get all members of staff out too. It's not only the bomb we need to be worried about – flying debris can travel.' I hear sirens in the distance.

'I'm not going anywhere,' he says, but his body says different. Already he is edging away.

'Go,' I say to him.

He runs a hand over his face. It shakes. 'Alright.' He turns, makes his way to a uniformed guard. They confer for a moment, then Baz heads into one store, the guard into the next.

Silence swells around me, sound reduced to a low whine of fear from Dolan and the increasingly rapid huff and puff as Orla attempts to control her panic. The air is thick with anticipation and the heat of it closes around my neck. The city ticks on beyond Henry Street. For a moment, my vision blurs. Mouth dries. Both Dolan and Orla watch me. Don't leave us. I check my watch. Hope that the bomb squad are close.

'Help is on the way,' I say to them.

'My arm—' Orla says, her face wet with tears.

'Keep breathing. Remember. That's all you have to do.'

She drags in a long breath and once more begins the rhythm of inhalation and exhalation.

I move towards Dolan, look up at the phone. Between the thin, pale bands of Orla's fingers, I can see it's set to live recording.

'Is this your phone, Mr Dolan?'

'Yes.'

I straighten. 'I'm not leaving. Just getting an update on when the squad will get here.'

I move away to call Steve.

'I've done a search on most of the social media platforms using the hashtag displayed on the piece of card at Dolan's feet,' he says, 'and nothing related to Dublin or Henry Street has come back. There's a couple of videos of the scene from the public appearing on Facebook but none coming from Dolan's phone.'

Orla lets out a small cry, tries to angle her body so that her hand can support her raised arm.

'Thanks Steve. Keep at it. I have to go,' I say to him then hang up.

I pocket my phone and before I can let myself think on it, position myself next to Orla, wrapping my hand around her upper arm to take some of the weight.

'Thank you,' she says.

The lump in my throat makes it difficult to answer, so I aim for a reassuring smile then scan the horizon for the bomb-disposal unit. A truck sounds its horn in the streets beyond. The whip of helicopter blades drums above. I pick out the beep of a pedestrian crossing. Some way off, I see Baz in the doorway of one of the stores. He gives me a signal to say the shop is empty. The weight of what is happening, what could happen, what is about to happen, lowers onto my shoulders and I feel a sadness creeping in and through my body. Then as I watch my partner hurry down the street to where the gardaí are manning the road, loneliness trails in, darkens the edges of my mind.

I should be happy that Baz is out of harm's way. Our role here is, after all, to protect the public. That's what he's doing. Right? Because I've never known him to back out when things got tough. If the job demanded a risk, we took it together or at least knew the other would be there for the catch should we fall. In the last couple of days, there's been flashes of the usual Baz, committed, and chasing through every thread to look for

146

probable leads and then it's like he's half-here, one eye fixed on something out of sight and ready to walk away from it all in an instant. I sense new lines being drawn up, risks re-evaluated and I see again the small movement of Gemma's hand against his chest.

A cry chokes in Orla's throat and it summons a groan from Teddy. I clear my head, concentrate.

'You have brothers and sisters, Orla?' I ask.

'Brother,' she says.

'What's his name?'

'Fionn.'

'Older than you?'

'He's only eight.'

'Bet he's all over the football?' Sirens scream in the distance.

'He's up half the bleedin' night thinking about the All-Irelands,' she says, through gritted teeth. The narrow bands of muscles stand out on her neck.

'Will he go to the match?'

'We don't have the dough for that.' She gives out a pained smile. The colour is drifting from her face. She touches her tongue to her lips which have turned a sickly white. She closes her eyes for a second and I see the sheen of sweat glisten on her forehead. 'You really Teddy Dolan?' she asks Teddy.

'Yes,' he says.

'Cool,' Orla closes her eyes again, sways a little. I tighten my grip on her arm.

'Orla, take a breath.'

She opens her eyes. A wide blue gaze that looks right through me. 'I don't feel very good.'

147

I wrap my arm around her waist and she sinks against me. Teddy watches us, his expression frantic. I don't know how he's managed to balance on that crate for this long. What he must have endured over the last month that has his body churning out enough adrenalin to keep him focused. No fight or flight for him, only survive. Orla's breathing turns shallow, fast. My eyes are pinned on the phone. Her fingers twitch around it. I slide my hand further up her arm, try to ignore the cramping pain in the muscles around my shoulder.

'Orla, you have to keep standing,' I say. 'Please.'

'I don't think I can,' she says, and I can see the resignation on her face. Her fingers are easing off the phone just as the bomb-disposal unit shows up.

'They're here!' I say. 'Orla, Teddy – our ammunition technician officers have just arrived.' Relief floods through me at the sight of the bomb squad. They park some distance away. Get out and go to the back of the vehicle.

Orla lets out a long breath.

'They're here,' I say again. 'You'll be at home with Fionn talking about football before you know it, Orla. I need to go over and fill them in, just hold on a little more. They'll be with you very soon.'

Orla nods quickly. Wanting to push time on so that she can escape from this nightmare. 'I'm going to let go of your arm now to speak to the officers. Just a little longer, okay?'

I say to her.

I feel her body stiffen, the muscles in her arm harden. 'Yes. I got it.'

I ease my hand away from her wrist, my arm from around her waist.

'Hurry,' she says.

'I will,' I say. My phone vibrates in my pocket as I turn away. 'Steve, what've we got?'

'Live feed onto Facebook. The account is a sock puppet, we're doing what we can to try and trace it but it doesn't look hopeful.'

I try not to run, but the further I get from Dolan, the greater the urge to put as much distance between me and that bomb as possible. 'Might be good to alert Monica Dolan that we've found her husband before the media does.'

'It's already trending on social media.'

'Do it now. ATO have just arrived. Keep me updated with any change.'

'Will do, Chief.'

I hang up. The ATOs are unloading a remote-controlled robot from the back of the van. A woman, mid-twenties is being helped into a suit by a man. The suit is navy, padded down the arms and legs. He secures it at the shoulders, then lowers a stiff chest shield over her head.

'Detective Sheehan,' I introduce myself.

'Maggie Tierney,' the woman says. 'This is Harry,' she nods towards the man at her side. He's wearing a navy overall. A thick silver chain glints at the neck, head shaved tight. 'And Andy's in the back there.' A younger man looks up from a seated position at the rear of the van, laptop on his knees. 'What can you tell us?'

I glance at the robot, which looks like a miniature tank, three wheels on either side, a long metal arm with a two-prong grasp extending from the front. 'We've got a male standing on a crate.

A phone attached to a selfie stick putting out a live feed on social media. I can't make out a trigger function. The girl tried to grab the phone but stopped just as the man shouted not to move that there was a bomb. He was worried any movement of the mobile could set the bomb off. It looks safe enough to me for her to let go but I can't be sure.'

She frowns at that, squints over at where Dolan is standing. 'Probably the safest call until we get a look at it,' she says. Harry passes her a pair of binoculars. Pushing her light brown hair out of her eyes, she presses them to her face. 'There could be a trigger plate attached behind the phone where it's housed on the selfie stick. How old's the girl?'

'Thirteen. Fifteen maybe.'

'You seen any wires attached to the phones?'

'No. But there's a suggestion there might be a remote detonator. That someone watching might trigger it if anything's moved.'

She blows out a mouthful of air. Grips the edge of the armoured collar and buckles it to the front of her chest. 'Let's hope we can get her away at least.'

'We're ready to send Erica in,' Andy says.

'Go,' Maggie says. Harry offers her gloves and she pulls the first one on, clips the cuff to the protective suit, then holds out her hand for him to tug on the other one.

She walks to the back of the van, where Andy turns the laptop to her. Teddy Dolan and the kid grow bigger on the screen and I see the colour drop again from Orla's face as she watches the robot approach.

'What's happening?' she shouts, her feet turning on the ground.

Harry lifts a loudspeaker to his mouth to answer. I put my hand on it. 'May I?'

He glances to Maggie who nods and he hands the loudspeaker over.

'It's okay, Orla,' I say into the speaker. 'We just need to get a closer look. The robot has sensors attached so she can feed back to us how we might be able to get you out of there.'

I look down at the screen. Orla licks her lips, stares longingly off into the distance.

'She's going to run,' Maggie says, grabbing the speaker from my hands, cupping it between her palms. 'Do not move!' she shouts and Orla looks up as if she's been slapped out of a trance. 'You move, you're dead.'

I flinch at the baldness of her words. Watch the horror grow on Orla's face. She licks her lips once more, stiffens her arm and gives a tiny nod of her head.

'Was that necessary?' I ask.

Maggie gives me a look that asks if I'm stupid, then focuses on the laptop. She waits, watches as Erica moves slowly around both captives, sniffing out signals and sending information back to the laptop. 'I see the device. Metal casing. Round the top of his chest.'

Harry leans over. 'Radio signals?'

'Nothing,' comes the reply from Andy.

'No remote.' Maggie glances up at the surrounding buildings, searches the windows overlooking the area, then focuses on the computer. 'We know the drill.'

Andy looks up from the computer. 'We can try and see if Erica can disarm. Maybe to confuse the signal with a disrupter.'

'No disrupters,' she says. 'It could cause it to function.'

'If we can get him to remove the coat,' Harry says.

'Too risky, Harry.' She jogs her shoulders a bit. 'I got the short straw, didn't I? Crown me,' she says, and Harry reaches for a huge helmet from the back of the van. 'Picking up anything on the phone?' she says over his shoulder at Andy.

'Nothing. It looks clean,' he replies.

'Good. We should get the girl away at least.' She pulls the helmet down and fits her visor over her face. She tests the belt at her waist for the tools she needs.

'I'm ready,' she says.

She starts out. Her figure grows smaller as she moves down the empty street towards Teddy and Orla.

CHAPTER 13

I wake on the couch in my flat. The ringing in my ears has passed but the memories of yesterday swell slowly in my mind. I feel, again, the grip of Orla's hand on mine, tight and sharp around my fingers. The sting of grit in my eyes. The thump of the explosion. I see the shadow of Maggie Tierney's body starfish into a cloud of dust. And Teddy Dolan's white, stricken expression.

My right hand stings. Nothing more than a series of fine scratches. I know Orla will have matching injuries to hands and knees, the blast from the bomb not enough to knock us from our feet but the shock of it going off turning our limbs to jelly and sending us to the ground anyway.

Sitting up, I reach for my phone. Maggie is in hospital but she's going to be okay. Ruptured ear drums, torn retina on the right and a fractured wrist. Teddy, like myself and Orla, was already clear from the area of danger when the device went off. I didn't sleep well. My thoughts veering between the flash of the explosion and what this means for The Murder Box, if anything at all. No one could've anticipated that Orla would have tried to steal the phone and yet Teddy said that his instructions were to wait for the guards and I think of the phone and how it was likely a ploy to lead us to him before the device went off.

Between the crime scenes across the city and now this, it could appear as though our perp is a desperate narcissist who has lost control and is hitting out at random and with increasing frequency. But someone who has lost control is not the sense I get. We're being kept on a track, our investigation guided down some chute, the end of which is coming at us sure and fast. And if yesterday was a taste of what's coming our way, once our time is up, I've no doubt this killer has a big finale planned.

A milky morning light shimmers on the windows of the flat. A gentle rain is falling over the city. On the street below, shop shutters rattle open, a truck beeps into reverse. The flat is more or less back to normal. Keith, working off his feeling of guilt, pulled out all the stops to erase the crime scene from my bedroom so quickly. The smell of animal blood is gone, replaced with the chemical aroma of cleaners and fresh paint. Still, when I returned last night, I opened the bedroom door to collapse into bed and found myself closing it again. Something about the mood of the room has changed, a sense that whoever was in there, never fully left.

I shower, dress quickly. My mum, who caught the story of Dolan's dramatic discovery on the late news, told me down the phone that she'd almost 'collapsed' when she saw that I was there. She was 'frantic with worry' which she expressed in the usual way, with a lecture. This is Sharon Sheehan one-oh-one. The deeper she loves, the more she fears, the more she fears, the more you'll get it in the neck when you hurt yourself.

'At least you're alright,' she said. The last with a tiny upwards inflection, a signal for me to reassure her that yes, I was fine.

'We're all going to the Jervis tomorrow to get things for the baby. I know Tanya and your brother would be glad to see you,' she said. 'Can we see you for breakfast at least?'

A simple request that reminded me how far from normal a case can take you in just a couple of days. We're not even close to a foothold in this investigation and I'm not one to stop until I've a good sense of where we're going. But, as I spoke to my mum, my hand began to shake, followed by a tight sensation in my chest that crept round my ribs and I heard myself saying, 'Yes, I can get away for an hour or so.'

Hooking my bag over my shoulder, I turn to leave the flat. As I go to close the door, my eye catches on the curtain pole. I put down my bag and grab one of the stools from the breakfast bar. Placing the stool under the window, I climb up onto it then reach up and tear the strip of plastic free. I get down. Return the stool, scrunch the plastic in my hand and drop it in the bin. Pausing at the door, I look back over my flat, that one action, small as it was, returning to me some feeling of control.

Downstairs, I remove an umbrella from my bag and start out away from the flat on foot. The pressures of this case feel like a clamp around my skull. Time is slipping away from us, but it seems the more we push our faces to the glass, the less we see. I need a moment to pull back; no one sees the bigger picture, what's on the horizon, with their nose pressed too close to an investigation. Even so, somewhere in the back of my mind, I can almost hear the digits on that clock clicking down.

Turning towards O'Connell Bridge, I tilt the umbrella into the wind and navigate my way through puddles and people. I stop at the centre of the bridge, let a group of tourists pass and look out over the dark Liffey waters, down towards the curve of the Ha'penny Bridge. On the ledge, set into the pale grey stone, a brass plaque commemorates the death of Fr Pat Noise.

'He died under suspicious circumstances when his carriage plunged into the Liffey on August 10th 1919.'

A tragic tale. If it were true. It took Dublin Council years to realize that one of their most historic architectural structures bore a memorial to a fictitious character. But by then the hoax was already part of the bridge's story and people defended the plaque's position as if it memorialized a real person. Fiction trickling into reality.

My head aches from trying to separate fiction from reality in this case too. We should have something by now. Forensics should anyway. Four crime scenes across the city, a Murder Box calling card at each one. Perhaps, as Camille and Baz say, the best way to solve this is to play along. To enter some more case details into the website. Jack floated the idea to our commissioner, and it was a firm no, followed by a not so thinly veiled threat that should my mind even stray in that direction, I could pack my bags. I didn't like that. After the scene at my flat, it's more than evident that The Murder Box was not something sent to the Bureau in general but to me. Camille is sure if I hadn't been working the Dolan case, the killer would not have singled me out. If we needed a further link between Dolan and this game, then this was it, surely?

*

I get to the coffee shop and Justin waves at me from the corner. He's already a grilled breakfast down. Tanya eases up out of her seat to throw her arms around me.

'Frankie, thank Christ you're okay,' she says. She pulls away, looks me over, her hand going to her round stomach.

Justin gets up, presses a kiss to my cheek. 'You always had to have the most attention on your birthday,' he says. 'A day late, but no surprises there,' he adds with a smile.

Dad is working his way through a bacon sarnie. He lifts a ketchup-smeared fork in a wave hello.

Sliding my umbrella under the table, I unbutton my coat. 'Will you pass a tea there, please, Justin,' I say.

I sit down next to Mum, give her hand a squeeze. 'So it's baby shopping today, is it?'

Dad looks up. 'Are you able to join us, love?'

'I'm afraid not.'

'You work too much, Frankie,' Mum scolds.

Tanya leans back, gives Mum a raised eyebrow. 'Says the woman who can't sit still for the length of a cup of tea.'

'That's different. I've the dance fundraiser coming up and I'm organizing the rehearsals. It's not a hardship at all.'

'I've a case, Mum. You know I can't take time off when it gets going,' I say, plucking a croissant from a basket in the middle of the table.

Justin passes me a tea then slips an arm around Tanya's back. 'How long will this shopping take?'

Tanya smiles back at him. 'Buckle up, J, you're in for the long haul. I've the day off work and I'm going to use it. One clean swoop – that's what we want. Divide and conquer and by

157

four this afternoon we'll have everything we need for this one's arrival,' she pats the top of her stomach. 'So then,' she leans forward, tea cupped in her hands. 'Teddy Dolan, give us the story?'

'The poor man's been through the wringer,' Mum says. 'We shouldn't be poring over his predicament like it's meaningless gossip.'

Tanya sighs, leans back, disappointed.

There's a brief silence until Mum's curiosity gets the better of her. 'So, he's been held captive for all this time?'

I swallow a piece of the buttery pastry, reach for my tea. 'Looks like it.'

'Shocking altogether,' Mum says. 'Is it some kind of stalker, do you think?'

'Could be,' I say, knowing well that whatever I tell her will be halfway around Clontarf come teatime.

'A victim of his own success,' she says dramatically. 'The poor man.'

'How's the fundraiser going, Mum?' I ask.

A groan from Justin, and Dad focuses anew on his plate.

'We've no partner for Mrs Hogan,' she says, spreading jam across a piece of toast. 'Probably for the best. God knows she doesn't have the shape for it.'

Justin looks up. 'How about Eamon Keegan?'

Mum looks up. 'I don't think he's able—'

Interrupting, Dad says: 'Give the man a chance, Sharon, you won't know until you ask.'

The cup in Mum's hand lowers to the table. She sends Dad a hard stare that cracks like static in the air.

'What?' Dad asks, all innocent, but I see the twitch at the

corner of his mouth. He's good at the moment, my dad. The years after his retirement from the guards were some of the darkest for my family, when he was almost swallowed by depression. Now, the good periods are great, the bad ones more flat than bad, and on days like today, you'd wonder whether we'd dreamed up all those years, whether they'd happened at all.

'You cut in all the time,' Mum says to him.

'I don't.'

I butter my croissant, take a bite, feel the talons of Lydia Callin's case loosen their grip on my mind.

Drawing in a short breath, Mum says: 'It's like that time—'

Justin presses the heels of his hands against his temples. 'Mam.'

She raises her chin. 'Well, he's being rude, your father.'

Dad spreads his hands. 'Can a man not have an opinion?'

'No,' both Tanya and I answer in unison.

Wriggling out from behind the table, Tanya massages the bottom of her back. 'Excuse me, nature calls. Again.' She heads off in the direction of the toilets.

'You going to be talking to Dolan today then or what?' Justin asks, his eyes begging me to change the subject.

I wipe the tips of my fingers clean on a napkin, check the time. An hour. A flutter of panic. But I tell myself that it's been an hour well spent. 'Today. If he's up to it.'

'And apart from the finger, no other injuries?'

'He seemed whole enough. We won't know for certain until he gets the clear from his doctors,' I say. Removing my wallet from my coat, I pass a fifty-euro note to Mum. She passes it back and I pass it back harder. A familiar ritual. Then she nods and tucks it under her saucer. 'Thanks, love.'

159

'That's a bit suspect though, isn't it?' Justin asks.

'Nice try,' I say, throwing him a wink.

He rolls his eyes. 'Can't get anything out of you. Like a Swiss vault.'

I get up, bend to kiss Mum's cheek.

Tanya returns. 'You going?'

I turn, give her a hug. 'When do you start maternity leave?'

'Maternity leave? Me? I'll be walking straight from court to the hospital.'

'When this case is through, we'll do something, okay?'

'It can't be more than a few weeks more. Now that Teddy's back, I mean.'

'No. It won't,' I say, and Tanya's words follow me all the way back to the Bureau. It can't be more than a few weeks. It can't be more than a few days. The Murder Box has spelled that out very clearly.

The Bureau is settling into the usual morning mayhem when I get there. Paul collecting cases on the phone, sifting through relevant ones for us, sending as many out to other departments as possible. The unease of the past twenty-four hours creeps back into my limbs. A dull ache settles around my shoulders. I shift impatiently on my feet as Paul fumbles through the papers on his desk.

'All going smoothly, Ma'am,' he says. 'Some gang-related stuff that surveillance have taken. A domestic homicide on the south side that's gone to Harcourt Street,' he says, chancing a smile that says we should be pleased.

'I suppose that's good. Anything from forensics on the explosive used with Dolan?'

He reaches back to his desk, takes up a thin file and passes it to me. I open it, scan the contents but he gives me the shorthand:

'Homemade,' he says, quietly. 'They're working through the debris now but it could be days before they've got the forensic report compiled. They said it was pretty crude. It could have gone off at any moment or not at all.'

This shifts Dolan slightly away from the role of accomplice and more to the side of survivor. But finding what is likely to be Lydia Callin's remains on the same day Dolan appears wired up to an explosive tells me we've a connection there.

'How about the murder game website? Any conversation around Dolan or the body we found in Clonskeagh there?'

'Nothing,' Paul replies. 'Although Steve remarked this morning how activity on it seemed very quiet.'

'Quiet? Since when?'

'There was a significant drop-off of hits from seven yesterday evening.'

Too busy trawling through social media and news stories on the events in Henry Street. Was the reality of the game beginning to hit home for these players or were they sitting back in anticipation of what was coming down the line?

'Dolan out of hospital yet?' I ask.

'Yesterday evening. He says he's not ready to talk to us yet.'

'That's unfortunate for him.'

Paul gives me a look of confusion.

'We still can't fully rule out that he might be involved in this,' I continue. 'How come he wasn't the one found in couple of suitcases in a river?'

'I guess,' Paul says.

'He has motive,' I remind him, surprising myself that I've now come full circle to Baz's way of thinking. But in fairness, I never expected Dolan to return alive. That has changed everything. 'An affair that could have blown up in his face at any moment. Nothing like a bit of pity to smooth over a shitshow in your life. The best PR there is. Not to mention that he appears hours after we find remains that are likely Lydia Callin's.'

I know I'm letting my mood colour what I'm saying. Frustration at the mess of this case. The mass of information and not knowing where the pertinent details are or which to look at first. And here he is. A real witness and he won't talk. He was mute as a stone at the hospital. We pushed and prodded gently, like we were coaxing a wild animal out of a den. Except instead of food or comforting words we offered:

'Could you describe where you were held? Was the voice of your captor, young or old? Male or female? Teddy? I know it's painful, but can you tell us anything that could help us find out who did this to you?'

But no answers came. He stared fixedly between his bandaged feet down to the grey linoleum floor as we spoke, the only movement a rapid bunching of the skin around his left eye every time we moved, like he was expecting a blow from the side. All the while, the doc palpated around his ribs, his neck, his skull, under his armpit, occasionally hooking his stethoscope into his ears and moving the disc over Dolan's back, like it was a metal detector searching for answers that neither Dolan's body nor mouth wanted to give up. Eventually, I was pushed away by the doctor.

Whether Dolan is ready or not, if we want to catch his abductor then we need to be able to pick through the debris of his memories. As distasteful as it sounds, the victim is our most significant piece of evidence. And I know, because I've been there, that right now Teddy Dolan is at home rewriting every last painful memory, pushing his brain to wind its neurons around and beyond what he's just lived through, erasing, shifting, contextualizing the story until it holds a shape that he can live with. And we can't let him do that. Not yet.

I scan through the rest of the report then hand the file back. 'Thanks,' I say. 'When Ryan gets here, tell him to start putting together a surveillance plan for our players. Let's move all this up a gear. I'll be out for most of the day. I feel like listening to a few stories, even if no one feels like talking.'

'Detective Harwood is in his office,' Paul says.

I straighten, look over at Baz's door. I haven't heard from him since the hospital yesterday evening. He left as soon as he could after questioning Dolan. When he turned to go, there was a part of me that wanted to run up and grab hold of him as he retreated, to shake whatever was wrong out of him. I was disappointed but it stunned me how quickly that disappointment turned to hurt and anger. 'Where's Mullins?' I ask Paul.

'He's in the conference room, putting together copies of the case report.'

'Great. Tell him to get up to date on the Teddy Dolan situation and meet me front of house in two hours. Where's our list of players for The Murder Box?'

Paul reaches out to a folder to his right, opens it and extracts a spreadsheet. 'We got the timetables and routines for the two med students and the engineer as you requested. We should have the Film studies and PPE students shortly. There's also a list of gaming and role-playing clubs on campus.'

He hands it over. Photos of the five students and the names of local clubs and societies. Board games, chess, cards, video-gaming and larping.

'What is that?' I ask, pointing to the last word.

'Larping? It stands for live action role-playing. A series of games where you act out the gameplay. You become the character in the game, so to speak.'

I tip my head. 'Good research or are you speaking from experience?'

He reddens, shrugs his right shoulder. 'Research mostly. My sister was part of a club in school.'

'Didn't know you had a sister, Paul.'

'She died,' he said.

'I'm sorry.'

He shrugs, pulls at the neck of his shirt. 'It was a long time ago.'

'Yes,' I say quietly, 'but still. I'm sorry. Listen, thanks for this.' I go to move off, then add. 'Can you contact Camille Forbes for me, please? Ask if she could come in this afternoon. I'd like her to look over what we've got.'

'Yes, Ma'am,' he says.

CHAPTER 14

The rain has given way and the September light is gold and warm on the grounds of Trinity College. There's a lick of cool in the breeze and students are already trying out their winter coats as they walk in small groups towards their various meeting points. A couple of tourists follow a map across the courtyard, pause to take photos of the historic buildings. I perch against the cold granite of the campanile – the famous bell tower in the middle of the grounds. Twin maples stand on either side of the lawns, their leaves showing the changes of the season, bright yellow and burnt orange. Even though it's quiet enough, you can almost feel the new-term energy in the air; takes me back to that feeling of potential when I was studying. When everything was still up for grabs, or we were naive enough to think so, anyway.

We have five persons of interest. Five people who we are busy trying to link to Lydia Callin, but no matter how much we dig we can't find any crossovers between their lives and hers. Desperate to pull in some fresh evidence, I thought again to conduct a search and seize of all of their homes. Try to locate the boxes.

A phone call to Camille Forbes deterred me from that path. 'We bring in those boxes,' she said, 'these players will simply cover their homework with their arms. They're in it to win.' And she's right. Our monitoring of the murder box site has given us nothing that could prompt an arrest. If one of them is involved in Lydia's murder – or all of them – we've nothing that would induce them to talk.

She went on: 'If there wasn't a clock on the website, I might say go on as you are, proceed at your leisure but I'm sure you know that the clock brings about an end to the game regardless and they may know that it likely signals another victim. Until that last moment, to them, everything remains in play and your actions to intercept them make no difference. Go in on them, but go in softly.'

I look up in time to see Derek Cohen exit a side building, the security guard I asked to dig him out walking by his side. Derek keeps his head down, his gait quick, even and measured. He's not the tallest, maybe five six, dark hair, a beard filling out a narrow jawline. He's wearing a pair of black combats, trainers and blue hoodie that droops from one shoulder. The security guard points him in my direction and he walks towards me.

I push away from the campanile. 'Derek Cohen?'

He stops, pulls the strap of his laptop bag higher. 'Yes,' he says cautiously.

'Detective Frankie Sheehan,' I say, 'with the Bureau for Serious Crime.'

He glances around as if someone might overhear. 'Is everything okay?'

166

'I hope so,' I say. 'Think your man there said there's a café close by?'

'I have lectures.'

I smile at him. 'Already? Term has barely started and so busy.'

He looks back towards the square, to the entrance, and for a minute I think he might try to run. And I almost wish he would. Nothing says I've got bodies in the basement more than scarpering at a glimpse of the heat.

'It's this way,' he says.

We walk to a crowded coffee shop on the edge of the campus. I stop at the counter but he turns down my offer of coffee.

'Don't mind me, I need my caffeine fix whenever I can. I expect there'll be some long hours today. Not all of us have the time you students seem to have,' I smile down at him. 'Why don't you get us a seat?'

He doesn't bite, even though I know from Paul's notes, Derek Cohen is not one for downtime. He goes straight to work in the students' union bar in the evenings. The effects of that show in his grades. Derek Cohen is holding on to his place at Trinity College with barely a fingernail. I wait in line for coffee and watch him navigate through the packed tables. No one looks up. No hellos, how are yous. He finds a free table at the back of the room. He sits, puts his bag on the floor, then rests his palms on the table. After a moment, he reaches for his bag, rips a page out of a notebook, folds it and wedges it under the front leg of the table. He leans on it again. Then, satisfied, he waits.

Collecting my coffee, I make my way to him then set the drink down. 'Warm in here, isn't it?' I say and remove my jacket before sitting.

'Yeah.' He pushes the pads of his fingers along his hairline, wipes moisture away. 'Are my family okay?'

'I think so. Sorry, I should've said, I'm not here about anything like that.'

I watch to see if he relaxes with this information, but he pulls back a little, lengthens his neck, looks down at his hands. 'I should really get back. I've a tutorial.'

I tear the top from a sachet of sugar, tip it into my coffee, take my time stirring it. 'I didn't think you were due at it for another while,' I say, putting down the spoon. 'Hang on.' Removing my phone from my pocket, I scroll about on the screen a bit. 'Yep, that's right. Free for the next couple of hours. Then it's a molecular biology revision tutorial.'

There's a shifting nervousness in his eyes. 'Why are you here?'

'I wanted to talk to you about The Murder Box.'

He pulls at the sleeve of his hoodie. 'What about it?'

'When did you join?'

The corners of his mouth pull down. 'I subscribed a couple of weeks ago.'

I lift the cup to my mouth. 'Have you solved it?'

A quick frown. 'No. Not close. Sorry, have I done something wrong, Detective?'

I turn the coffee cup around on the saucer, let him stew. 'How did you find it? Was it through a friend or one of the clubs you go to?'

'Clubs?'

'Gaming clubs.'

'I heard about it on the SD Gaming forum. A few of us were talking about a murder-mystery game set-up and it came up.'

'And you subscribed after that?'

'I got a private message some time later inviting me to join.'

'From whom?'

He flushes. 'I don't know.'

'How long after your chats on the SD site did you get the invite?'

He shrugs. 'Five, six months.'

I take out my phone. Open up a search engine on the internet. 'Can you show me the SD Gaming site?'

He peers down at the screen then takes the phone. After a few seconds he returns the phone to me. 'There it is.'

Clicking through the menu, I find the site's forum. Along the header bar is a search facility. 'Show me the thread where you talked about a murder-mystery game set-up?'

He bites his bottom lip. 'It's no longer there.'

Half-expecting this answer, I put my phone away. If they are aware of the seriousness of The Murder Box then they'll have wanted to eliminate any trace of them discussing the concept of it. But I ask, 'Why is that?'

'Some of the members are pretty hot on their online footprint, so from time to time they'll ask admin to delete something.'

'Alright,' I say, giving a nod of understanding.

He shifts in his seat, looks down at his hands. 'Sorry, Detective, is there something wrong here?'

I take a sip of coffee. 'I've a few questions concerning an ongoing investigation.' I leave a beat for that to sink in. Then, 'So, you talked through the idea of a murder-mystery game with a group of individuals on the SD Gaming forum, then six months later you get an invite to join The Murder Box. Have I got that right?'

'Yes.'

'How many of you?'

'Six.'

I tally this against the names of the players given to me from Steve. We're one short. Another if you count me but Derek doesn't know I have accessed the site or that I have a box. Or at least, he shouldn't know I'm there among the other subscribers. 'On that day you subscribed to join and the day after you received a package. What was in the box?' I ask.

'Details on the murder mystery. A case of a missing woman .'

'No name?'

'Lydia Callin. Said that she'd been missing for a number of weeks. We were given a last sighting and a post-mortem report. A couple of other pieces of evidence.'

'Such as?'

'Photos of clothing. A picture of an earring. I worked out the first stage of the game and was given a couple of other pieces of evidence. It's tough though.'

'What other pieces of evidence?'

'A new suspect. Erm,' he pauses not wanting to go on. 'What's going on, Detective?'

'A new suspect. There are numerous suspects?'

A wry smile. 'Have you played a murder-mystery game before, Detective?'

I smile back. 'Some might say it's my day job.'

He gives in to a small laugh. 'Anyone playing could be a

suspect. And on top of that I was given a potential ex-boyfriend.'

He flushes at that.

'Were you given a name for this ex?'

The colour in his face deepens. 'No.'

I take a slow drink of my coffee. 'Doesn't seem like much to go on.'

He picks at a flake of skin along his thumbnail. 'There was a photograph of him getting into a vehicle outside that exhibition he was at.'

'Exhibition?'

He swallows. Looks down.

I lean towards him. 'Are you talking about Teddy Dolan?'

He keeps his eyes down. 'Yes.'

The reason for the silence on the murder box website yesterday evening through to today becomes apparent.

'You didn't think to report that?' I ask.

He shrugs. 'It's a game. I didn't think the photo meant anything. There's thousands of Teddy Dolan online – it's very easy to manipulate images with the right programme. The game said it would give an authentic experience and that's what we're getting.'

I swallow down the retort that Teddy Dolan's abduction was not a game. 'I'll need a copy of that photo.'

He nods quickly. 'Sure.'

'How about the missing woman? Lydia Callin?'

'We were told she left her flat in South Circular Road, went out and was found murdered,' he says.

I reach up, massage the old scar at my temple. Feel the ribbon of tough tissue just under the surface and try to unpick what

171

he's saying. If the victim is considered a player that adds another digit to our five. It would tie up with Derek's account that there were six of them expressing interest in a murder-mystery game. I ask him how many of the usernames now participating on the murder box site he recognizes from his chats on the SD Gaming forum.

He pauses but it's not because he's unsure, the question makes him shift in his seat. He touches his tongue to his bottom lip. 'There's lots of subscribers but, including me, I recognize five usernames from the SD forum,' he says.

'Someone didn't join?'

'It looks that way.'

I turn to a fresh page in my notebook, pass it across the table. 'Could you put down all the usernames you talked to on the SD Gaming site please?'

He stares at the blank page for a moment, then takes a pen out of the front of his bag. 'I'm not sure I can remember of all of their usernames off the top of my head.'

'Do your best,' I say.

He bends his head and writes down the list. 'I think that's right,' he says when he's finished.

'Which one didn't subscribe to The Murder Box?'

Leaning over the table, he places his finger beneath one of the names. LC_gxmer91. 'This one,' he says.

I stare at the name. The first two letters, the initials LC, point to our victim. Lydia Callin. I swallow.

'You didn't think it strange when all of your friends sign up bar this one?'

'We're not friends,' he says sharply. 'We don't know each

other. We just formed a private group on the SD forum because someone asked about gaming at Trinity. We got chatting from there. On the internet only.'

I pinch the bridge of my nose. 'You see, I find that really hard to believe, Derek. All of you attend the same Uni, probably go to the same gaming clubs and you're telling me you've never once revealed your identity to each other in real life?' But as I say this, it occurs to me that Lydia Callin is the only one of their original group that wasn't attending Trinity. It might suggest he's lying about the reason they gathered online. Perhaps, the truth lies closer to the fact that they were all interested in the idea of this murder mystery.

His mouth twists, disgusted at the thought of meeting the other players face to face. 'No.'

'Why not?'

He looks down, snatches a breath. 'We agreed we'd stay anonymous. It'd ruin the banter online or something. And then when the box arrived, it felt even more important to remain behind our online aliases, to stay within our roles.'

He glances over my shoulder, out over the packed café, the groups of students gathered and chatting, laughing. A tutor sitting near the window is writing furiously in a ring-bound notebook. 'Sorry, detective,' he says, lowering his voice and bringing his gaze back to me. 'I'm getting uncomfortable. Why are you here?' And I think that Camille Forbes is right: none of these players will want to give up this game. He reaches up, scratches the side of his jaw. 'Is it to do with Teddy Dolan – because honestly, I don't know anything more than this game, and really, that isn't a lot.'

'Lydia Callin, the named victim in your game,' I say keeping my eyes fixed on his face. 'Her body was found yesterday.'

He gives out a short laugh. 'What?'

'Her dismembered remains were discovered in two suitcases in the River Dodder near Clonskeagh.'

His dark eyebrows draw down. 'Fuck.' He swallows, then leans forward to study my face. 'Are *you* part of the game?' He looks over my clothing, the dark camo-green of my blouse, the stiff padded shoulders of my jacket. 'Can I see some ID?'

Removing my ID from my inside pocket, I lay it on the table between us. He spends a while studying it, then runs a hand over his face and squints across at me. 'Is this real?'

'I would think real enough for Lydia Callin.'

'Jesus.'

'Derek, where were you on the tenth and eleventh of August?'

'I was away with my family. A week in Galway together before I started back here.'

I take out my notebook, pass it to him again. 'Would you mind giving me the name of your parents, or someone who could verify that.'

'Why?'

'If you've an alibi for when Lydia Callin went missing, it allows us to rule you out.'

He writes down his parents' names, their address.

'What did you do after you returned from your holiday?'

'I'd a few weeks off, then came back to digs the week before term. The degree is intense. I wanted some time to get settled and I've work at the union.'

'You're on Hanbury Lane? Is that right?'

If he's surprised that we already know where he lives, he hides it well. 'Yeah. In the direction of the Guinness factory.'

Finishing my coffee, I place the cup and saucer to the side. 'Tell me, besides your group, do you know the other players in this game?'

'No.'

'How many would you say there are?'

'Eighty-odd.'

I drum my fingers on the table for a second. 'That's the thing – it turns out there aren't. In fact, there is only your group of five.' I leave me out, not wanting to give away my position just yet, and Lydia, although I know for the game's sake we are both considered players. I watch for any change in his expression that registers my omission.

His eyes darken and he gathers up his bag, slides free of the table. 'Oh no, I'm not doing this. I haven't done anything wrong.' He stands. 'Shouldn't you be reading me my rights or something?'

'Should I?'

'Look, I'm sorry if a person is dead, but I'd nothing to do with it. And even if what you're saying is true, people do this kind of thing all the time, what we're doing. They research murder cases. Armchair detectives,' he says. 'That's what they're called.'

I lean back against my seat, look up at him. 'The law doesn't look too favourably on anyone who interferes in an investigation.'

'Fuck this,' he says.

I turn, watch him stumble and apologize his way through the other students. All of whom barely acknowledge his passage through the room. His bag slips from his shoulder multiple times until finally he gives up hoisting it into position, balls the strap in his hand and disappears out of the café. And I hope that Derek Cohen does exactly what I think he'll do.

CHAPTER 15

I come away from my meeting with Derek Cohen feeling, for once in this investigation, like we might have nudged ahead. Ahead of what, I'm not sure. But we're no longer testing ground not knowing where next to step, we've leads to follow and by this evening, hopefully, a plan to execute. Sitting in the car outside the Bureau, I wait for Mullins to join me. The rain has returned and is tipping down on the roof. The kind of rain that drives in straight lines and rolls in sheets over the windscreen. I pick out Mullins making his way quickly towards the car, shoulders crouched, head ducked beneath his rucksack which he holds over his head.

He opens the passenger side and drops into the seat. He shakes his rucksack out then barely taking the time to close the door, removes his notes from the bag. He lays them out across the dashboard explaining to me as he goes what he's been working on. Mullins has done his homework, I'll give him that. He's read through every document he can on geographic profiling. He spreads a map of the city across his knee. Taps on Teddy

Dolan's address. It's well outside our circle of play. Sitting along the coast, cocooned by solid, comfortable houses and facing the cool front of the Irish Sea.

'According to the geoprofile of this case, if we think of his home,' he says, 'and where he grew up, he's out of the zone, unlikely as the killer but also unlikely as a victim targeted in The Murder Box.' Then he drags his finger down the map. 'But if we look at where he works, here, just south of Donnybrook, then he's in the game.' He stops abruptly.

Just a little north of Clonskeagh. 'I think it's time we pushed Teddy Dolan for a few answers,' I say.

Mullins is still in his first-day suit. I'm thinking the newbie vibe he exudes just might come in useful here, persuade Teddy Dolan he's got the softer end of the questioning.

The rain is still going when we park up outside Dolan's. I turn off the ignition and reach into the back seat for my mac, indicating the footwell at Mullins' feet where there's an umbrella. He collects up his papers, slips them back into the rucksack, retrieves a small hand-sized notebook and slides it into his breast pocket.

He reaches for the umbrella, holds it out between us. 'Don't you want it?' he eyes my hair.

I push out of the car. 'I'm good.'

He opens the door, puts up the umbrella then steps out under it. 'Are they expecting us?'

The curtains are drawn in the windows of the Dolan home. The gates pull back before we've a chance to ring the call button. I look up, spot the new camera looking down on us from a metal pole inside the garden. We walk up the short drive. Sodden, rust-coloured leaves cling to the ground. We move around a rose bush that has fallen like a swooning lady over the edge of the kerb; hot pink petals spill over the dark tarmacadam of the driveway. There's a note stuck over the doorbell. Do not ring. Mullins looks at me expectantly, then reaches for the bell, but I hold his hand back and after a second or so the door edges open. Monica Dolan stands before us, blonde hair pulled back into a chic ponytail, lemon cotton sweater rolled up to the elbows. Her wrists glint with silver bracelets as she pulls the door inward.

'Hello, detectives,' she says, stepping back to allow us in. 'Sorry, I don't think we've met?' She extends a hand to Mullins who fumbles with the umbrella, shaking it outside, tries then tries again to get it closed. Eventually, he drops it on the ground, wipes his palm over the bottom of his jacket then shakes Monica's hand.

'Detective Smith Mullins. Nice to meet you, Mrs Dolan.'

Monica gives him a bemused smile and maybe it's that or the fact that she's not wearing make-up that lightens her face, so she appears younger than the previous times I've met her. There's less of a performance to her movements. But she looks tired and dark smudges tell of sleepless nights beneath her eyes. When she turns to close the door, she puts her full weight behind it, leaning both hands on the wood. She gives the handle a rattle to check that the bolt has shot through, then, satisfied, slides a door chain home.

'The family liaison officer has just left,' she says. 'So he's tired. We both are.'

'That's understandable.' I give her a reassuring smile. 'How are you?'

She runs a hand over her hair. 'Okay, I think. Just glad it's over.' And there could be a warning in that. Monica making it clear that for her, this is the end. If that is what she's hinting at then we have to wonder why she's not interested in finding out who abducted her husband.

'We've a few follow-up questions. We'll try not to impose for too long,' I say and feel Mullins stiffen beside me, confused as to why I'd lead her to believe that we're anything but finished with this case.

'Alright, just remember he's been through a lot,' she says, giving each of us a firm look.

We follow her, as Baz and I did before, down the wide hallway, Mullins' head tipped back to take in the chandelier and space overhead. There's the skip of classical music coming from the other side of the house and the scent of fresh coffee in the air. She opens the door of the living room. It's dark. Not blackout dark but muted. The curtains are pulled and the room smells musky. On a chair in the far corner, I see two pillows stacked on top of a folded blanket.

Monica follows my line of sight. 'Teddy felt easier sleeping down here last night.'

'Stop talking about me as if I'm not here,' his voice comes from the direction of the sofa. He sits up carefully from a lying position. Ruffles a hand through his hair, then reaches out to a glass of water on a magazine table at his side.

'The detectives are here,' Monica says and goes to the window.

Her hands are on the edges of the curtains, ready to throw them open.

'Leave them closed,' he says, then adds, 'please, love.'

She does as he asks, turns back to us. 'Tea?'

'Not for me, thanks,' Mullins says a little too brightly.

'That'd be lovely,' I say and she all but runs from the room, closing the door with a gentle click as she goes.

I take a seat in one of the chairs across from Teddy.

He's dressed in a pale grey tracksuit. He's shaved. Had a haircut. But his face is puffy and pale. Now that I'm closer, I can smell the bitter scent of stale booze. 'Your man has just left. He poked around up here a bit,' he taps the side of his head. 'But I can tell you what I told him, which is not much.'

'Can you tell me about the phone call you had with your wife on the night of the exhibition?' I ask, aiming for an easy one to get him comfortable.

He turns the glass of water in his hand, looks down into it. 'She was booking flights for a golf trip. We talked about what time would be good with filming and all. Then chatted a bit about what we'd planned for the weekend.'

'What was that?'

'We decided a quiet night in. My schedule had been kind of hectic. Hers too. We were going to get a takeaway. Just a pizza, couple of bottles of wine and watch a movie.' He looks up. 'Living the life, as they say,' he laughs, it gets stuck in his throat and he downs a mouthful of water. Then he focuses on me, his expression changing from bitterness to concern. 'How are you, though? I mean, the explosion. Fuck,' he beats the heel of his hand to his forehead. 'That can't have been good? And that girl? Jesus.'

He rocks a little, only stopping when the water from the glass sloshes over his hand.

'I'm fine. A few scratches is all. Thank you. Teddy, can you tell me how you got to Henry Street yesterday?'

He looks at me, I think, with not a small degree of panic, like he's not sure how he's here, in this room, with us. Teddy Dolan is teetering right on the edge of reality.

But he answers. 'We drove. Parked up a bit from the street. I got out and went on my way.'

'Can you be more specific about where you were dropped off?'

'It wasn't far. I don't know. It's all a bit of a blur, I can barely remember going to the hospital after it all. The doc said it's shock.'

'Take your time,' I say and wait.

He looks down at his knees, his head shaking slightly from side to side. 'It looked like the back entrance to the shops, you know, where deliveries might be deposited. There was a . . . a building, small, on one side,' he says. 'Had barbed wire on the roof.'

'What else do you remember?'

'They covered my head, then when we stopped,' he says. 'They cut my hands and feet free. Told me to sit up, put that thing around me, then the coat. They told me to get out of the car, then I felt them put another belt around me which was the harness for the phone,' he pauses. 'They put the crate in my hands and gave me instructions on how to set myself up. Then I was to face the wall. Count a full minute before I took the hood off. I was to put the hat on, well over my eyes and walk to the top of Henry Street. They said they'd be watching and if I made a run for it, they'd . . .' he breaks off, rubs a hand over his face. 'I heard them drive away.

Counted through a minute. Came out the top of the street, saw I wasn't far off Henry Street and . . .' He looks up at me, his dark eyebrows down over his bloodshot eyes. 'that's it.'

'You said yesterday that you didn't know who they were? Any ideas now?'

He shakes his head. 'I'm sorry. The whole experience is so hazy. They were putting something in my food or the water, I don't know which. I spent most of my time asleep or unconscious, I don't know. They never spoke to me. They used a text to speech app or something if and when they did speak. The voice was automated. I never saw whoever it was.'

'How about the vehicle? How long did the journey take?'

'It wasn't a car, I don't think. Felt too spacious. A van maybe or a family estate. I don't know how long we drove. Could've been ten minutes, could've been two hours. Time was difficult for me to hold on to.' He blinks. Hard. His hand twitches around the glass and, for the first time since sitting down to talk to him, I notice the bandaged finger. He catches me looking at it, tucks that hand under his leg. A shimmer of sweat glazes his forehead. Just above the neckline of his grey sweater, I see the rapid movement at the base of his throat as his breathing increases. He puts down the glass, coughs into his fist, tries to get a bit of control on his emotions.

'I just wanted it over,' he says after a while. Quietly. Like ash floating through night sky. And something in him seems to still. His breathing slows. A tear runs down his face. He tips his head back and lets out a breath. It looks like relief. The thin skin of his eyelids flickers and he raises dark eyes. 'Whatever was going to happen, I wanted it to happen.'

183

'But you held on,' Mullins says suddenly, and I give him a look of warning that tells him not to push.

'It was only when the girl, Orla, began circling me that I . . .' he trails off.

'Teddy, can we go back to the car again?'

He inhales a deep breath. 'Sure.'

'How many people were with you?'

He's back to studying his knees. 'I've been thinking about it. I'm pretty sure there was just one. I remember hearing just the one door closing at the front of the car. And when they moved me, one hand grabbed my arm, and the other held a knife to my throat.' He blinks hard a few times then looks up quickly as if he's just realized something. 'I got the sense they were taller than me. I know that doesn't help much but it's all I've got.'

'A knife?'

'Yes, the knife was always there,' he touches his fingertips to his neck.

'On the night of the exhibition. What happened?' I ask.

'I'm really trying to remember, but I can't. I'd gone out to call Monica. I hadn't been feeling well, I was tired and wanted to go home. After that . . . I really don't remember anything.'

I think about the photo Derek Cohen told me about where Teddy is getting into a car after the exhibition. We've no idea if it's authentic. Nothing to verify it besides Dolan who has some serious holes in his memory. 'We'd some information that you were seen getting into a vehicle? Do you remember that?'

He thinks for a while and I see his frustration that he can't bring the memory forward. Or won't.

'I'm sorry. No.'

He stares off into nothingness and I leave him there for a while. Listening beyond the sounds of the room, I think the tea has been forgotten and instead Monica Dolan is likely pressed up against the door trying to pluck anything from the story her husband is relaying. We're not the only ones who want answers.

'Teddy?' I ask quietly.

He passes a hand over his mouth. 'Sorry. Yes.'

'Where did they hold you?'

'Lower floor or a basement. I think I was still in the city. I could hear traffic and sometimes I thought I heard people moving. Like above me,' he raises an arm, makes a circle in the air above his head.

Immediately, I conjure up what type of houses across Dublin would accommodate a basement. That might suggest his abductor was working most of the time or that they had a family they needed to get back to and Teddy was being kept in a separate property to the perp's home. Or we're looking for someone who lives alone.

He goes on: 'I was in and out of consciousness for most of the time there. It just felt like I was constantly waking from a black sleep. My hands were tied with cable ties. There was a bed, or a mattress for me to lie on. Food was brought in once a day. Erm, a few packaged sandwiches like you buy in a shop. Biscuits. And bottled water.'

Food bought at a convenience store, perhaps? We could be looking at a location with a shop nearby. Which doesn't exactly narrow things down in a city but if we manage to root out a few proposed locations then we've at least 'shop within walking distance' to check off the list.

185

Mullins jumps in, tries to get more information on what the location looks like. 'How about windows?'

Teddy half-turns towards the sound of Mullins' voice. Closes his eyes briefly. 'One, I think, high up on the wall but it was boarded up.' He coughs into his hand, stretches for his water then takes a long drink. 'Sorry, I'm very tired.'

'You're doing really well,' Mullins says. 'We've just a few more questions.'

'Okay,' Teddy replies.

I shift to the edge of my seat. 'What does the name Lydia Callin mean to you?'

His body freezes. Just a second. Like a little zip of energy has charged up his spine. I watch his face for a reaction, for anything that tells of his involvement with Lydia but all I see is exhaustion. I think he's going to give us another shake of his head and claim that he doesn't know or remember but instead, he meets my eyes and says: 'You know about the affair.'

'Her flatmate told us,' I answer.

'I met her last year. Monica and I, we were going through a rough patch. Or I should say, she was. I was acting the maggot and she was on my back about it.' He pauses. 'You ever get to a point in your life where you look back on something and don't recognize yourself? Where you can't believe that truly, truly to the core of your being, you're a fucking arsehole. Rotten and dirty and barely earning yourself the title of man.' He shakes his head at the ground.

Mullins is busy with his notebook, practically ready to write Dolan's biography, so I clear my throat, then prompt: 'Lydia?'

Bringing his gaze back to me, he rolls out his right shoulder

186

as if he could shrug off her name. 'Sorry, yes, we met a year or so ago. It wasn't quite Christmas, around Halloween perhaps. I remember that the evenings were dark when I came out of the studio. A friend, one of the production team, fancied a drink, but we wanted somewhere off the beaten track. She was behind the bar. I stayed late,' his mouth turns down. Disappointed at himself. 'She wasn't loud or in your face or particularly sophisticated, but she had this calm energy. Like she really knew herself. You meet those people, don't you? People who are just really sure of themselves but in a quiet kind of way.'

'You were intimate?'

He reaches for the water again. 'Yes.'

'How long did you see each other?'

'Up until the start of summer.'

'June?'

'Probably May. I can't recall the exact date.'

'Did she think you would leave your wife for her?'

'No,' he says firmly.

'How do you know?'

'We both knew that was impossible from the start. She knows how the world works. She was as eager as me to keep things quiet.'

He gets up suddenly, walks across the room. Wanting to get out from under my questions. He goes to the window, pushes the curtains open a fraction. Squints out at the grey day. 'Why are you wanting to know about Lydia?'

Mullins gets there before me. 'We're following a line of inquiry, is all.'

The curtains close again and my eyes take a second to adjust to the darkness.

I ask the question we came here to ask, hoping we've done enough softening around the edges that it doesn't shut Teddy down altogether. 'When you broke up in May, was that the last time you saw her?'

He doesn't get to answer. The door creaks and Monica appears, a tray in her hands, four mugs balanced on it.

'I'm sorry, I couldn't remember who said they wanted tea and who didn't.'

Teddy creeps back to the sofa.

Mullins gets up, takes the tray from Monica and sets it on the table.

'Thank you,' she says, taking a mug and sitting down next to her husband. She rests her other hand on the his knee. 'How are you feeling, darling?'

'Fine,' he says.

Mullins sips the tea, flinches then blows at the hot surface before putting the mug on the table.

'Detective, would you mind?' Monica asks, pointing to a shelf below the table.

'Of course. Sorry,' he replies, flushing. He reaches out towards a stack of ceramic coasters.

'Monica,' I say, 'last time we spoke, I asked if you knew of Lydia Callin?'

Her hand tightens on her husband's knee as if to hold him in place.

'It's alright,' he murmurs.

She flares her nostrils at me. 'Is she involved in this? Did she have something to do with Teddy's disappearance?'

'As we were saying to Mr Dolan,' Mullins begins, 'we are simply following—'

But Monica Dolan isn't as easily talked down. 'My husband has been through enough. Do you understand that? I, he, neither of us ever thought he'd come back alive. But here he is. If that woman has had anything to do with this, then we need to know. You don't get to ask your questions without answering a few of ours.'

'Mon, they're just doing their job,' Teddy says.

I swallow down a mouthful of irritation, if she'd been straight with us from the beginning, maybe Lydia Callin would still be alive or at the least we'd have had a clearer picture of her husband's activities. I say: 'Unfortunately, we found Lydia Callin's body yesterday morning.'

The colour drops from Teddy's face. 'What?'

I leave him with that information for a few seconds. I can almost hear it clacking through his thoughts, knocking down one after the other until he gets to what it could mean for him. That his affair could implicate him in murder. That if this got out, the legs of it would run across the headlines for weeks, flattening what career he has left.

'We're in the early stages of our investigation but we do need to follow the leads we have,' I say. 'We want to rule both of you out. But to do that we need you to cooperate.'

'Lydia's dead?' Teddy breathes.

Monica is on her feet. She glares down at me, pointing at the door. 'Get out.'

'Mon!' Teddy says.

'No, Teddy. I've been through enough. I'm not having your bit on the side becoming part of this story.' She turns to me, eyes wide with rage. 'You – stop this line of inquiry. This is some kind of fucking publicity stunt for your department, isn't it? Wanting a few more weeks in the papers. Hoping for a promotion. Understand me when I say that if you make this bad for us, the only line you'll be investigating is the line at the post office when you pick up your dole.'

There's a scuffle beside me as Mullins gets to his feet and goes to the door. Teddy has his head in his hands. The room is quiet for a moment. Mullins looks between Monica's worried expression, Teddy's bent head and me.

I lower my voice. 'I guess we could always take this down to the Bureau.'

Teddy's hands peel away from his head. 'No.'

'We have an investigation to conduct, Teddy. We need answers now, not when you feel like giving them.'

Monica makes some kind of noise that sounds like a swear word hissed through gritted teeth. 'This is what that bitch wanted.'

'How so?' I ask.

'Oh, come on. A twenty-two-year-old nobody and my husband? He's a star. He breaks up with her and somehow she's managed to inveigle her way into our lives again.'

'She's dead, Mrs Dolan. Murdered.'

She closes her eyes, takes a long, slow breath in through her nose, holds it a beat before releasing it, spreading her fingers at her sides and forcing her shoulders down. She sits down again.

I look to Teddy, ask him again when was the last time he saw

Lydia. And Monica's right arm gives a little involuntary twitch where I think for a second she's about to hit him.

'When we broke up,' he says.

'They don't need to know this, Teddy. Detective, you'd understand, if you worked in the world we do, that people will do anything to get their name alongside you in a paper. Teddy is safe now. That's all that matters. And I'll be doing – *we'll* be doing everything in our power to shut this whole thing down as soon as possible. We won't have this following us around for the rest of our lives.'

And I see now what Monica Dolan is about. She knows her husband did not stop seeing Lydia Callin in May. Knows that there's a possibility her husband's most recent affair could come out and take centre stage in what should be their combined story of survival. A story that would mean her husband could reclaim his career. But another affair hitting the gossip columns pours water over whatever embers of public sympathy Teddy has earned. Mullins is on the same line of thought; he's barely moved at the door, transfixed by what Monica is saying, his head tipped a little, taking in every strained key change in her voice.

I say to her: 'How about you? When did you last see Lydia Callin?'

She pulls her chin in. 'I didn't. I never saw her.'

There's a groan as Teddy unfolds his body, rolls his head back on his neck. Then he pulls himself upright, rests a hand on his wife's arm and whispers, 'I'm sorry.' Then, to us: 'The last time I saw her was on the first of August. It was a Thursday. We met at her place when her flatmate was working.'

Something in Monica seems to diminish, whatever string had been holding her up over the last month has finally been cut.

Teddy turns to his wife. 'I'm so sorry.'

Mullins is quiet when we get back to the car. I start the ignition. 'What's up?' I ask.

'Nothing. Just thinking.'

I push a raindrop out of my eyes. Remove my phone from my pocket, open it, expecting a message from Baz asking how we're getting on, but there's nothing. I send him a quick text, ask how *he's* getting on and hit send. 'Best to think out loud when you're on a case,' I say to Mullins. 'Don't be afraid to say what you feel is happening.' I throw him a smile.

'He last saw Lydia Callin on the first of August. That was the day before he went missing. Only nine days before Lydia went missing.' He takes a breath. 'Why haven't we searched his house. For the murder-mystery box?'

'You that desperate to get on Donna Hegarty's bad side? Have a yearning to go back to traffic?'

He stares out at the Dolan home then back at me. 'He has motive. As does his wife for that matter.'

When I was standing in Henry Street waiting for that explosive to go off, it never felt to me that Teddy was putting on that fear. I smelled the stench of urine on his clothing. The sweat from his skin.

'You don't think he did it?' Mullins asks.

'If that box of tricks hadn't landed on my desk pointing a much too obvious arrow at Teddy, then I'd be right there with you.'

He takes that as praise and a flash of pride crosses his face. 'He lied about when he last saw her initially.'

'I think that was more about hiding it from his wife.' I start the car, check the GPS on my phone. Next on our list, Ashley Noone. Twenty-year-old med student. Only child whose parents have invested heavily in their darling daughter's future. All college payments from Daddy's account, a nice little allowance set up and a part-time job at her auntie's sandwich shop to keep the feet on the ground. 'We've got a strong connection to the cases now, yes. We've verification of the affair – but why would Teddy put himself right at the centre of Lydia Callin's murder by creating a murder-mystery game? It doesn't make sense. We need more. And although time is not on our side, luckily we've plenty of people to get information from,' I say and pull away from the kerb.

Mullins gazes out the passenger window. Teddy Dolan clearly still on his mind.

'Perhaps you're right,' I concede. 'If we get a warrant signed today and find a box in his house, then that would do very nicely.'

'That's what I thought.'

'Okay then.'

He looks at me expectantly.

'Well, make the call – or are you wanting me to hold your hand for that too.'

He takes up the phone. Excited. I half-listen as he talks to Paul, arranges the warrant, then for a couple of SOCOs to go out to the Dolan house as soon as possible. And I can almost hear the creak of the hinges on our money box. He gives instructions on what they should be searching for and I'm impressed by the detail he provides: phones, laptops, tablets and The Murder Box – he pauses – receipts, in coat pockets, public-transport tickets or cards.

'Is that it?' I hear Paul say with an uncharacteristic note of sarcasm.

There's a pause as Mullins rattles around his thoughts, makes sure he's pinched every thread. 'Yep, that's it. Thank you, Paul.'

'No worries.'

Mullins hangs up. Pleased with himself. 'Where to now?'

I turn right at the RTE studios towards the city centre. 'We're off to get the lowdown on how Ashley Noone spends her day.'

CHAPTER 16

End of lunch hour and Ashley Noone folds a paper bag around the last bread roll of her shift. She passes it over the glass counter, a quick smile to the customer in front of her who dumps a handful of coins into her waiting palm before dipping her chin to continue a phone conversation. The customer tucks the roll into her bag, plucks too many napkins from the dispenser and leaves without a thank you. If Ashley wasn't so tired she might've called after her, soaked her voice with acid and shouted 'you're welcome' at the closing door.

Instead, she pulls the plastic gloves from her hands and reminds herself why she's stuck here, pushing egg mayo into sandwiches for people she wouldn't normally even speak to. Her parents remind her every week that she needs to be grateful. Her aunt has made a nice little packet over the last decade with these delis. Small corner pop-ups, and now two vans. Ashley drew the line with the suggestion she could work in one of the vans. However much she hated working in the shop, it was better than being cold and surrounded by stinking vats of congealing food. She dumps the gloves into the bin and drags the hairnet from her hair, goes to the door and flips the sign to 'Closed'. They always have a twenty-minute break once they get over the main rush – not so long they'll lose business, but enough for them to have a quick smoke and to force themselves to eat through their lunch.

She finds Suzanna out the back where there's a stingy little yard. In time, some rich eejit will come along, buy up this shop and squeeze an even stingier house in here, then smack an outrageous price on it and some bigger rich eejit will come along and buy it. She lights up a cigarette, sits on a stool. Suzanna crosses her legs, the bony angle of her knee acts as support to the hand holding her coffee, the other arm is held out straight from her body so that the smoke drifts off and away from her hair. They sit together silently until they've finished their cigs, then drop them into an empty takeaway cup.

'Fucking wrecked,' Suzanna says. 'I've another shift tomorrow.' She slides Ashley a bit of side-eye. From time to time, Suzanna has a real problem with Ashley's situation – that she's more control over her hours and as long as she clocks up fifteen or so throughout the week, her aunt is happy enough. For Suzanna, this is her job, not something to be worked around college studies, and once in a while she likes to test Ashley, to make sure she respects that, that she's not looking down her nose at her, thinking she's better.

Ashley's dealt with this kind of a bullshit all of her life. Especially from women. It's fucking exhausting, playing down who she really is. Either acting dull or stupid so that they don't feel threatened or jealous. There's nothing she can do about her looks, nor would she. She's blonde, fine-boned, big-eyed and fucking happy about it.

'You see they found Teddy Dolan?'

'Yeah.'

'And now they've found some other girl's body.'

Ashley removes the wrapping from a sandwich, takes a bite and almost gags. Possibly one of the worst things about working with food is that you have to eat it afterwards. 'Didn't see that.'

'There must be some connection,' Suzanna says. 'Weird though.'

She has to stop herself from rolling her eyes. Not much weird about crime in this city. This is Suzanna all over. You can't open a newspaper without seeing the details of some new murder shoved into the corner of a page. There was a time when murder made front-page news. Now the headlines are reserved for political, financial or celeb scandals. Life and death don't sell like they used to. It's so like Suzanna to read more into this girl's death because, to her, murder isn't enough. She is an absolute hound for conspiracy theories. Over the last year, Ashley's heard them all. But still, Ashley can't help asking her if she has a copy of today's paper so she can check it out herself. Maybe there is something. Suzanna roots around in her bag, passes her the paper.

'Saw it on the local news this morning. It must be in there somewhere,' she says as Ashley turns through the pages. But it is isn't. Of course it isn't.

'What you doing after your shift?' Suzanna asks when Ashley passes the paper back.

'I have a tutorial.'

Suzanna shoves another cigarette between her thin, flat lips and replies out of the side of her mouth. 'I know where I'd rather be,' she says, then lights up behind her cupped hand. 'How's uni going, anyway?'

Ashley wishes she hadn't made the mistake of oversharing with Suzanna last year. It's the part of her own personality that she most hates. The constant urge to tell people that little bit too much about her life in order to trade herself into their good graces. She should know better. Experience has shown her that women take one look at her and decide she's the enemy; throw in the fact that she has money behind her and she really doesn't stand a chance.

She swallows the last bite of her sandwich, rolls the wrapper into a ball and stands. She pauses, looks down on Suzanna and answers her question.

'It's going well,' she says. She watches Suzanna pout at that, not wanting to hear that once more life was handing Ashley an ace. 'Very well, actually,' she twists the knife. 'You might say, I'm killing it.'

Ashley's tutor, Lang, clicks the top of his pen, makes some notes on his clipboard. 'Too much water, Tilly. Get rid, start over,' he says to one of the students. He barely contains his anger.

Ashley watches him try to ease the tension from his jaw. Tilly, clearly mortified, takes her tray of specimen tissue and walks it to the clinical waste bin.

'Get a move on,' Lang growls from the top of the room. He plucks an orange from his desk.

In a minute, he'll walk to Ashley's bench, stand behind her and watch her from over her shoulder. All the while, she'll hear his fingers dig through the orange peel, the scent of citrus growing. She hates when he does this, hates that she can feel the warmth of his breath as it crawls over her hair. He'll be waiting for her hand to shake while she works on the heart tissue, wanting her to forget a step in preparing the specimen on the slide. But Lang doesn't intimidate her. She knows exactly what she's doing. Has been practising this very skill on lamb's kidneys whenever she's had a free hour to use the labs.

The first bloom of citrus rises to her nose, but she won't be thrown off. She unclips the block of paraffin wax from the case. Inside is the dark blot of lamb's heart tissue she's examining. She thinks about what this means for later. How much she should give away to the other players in her group. There's at least one who'd have the skills to do this properly. And she's examined the slide in The Murder Box; the cut of the tissue was much too thick.

She fits the tiny block of wax to the front of the microtome. This one is a rotary microtome. A machine, somewhat more sophisticated and delicate than your meat slicer at a butcher, but something about turning the handle at the side and collecting the fine slices of specimen from the front makes her think of prepping in the sandwich shop, where her job is to pass a roast ham across a blade and collect the slices beneath before lunch hour.

She touches the tip of a cocktail stick to one of the delicate, translucent slices. Then carries it to a waiting tray of water, where she gives it enough time to un-wrinkle, then she takes a slide from the side, keeping her movements clinical, decisive but never breaking concentration.

Behind her, Lang shifts his position and for a second it gets to her and she freezes. She has never seen him do this with any of the male students and the thought makes her grit her teeth. She has a sudden vision of spinning around and driving the glass slide into her tutor's neck. She won't; she's human, after all, and would regret it immediately. But there would be a moment, the length of an exhale, perhaps, where she'd enjoy the startled widening of his eyes, the desperate grapple of his fingers at his throat. That would feel good.

'You might want to change that slide,' he says suddenly.

She breathes out. Spell broken. She's pinching the slide, right where the specimen is due to go and he's right, she has smeared the surface with her own skin cells. She puts it to the side, takes up another, dips it in the water next to the floating tissue and feels a surge of achievement when it clings cleanly and smoothly to the surface.

'Nice work,' Lang says. He lingers a beat too long then returns to the top of the room to deposit the orange peel in the bin.

Not that there is ever a good time to admit this in a murder investigation, but I'm enjoying the day with Mullins. I miss having Baz here but Mullins did well in the Dolan house, kept his mouth shut when he was supposed to, and he has an ear for how to parse a difficult question. Not every detective can do that. You don't know how a witness or victim might react when you're talking to them. Some want to get their story out as quickly as they can, some part of them hoping that to unload is to unburden. Those ones give you a jumbled mess of information, timelines mixed up, the pieces the wrong way around, random names thrown in for good measure. 'Then Rita came in—' but you need to let them run that rope through their hands until they get to the end. Other witnesses, you have to tease the story out of them. When you do finally get them on the move, the wrong question at the wrong time can throw them right off and you end up missing something vital.

'That's something,' he says now, tearing open a sachet of brown sauce and squeezing it over a breakfast sandwich. It's almost five o'clock. Using the empty wrapper, he spreads the sauce over the bread then presses the sandwich closed. 'She'd have had the opportunity to get that slide made up. Who was the other med student in the group?'

We're fresh from talking to Ashley Noone's tutor, Dr Lang and are parked down Clonmel Street, along the old stone walls that border the Iveagh Gardens. It's just over six months since a man killed himself in front of witnesses in the park's sunken lawns, but it feels to me like a decade ago. Despite the height of the walls and the buildings around us, a stripe of yellow sunshine escapes the overhead clouds and beams through the windscreen. I pull the visor down, reach for my coffee on the dashboard, turn through the list of students' names given to us by Dr Lang. He was reserved in his praise of Ashley Noone, a note of begrudgery in his voice.

'She's very focused,' he said. 'She'll do well in a research setting down the line, I'm sure.'

He was hitting sixty with a reluctant knock, his hair slicked straight back from his forehead, glinting with the tell-tale sheen of black dye that glowed with a hint of burgundy under the office lights. It did little for his ruddy complexion. He wore a black turtleneck that rose to his jawline and he finished every sentence with a kind of sly, self-satisfied smile.

Ashley Noone had not headed home over the summer months. She had studied. Lang said he'd warned her about burnout.

'But she wouldn't listen,' he said. 'She's not the most receptive of students. I get the feeling she thinks she's something to prove. It can be the case with some of the females I teach. Hard to believe in this day and age. I try to encourage them to be as they are. One's allowed to embrace your sex and be successful, no? Is she in some kind of trouble?' he asked, a frown of concern on his brow.

'Harrison Lloyd,' I say to Mullins' question. 'Lucky for him he's on the B module and won't have to endure Lang until next term.'

'So, Ashley could be the one. She'd have the skills to put together the histology slide. And the time. As he said, she's been here all summer, practising, using the labs.'

'Abigail, our pathologist, says the slide in The Murder Box was clumsily done. The tissue sample wasn't prepared correctly. It was so thick they couldn't view it under the scope as was,' I say.

I unwrap my sandwich. Cheese and some kind of tomato pesto. I bite into it and the cheese sticks to the roof of my mouth. I wash it down with more coffee.

'Are you worried Lang will say something to Ashley?'

'Won't matter if he does. Besides, Lang's not about to give Ashley any warning about what might be coming. He'll be there with his fake smile and his polo-necked fucking shoulders for her to cry onto when her world begins crumbling.'

'You thought he was a creep?'

I chew through another bite of the sandwich. 'You didn't?'

'A little eccentric, perhaps.'

I shake my head. 'How nice it must be to look through the prism of a Y chromosome.'

'What?'

'Never mind.' I fold the other sandwich back up in its wrapping, swallow down enough coffee to wipe the taste from mouth and memory and put it away. 'Come on, we've got some screen time to clock up.'

He frowns at me. 'Screen time? Aren't we going to check out the remaining players?'

'We are,' I reply and when he still looks confused, I add: 'You'll see.'

The search of Dolan's house took all afternoon and a good part of the evening and raised no flags. Between that and the surveillance we've planned, it's only a matter of time before either Jack or Donna puts a lid on things. I'm hoping that we'll be able to keep the eyes we have on all the players for at least twenty-four hours. There's a good chance they know as much as we do about Lydia Callin and her murder, but if what Camille Forbes says is true, then one of them is our killer. Now that we have their IP addresses matched to their usernames, Steve has managed to gain access to the private chat rooms on the murder box site and although they've been quiet the last day or so, since this morning there's been a flurry of activity. My conversation with Derek Cohen did what I expected – sent him running to his small network of murder-mystery players to ask if they could all meet in person. Ashley suggested her place, as we predicted, seeing as she's the only one of their group living alone. Ryan said the surveillance team baulked at our plans. Months, they said, that's what they needed to get in and out cleanly. But we don't have months. We need to know what these players know, and quickly.

'The last of the surveillance team left Ashley Noone's premises at five-thirty,' Steve tells me. 'I've the feed set up in the viewing room off Interview One.'

Tension eases from my shoulders. Ever since Neve Jameson walked into my office, a growing panic has been coiling around my spine. Not helped by the surprise of Teddy Dolan's reappearance on Henry Street or the happy splash of pig's blood across the walls of my own bedroom. We still don't have a prime suspect and it makes me anxious. I don't like to hunt what I can't see. Normally, with the mountain of information we have, a body, an entire box laying out our victim's last movements, witness statements, Dolan practically returned from the fucking dead, I'd be ready to leap to the next lily pad. Be able to cross some of that information off the list. Instead, we're drowning in it, all pieces still in play and no idea where it's going next.

The office is slowing for the day, Paul gathers up his coat and bag, touches each of the items on his desk as if for luck, then turns his screen off. He lifts a hand in goodbye and makes his way to the door. The overhead lights dim, the faces of the remaining two or so members of staff picked out by the glow of their screens. Ryan is slumped in his chair watching the Clonskeagh CCTV footage.

'Make sure you take a break,' I say to him.

He looks up, surprised to see me. 'Hey, Chief. Will do. Harwood's on his way in.'

'He say where he was?'

'Following up on a lead, I thought.'

I flick a glance at my watch. It's almost six-thirty. 'Okay, well, tell him to join Steve and me when he gets here.'

I go to the viewing room, try to push thoughts about what might be going on with Baz out of my head.

Steve looks up when I enter. 'The camera is positioned below the TV here, to the right of the desk,' he says and clicks the mouse. The screen fills with the main room of Ashley Noone's apartment. 'Good view of the dining table, partial view of the entrance and exit towards the kitchen.'

It's better than I'd hoped. 'How's the audio?'

'Seems to be working alright. She got in. Took some shopping into the kitchen. Was off screen for ten minutes but there was good audio there. Could hear her unpacking. She laid out the dining table with some snacks and it seems like she's in the bedroom at the moment.'

I pull up a chair. Sit down.

There's a knock on the door. Baz. He throws us a smile in greeting and I feel a rush of relief.

'How we doing?' he asks, removing his coat and folding himself into a chair.

'Hoping they'll be here soon,' I reply.

I look him over. He's shaved. Hair swept to the side. Fresh shirt. 'We missed you this morning,' I say. 'Where've you been?'

He rubs a hand over his ear. 'Yeah, heard it was full steam ahead. You went out to Dolan. Did he talk?'

He knows me well enough, knows any detective well enough to understand that it hasn't slipped by me that he's not answered my question. But I don't ask again. 'He did. He doesn't remember much. We'll have to wait for blood toxicology to come through but it sounds like he was drugged for most of his captivity. He says he had no idea who was behind his abduction.'

'Was he sleeping with her?' he asks, meaning Lydia.

'Yes.'

'Hmm,' he says. He reaches out, takes up the surveillance report. Reads through the names of our suspects. 'Do they know we . . . you . . . received a box?'

'They shouldn't.'

Ashley appears on the screen. She's changed into light blue jeans and a red check shirt. Her blonde hair is loose around her shoulders. She draws the curtains, finds a lighter over the mantelpiece and lights a couple of candles on a low table in front of the sofa. She kneels down, removes a red box from beneath the table. The Murder Box.

CHAPTER 17

Ashley has just enough time to set out the game's pieces before they arrive. They being the other players. She looks over her flat. A couple of candles are burning in the middle of the coffee table. They give off a pleasant floral scent. She's plumped up the cushions on the sofa. Her desk, near the window is clean of the usual empty Coke cans and crumpled crisp packets. Pencils, pens tidied away, laptop closed. Her textbooks are stacked in a pleasing pyramid shape from largest to smallest. She loves this flat and can't imagine that in a couple of years she'll be forced to let it go. Return it to her aunt who occasionally likes to drop by unannounced as if she lives here.

She goes to the bedroom, searches through her make-up, then applies a dusting of highlighting powder over the crest of her cheekbones and along the underside of her eyebrow. She doesn't want to overdo it. She knows all of these people from their online personas, but she also knows that counts for very little. She's only this afternoon learned their real names and she's not sure whether she should be meeting them. But as the wheels are already in motion, she's not going to let them pigeon-hole her into the role of dumb blonde.

The bell goes and she steps out of the bedroom, gives the living room a final glance, then opens the door.

'Hey, Harrison Lloyd,' the guy standing in her doorway says. 'Ashley?'

She smiles back. 'Hey. I think we've actually met before?'

'Same anatomy group last year,' he says, an English accent ticking every syllable.

She widens her eyes. 'Right.' Of course she remembers him. Looks-wise, he's difficult to miss. She steps back. 'Come in. There's snacks and drinks on the table.'

He's stuck to nerd chic: Converse, loose jeans hanging from his hips, a hoodie, the neck of a white T-shirt underneath. But he's tall, 'fit', as Ashley's friends like to say, meaning half of them want to fuck him, half of them probably have. But Harrison's first love is games, his second love is crime – everything else slips from the sides. He'll be straight into a degree in criminology when he's through med school or developing new forensic techniques in some government lab somewhere.

For a while, in first year, he was obsessed with forensic linguistics or so he told them online. This information came from the mouth of his avatar, on screen. When they formed their little chatroom on the SD Gaming site, they agreed that they would stay in character, that had been the deal. They'd never strayed from that. But tonight's different. The only reason they were meeting face to face was because shit just got real. It was Derek who suggested they step out of the dark, saying that the game might be proving more real than they'd thought. If they

208

were dealing with a real victim, if Lydia Callin had truly been murdered, then at least one of their group knew Lydia in real life. And the reason for Derek's call to reveal their identities became clear.

She didn't think they could give up. In fact, she was sure they couldn't. You don't leave the magic circle until the game is done. When they talked about creating a murder-mystery game none of them thought it would actually come to fruition. Or at least most of them didn't think it would happen. Then when the invite came through to join The Murder Box, Ashley imagined she knew what she was signing up for. Imagined that yes, it would look real, might even play out in the real world in some way. There would be actual physical evidence they could pore over, real witnesses to talk to, psychology they could analyse. Proper sleuthing. But all invention at the end of the day. At no point did she think the victim would be real. They'd all noticed that one of their group never crossed over and subscribed to the box. And they would have been stupid not to put the initials in the username, LC-gxmer91, against the name of the victim in the game – but that was part of the illusion, wasn't it? Every murder mystery has a victim. She admits, the worst might've crossed her mind for a moment. But thinking about the reality of something is very different from actual reality. All in all, when Derek suggested the victim was real, she'd been disturbed but she also noted that she felt excited. She imagined it was exactly how real detectives felt when a case landed on their desk.

James Mayfield arrives next. She recognizes him immediately from around campus. He passes her a bottle of organic wine. He looks nervous as hell, wearing a stupidly tight suit-and-tie combo he looks like he's had since his school days. Online, he is quiet and awkward always needing to clarify his meaning and over-apologizing. If she had to choose from a line-up the person behind the online persona, she would point straight to him. He almost matches Harrison for height but somehow seems smaller There's a delicacy to his movements, an ethereal quality. When he speaks he traces the air with long, slim fingers, raises the plump pout of his mouth to accommodate the soft lisp of his tongue against his front teeth.

He shuffles in the door, stands in the way and the next guest who is coming through behind him has to tap his shoulder for him to move aside. He presses a palm to his tie and almost falls over the coffee table. 'Sorry, sorry,' he says and Ashley bites down on the back of her tongue.

She moves around him. 'Pippa?'

'Hi,' Pippa says. She has glossy black hair that's straightened to just below her ear. Sharp brown gleaming eyes and a pleasing smile. 'Yes, that's me. Thanks a million for hosting. Ashley, right?' She extends a hand. No girlish air kisses for Pippa, Ashley notes.

She shakes Pippa's hand, feels a rasp of rough skin against her knuckles and remembers that Pippa's a third-year engineering student. From what Ashley's gathered, Pippa's more on the board-game side of things. James introduces himself and Harrison turns from the table on the other side of the room, where he's helping himself to the bowls of snacks, jellies and crisps. His mouth is full, but he manages a quick 'Hi' in Pippa's direction.

They settle around the table like flies on fruit.

'Is Derek here yet?' Pippa asks.

210

'He's running about fifteen minutes late. Drink?' Ashley asks.

'Why not?' Pippa replies. 'White wine, please.'

James shakes his head, pats the absence of any stomach and says, 'Not for me, thanks.'

'Water?'

'Got some, thanks.' He retrieves a small silver flask from inside his jacket.

'Seriously?' Pippa laughs. 'There gotta be whiskey in that.' She snatches the flask from him. He reaches after it, but she's too quick. She unscrews the top and sniffs. 'Jesus Christ, man. Water? That's not right,' she says, her expression pulling together in confusion. She replaces the lid and hands it back to him.

His face is crimson. Ashley can almost feel the heat coming off it. 'Coming right up with that wine, Pippa.'

She goes to the kitchen. Opens the white and carries it back to the table. She fills Pippa's glass then sits.

Harrison has started on beer. Ashley has a wine in front of her, but she's watered it down. She needs to keep her wits about her. In the middle of the table is The Murder Box. She's laid out the case board. But she's not shown every piece. She's made notes on parts of the case file and she's not about to share them with everyone. She's not an idiot.

In fact, the first thing she'd done when Derek had implied their victim was real was open her computer and search all past posts by LC_gxmer91, but they had been deleted. Another search of Lydia Callin's name online and she landed on a Facebook page. It was set to private and on a whim she'd sent a friend request. There'd been no reply, but then it'd only been a few hours. She couldn't find any other mention of Lydia Callin online.

She removes her phone from her back pocket, checks the time. Where the fuck is he?

'Do you think the victim is really an actual person. Murdered like?' James murmurs. Even though he's not the loudest, the very fact of his meekness commands attention.

Pippa looks around the table. 'Maybe we shouldn't jump in before Derek gets here.'

'Is it part of the game, do you think?' Ashley asks, trying to hide her concern behind the bowl of her glass. 'He could be messing with us?'

'Everything's part of the game,' Harrison says.

Ashely knows the rest of the players are curious to know where Derek got this new information. It's clear he knows a lot about what the game really involves. He must know how that makes him look. Guilty.

'Should we share home addresses?' this from James.

'Why would we do that?' Harrison asks.

'Might be another clue we could use. The police call it geo-profiling,' James replies.

'It's bad enough that we're here, talking about the game as if it's an entity that's outside this room,' Harrison says. 'Sharing personal details will fuck it all up.' Harrison is the only one that doesn't want to be here, Ashley thinks. She watches his expression, tries to decide whether it's an act or if he's really that bothered. He can't object too much. He's here, after all.

'You know mine,' she reminds him.

'And whoever the murderer is knows,' Pippa replies. 'The boxes were delivered to us.'

They all exchange cautious looks. Because the answer to this

212

game could be in this room. That's how it goes. The killer plays along. They work out who's responsible. To win. No one really discussed what would happen if they lost. It didn't seem relevant when the idea was floated. And it was just an idea. No one imagined that six months later they'd all be presented with a subscription to a murder-mystery game. But they all jumped on board. Logged on to the site. But none of them, as far as Ashley knew, thought they'd be dealing with a real murder.

She should be more worried. There is a clock on the game. Dated to end in days. They all know what that means. It's game over and start over. Would that mean another victim? Another victim from this room? They should all be worried. But there's none of that.

'Come on, Harry,' Pippa goes on. 'You're telling me you're not going to immediately hunt down the addresses of everyone in this room now that you know our names?'

Harrison scowls at her and takes an angry swig of his drink. What a tool, Ashley thinks. Now that she knows his name, it'd take less than an hour to find out his address.

'They've set this up, right?' Pippa says. 'The killer. I'd say it's very much within the scope of the game to sit here and even that playing field. I'll start,' she says. 'Ranelagh. Two housemates.' She smiles at James.

He clears his throat. 'Rathgar,' he says.

'With your parents?

'My mother. My dad's dead,' he says, then clamps his mouth shut before he gives away more.'

Pippa stretches back, looks at him as if this information says everything she needs to know about James Mayfield. 'I'm sorry. Siblings?'

He shakes his head.

Pippa pushes a lock of hair back from her forehead then turns her gaze on Ashley. 'What's the rent like here, Ashley?'

Ashley knows what Pippa's doing. She tells herself she doesn't need to win this person over. She only needs her respect. She won't be coerced into admitting that this is not her flat.

'Manageable,' she settles.

'You must have a grant or something?'

'Give it up, Pippa,' Harrison says. 'We're not here for you to put us in the hot seat.'

'Only the guilty don't answer questions,' she clicks her tongue at him. 'Just saying.'

The door goes and Ashley, grateful for the interruption, answers it quickly.

Derek Cohen pushes into the room at speed. 'Sorry I'm late,' he says. 'Everyone here?'

'Yes,' Ashley replies. 'You want a drink?'

'No thanks. Sorry, Ashley, right?' He grabs her hand and shakes it, then walks by her, straight to the table. She tries not to be offended by his brusqueness and quickly introduces the rest of their group.

'Good to finally meet you all in the flesh.' He settles his laptop bag in front of him. Eyes the game's board or case board that Ashley has placed on the table, looks like he wants to ask a question about it, but swallows it down. 'We're in trouble,' he says. 'A detective came to the college today. Walked me right out of a tutorial.'

'Fuck,' Harrison says, but with more of marvel in his tone than fear.

Ashley sips her wine.

Pippa's fingers start up a drum against the armrest of her chair. 'What did you tell them?'

Derek pauses, choosing his words carefully. 'It's what she told me. They found a woman's body in the River Dodder, near Clonskeagh. Hacked to bits. Packed in suitcases. It's Lydia Callin.'

There's a part of Ashley that's horrified by the reality of it, but there's also a part of her that wants to take notes on what it is exactly this detective said about their victim. She eyes the histology slide on the table.

'So it's definitely real?' Pippa asks.

'Yes,' Derek replies.

Silence spreads out between them. Ashley looks around the room. What strikes her is that none of them object to this information from Derek, not one of her fellow players comment on how it can't be true.

'We haven't done anything wrong,' James says suddenly. His voice surprisingly strong. Out of everyone, she would have expected him to break down once things got a bit rough.

'That may be so,' Derek says. 'Well, I certainly haven't.'

Pippa says: 'Likely story.'

'She asked me for an alibi,' he says, leaving a slight pause, implying that they should all have theirs up their sleeves. 'About the tenth and the eleventh.' He reaches out and points to the timeline laid out on the case board. 'But also the weeks before?'

'Of August?' Pippa asks.

'Yes.'

They're all listening now.

'How did she know to talk to you or indeed any of us?' Pippa asks. 'She couldn't have accessed the site. No one can access the without the right codes.' She doesn't hide the suspicion on her face when she stares at Derek.

He pulls back, picks at the cuff of his hoodie. 'She said she heard about the box.'

'Fuck,' Harrison says again, pushing his hands through his hair. 'How? Someone must have told them?'

'Don't look at me,' Derek says. 'She went on about some crime scenes, break-ins, like set-ups around the city. There was a Murder Box card left at each one.'

A look passes around the table.

'That's not in the game,' Harrison states.

No one replies at first, then Pippa says. 'Break-ins?'

'Like fake murder scenes. She said there were four of them.'

Pippa frowns. 'Well, someone here knows about them. What is this?' She glares at Derek.

'I've no idea. I'm just repeating what she said. I could've kept this to myself, you know,' he says.

'You fucking asshole,' Harrison says. 'If you've been messing around and using the game to scratch some disgusting itch, then I'll—'

'You'll what?' Derek returns. 'Kill me?'

Harrison leans across the table. Face growing red. Fists clenched. Ashley rolls her eyes.

'Shut up,' James says. 'If none of us knew about these scenes, then they're not for us. Your detective said, didn't she, that they weren't real murder scenes?'

Derek is sulking but he nods.

'Well then, I'd say they're designed to keep the police busy while we solve this thing,' James says. He folds his arms neatly across his chest. 'A nice little red herring, if ever I saw one.'

Time ticking on. Ashley asks. 'So, what's next?'

'The detective said that the victim had been stabbed,' Derek says. 'Heart removed. I think the postmortem report we got probably compares well. But I'm not about to tell you where my investigation is going next, Ashley.' He stops, considers the case board again. 'Unless you want to trade something?'

And there it is. Confirmation that not one of them around the table is interested in backing out of their game.

Before answering, Ashley takes a moment to assess the mood in the room. 'If everyone else is up for it.'

Harrison sits back. Nods. 'Alright but no questions. Just an offering up of a single piece of information.'

'Sure,' Ashley says.

Derek shrugs in agreement.

'Sounds good to me,' James agrees.

Pippa stops drumming on the arm of the chair. 'Now, this is getting good. Come on then.' She reaches into her pocket and removes a notebook.

Ashley wants to get up, not wanting to be under such scrutiny. She makes the move to do so but knows that as much as that might cloak her own reaction, it will also prevent her from seeing theirs. There's been a few trades between the players on the game's site, the occasional exchange of ideas and theories about what has happened to Lydia Callin, but that was different. It's easier to add tone, to frame your answer from behind a screen. She's done it herself. Pretended not to have a clue when she's had her hunches.

It was James who fell for that one first. When she threatened to back out because she was hopelessly stuck and she'd nothing, not even the victim's last movements. He'd messaged her, reminded her that there was a chemical found on the back of the victim's hand. He'd basically told her to look for a nightclub stamp. Then after that she thought about where Lydia Callin could have gone. And had drawn a blank. It was about then she understood that there were two ways to tackle this mystery: look into the victim or look into the suspects. And if that failed, she'd discovered another way to root out the solution to this game without getting too dirty, Derek wasn't the only one who'd had contact with the detective and Ashley planned to use anything the guards gave her to get ahead.

Turning back to the table, she reaches across, picks up the sealed histology slide, the dark fragment of tissue trapped beneath the glass.

She holds it up to the group. 'This specimen wasn't cut with a microtome.'

Pippa all set to write down her tidbit of information, looks up from her open notebook. 'What the fuck is a microtome?'

'No questions!' Harrison says.

'Well, come on to fuck. It has to mean something,' Pippa says. 'I mean, you might as well say the victim wasn't born on a Tuesday.'

'Actually, she was,' James murmurs, keeping his head low.

They stop arguing. James feels the collective glare and glances up. 'What? She was.'

'You better give us something better than that, James,' Derek laughs.

Straightening his already straight tie, James places both palms on the table then slides them apart as if he's measuring something. 'It will surprise no one that I'm more interested in the psychology offered here—'

Ashley frowns at that. James shouldn't get away with giving some woolly profile on the killer. Her information was illuminating for anyone with access to an internet search engine. No one who has paid attention during a med degree would slice through a specimen the way that sample on the slide was done. Her microtome clue was top notch. Even Pippa will work it out. But the psychology of the killer. How is that a revelation? Any of them could fit the bill on this case. They were all players in a mystery game that involved a real victim.

James clears his throat. 'The killer is between twenty and thirty-five years, likely childless, no doubt educated, selfish, but he might hide those aspects of his personality in order to be liked or to fit in. They are narcissistic. Grandiose. Family life might be difficult. Not necessarily financially, but strained emotionally. Parents divorced or separated. They feel hard done by. Owed by society. Victim choice will be significant—' Ashley takes a gulp of her wine. 'Perhaps in an emotional way or that the victim reminded them of something. I'm still on the fence with that. Might as easily be they'd access to them in a way that was convenient, knew their haunts, movements.'

'More or less rules out Teddy Dolan,' Harrison says. 'What's Dolan about, anyway?'

'I thought we said no questions?' This from Pippa.

'Don't know,' James says, despite Pippa's objection. 'Who was it who got awarded the photo of him from the game's site?'

'Me,' Derek answers. 'Think what you like, but after yesterday's news, I'm saying that photo is the genuine article and means something.'

James thinks on this for a while. 'Huh. You could be right.' Then, after another moment: 'Why if Lydia Callin's body has been found has there been no mention of it in the press?' He pouts in Derek's direction. 'Especially if there's a link with Teddy Dolan.'

'They keep quiet about cases like this sometimes. Don't want to give the killer a heads up by information getting into the wrong hands,' Harrison chips in.

There's a beat of silence after this, then James turns to Derek, his voice a whisper of revelation: 'Your detective doesn't want us to know how far they've got.'

Ashley helps herself to a top-up. She's had enough of James Mayfield. 'It's not unusual that they'd hide sensitive information from the public,' she tries to wipe the tartness from her voice but fails.

'See?' James says calmly. 'Grandiose.' The others laugh and Ashley wishes they'd leave.

'Next,' she says.

They all look at Harrison. He smiles. The kind of smile that's probably opened doors for him all his life. The kind of smile that could let you get away with murder.

220

He turns the histology slide in his fingers. 'There's no exhibition on Greek mythology in the National Museum of Ireland.'

Everyone waits for more. But he looks up. His smug smile widening.

Pippa throws up her hands. 'Oh, come on!'

'What?' Harrison says.

'Are we just pulling stuff out of thin air now?' she gives a frantic look to Derek, beseeching him to qualify what serves as a clue and what doesn't.

'You have to give us more than that, Harrison, to be fair. Something we can use,' Derek says.

Harrison hooks his hands behind his head. 'If youse haven't followed up all the leads we were given, that's not my fault.'

Derek won't be shaken off that easily. He leans forward, examines Harrison's expression. They're all watching now. 'You tampered with something. Where? What? You're supposed to leave any clues where you find them.'

'Who says?' Harrison replies, raising his eyes briefly.

'The rules of any game, you fuck.'

Harrison shrugs. 'I didn't read anything like that in the instructions.'

The skin around Derek's mouth grows pale, his nostrils flare. His fingers are curved like white bows against the table, as if he was about to carve deep grooves in the wood with his nails. Harrison licks his lips, looks uncertain, but he doesn't relent.

'Give us more,' Derek growls.

Harrison's body jogs in his seat as his knee bounces under the table. The colour in his face deepens, spreads down his neck. Ashley meets Pippa's eyes. The atmosphere in the room thickens. Everyone still as statues, not wanting to be the first to kick the domino that will launch both these men at each other.

Finally, Harrison sniffs, drags in a quick breath and straightens. He levels Derek with a glare. 'At the newsagent Lydia went to, a flyer behind the counter caught my attention. It was about an exhibition on Greek mythology at the museum. The only reason it caught my eye is that the exhibition was dated tenth of August which obviously matches up with the date Lydia Callin was murdered. I took it so I could verify with the museum. It was a guess that it was worth anything but it paid off and all I'm giving you is: "I am the son of night and darkness, the twin brother of sleep",' he says, then lifts his chin, looks at each of them individually. 'That's it.'

Cryptic shite, Ashley thinks, deciding that there's no way Harrison has the sophistication to put together a game like The Murder Box. 'Derek?'

Derek holds his glare on Harrison for a second longer, then he too moves on. 'I think I've given up enough this evening. I told you the case was real. That the guards have opened an investigation. I'm done.' He turns to Pippa. Waits for her contribution.

Lifting the case board from the centre of the table, she clears the pieces from it then turns it over. She rests a fingertip just below the bottom right corner where there is a tiny number seven, painted onto the red gloss in gold.

The chairs screech on the wooden floor as both Harrison and Derek get up to look down at the tiny figure. Ashley and James are the only ones who don't move. Ashley had noticed the number a week ago. She resents the attention Pippa is getting.

The instructions had clearly stated that every aspect of The Murder Box was to be assessed. Ashley had taken that literally. An issue number is what she'd deduced. She'd already worked out that their little group was coming up short.

'There are two other players,' Derek breathes. 'I didn't even see that.'

'This means that the killer might not even be here?' Harrison asks.

'I wouldn't necessarily say that,' Pippa says. 'The victim is a player in most murder-mystery games remember which brings us to six.'

'That leaves one more,' Ashley can't help herself.

James slides carefully away from the table. He scans the room, his gaze extending to the crowded mantelpiece, the television, the light fixtures above before he points a look of accusation at Derek. 'And I'll bet the other is your detective,' he says.

CHAPTER 18

They leave quicker than they arrived. Any camaraderie between them gone. James is tense as a bow string as he goes.

'I say when we're ready to have the chats, it's with our lad, James, there,' Baz says. He reaches down to the food delivery Paul organized before he left.

'Agreed,' I say.

Baz examines it, then looks up. 'Sandwich or pasta?'

'What's the sandwich?'

'Cheese.'

'Pasta, please,' and I catch the cardboard tub he throws towards me. I read the label Organic Deliveries printed on the front, sun-dried tomato pesto fusilli. 'Thanks.'

Steve clicks through the footage, checks the audio to make sure we captured it all. 'Should we seize their boxes?'

I stifle a yawn. 'Let's see where each of them goes with their own investigations given the information they've just shared,' I reply.

There's a knock and Jack Clancy is standing in the doorway.

He takes in the scene in front of him. Glares at me, then at the screen where Ashley Noone is unhooking the camera from behind the television.

'They've just left,' she says into the feed.

'Okay, Ashley. Our team will be there to clean out the equipment in the next hour,' Steve replies. He turns off the audio then turns to me. 'You sure we can trust her not to say anything?' Steve asks.

When we looked into Ashley Noone's movements on the evening of the tenth we confirmed that she was at an evening seminar on Electro-bio-imaging at the college. In the end it was her tutor who eventually confirmed her attendance, saying suggestively, 'Yes, she was there with me.'

I say to Steve: 'She doesn't want to give up on this investigation any more than we do,' I say. 'She'll stay quiet.'

'What the bleeding hell is this?' Clancy says. 'Frankie,' he raises his eyebrows at me, widens the door, indicating that he wants to speak to me alone.

Grabbing my pasta, I get up slowly. Give a nod to Baz for him to take over, alert the engineers to go in and retrieve the camera and audio devices from Ashley's flat.

'My office?' I say to Jack when I step outside of the viewing room.

He follows, closes the door firmly.

I lean against the radiator on the far wall, press my palms against the heat. 'What's up?'

'What's up!' he asks, incredulous, eyebrows near popping from his forehead. 'You brought in surveillance?'

'Yes.'

'Why didn't I know about it?'

'I wasn't aware I had to run every turn of this investigation by you.'

He wags a finger at me. 'No. You don't get to do that. You know why you didn't tell me. How'd you even get this organized so quickly? Surveillance projects take planning.'

'And we planned it. Quickly.'

He opens his mouth. Closes it again. Colour growing on his face. 'The commissioner won't like this.'

A gentle tap on the door and Helen bursts into the room. 'Oh, sorry, Chief. I didn't know the assistant commissioner was here. Hello, Sir.'

Jack walks to the window.

'What is it, Helen?' I ask.

'Here are the searches,' she says and leaves a blue folder on the table.

'Thanks.'

She glances uncertainly at Jack's back, then at me, but whatever she reads of the tension in the room, she doesn't remark on it.

'If you need anything else,' she says, 'I'm off now but Mullins will continue working it.' She reverses out of the room and when the door clicks closed, Jack turns. If I thought the brief interlude would lessen his temper, I was wrong. The blood is up on his face like a red flag.

'It was a short operation,' I say. 'The surveillance department owed me. Adrian Redmond. Remember him? I called in that favour.'

He nods. 'Favour,' he says, feigning understanding. I brace myself. 'We're not the bleedin' mafia. We don't work on favours.'

226

I push away from the radiator, sit at the desk and begin checking the reports for the day. 'Don't we?'

I don't look at him, but Jack knows exactly what I'm talking about.

'You're to pull this operation,' he says. 'Now. That's it. She'll go spare when she hears about it.'

'She needs to keep her nose on her paperwork and out of how we run our investigations. It's my neck on the line here, Jack, of which she's all too fucking happy to remind me when things go to shit.' I lower my voice. Fuck it. 'We kept the fires lit on Teddy Dolan's case with next to fucking nothing coming in. For a month. Lydia Callin's barely through her autopsy and I'm already being warned about budget.' How the tables have turned now that our victim is neither celeb nor commissioner's nephew.

He reaches for a pleading tone, but I can hear the barely disguised anger in his voice when he speaks. 'And what have we learned from that, huh? More money, more time does not always mean better results, Frankie. We got no further, despite the extra dough. Instead, we got Dolan in Dublin centre strung up like a turkey with a fucking explosive strapped to his chest.' He huffs a few times, the colour in his face returning to something like normal. 'Lessons have to be learned.'

'Funny how that learning is only ever applied to cases like Lydia Callin's.'

Hands on hips, he gives me that one, sighs and nods in my direction, suddenly looking exhausted. 'Christ,' he says, rubbing a hand against his chest. 'We're creaking like an old ship on rough seas here, Frankie. We can't be using every resource the Bureau has on one case.'

'Let me do my job, Jack. It's why you put me here.'

Quiet then. Finally, he gives a stiff nod.

'If Hegarty doesn't like it, she can fire me,' I say.

He gives me a warning stare, but after a second, closes his eyes and nods. 'No wonder she bloody hates you.'

I smile, knowing I've won this one. I tidy away my papers, slide them into the drawer. 'She doesn't hate me,' I answer.

'Huh,' he huffs. 'You sure?'

Getting up from the desk, I lead him out of the office. 'Hate is far too crass a word for Donna Hegarty. Deplore, that's what's she'd say.'

When Jack leaves, I open the pasta then turn my attention to what Helen has put together on our players' comments. It hasn't taken her long to find Harrison's 'son of night and darkness' clue. Turning the fork through my dinner, I look over the contents of the printouts, still warm from the computer. It's from Greek mythology, a reference to the old god of death, Thanatos. Between mouthfuls, I scan through the pages. Thanatos, son of Nyx, the god of night, and of darkness, twin brother to the god of sleep, Hypnos.

What's bothering me is how whoever planted this clue knew that Lydia Callin would happen to stop into the shop for cigs before going out. They'd have to have known. Otherwise, how would any of the players pick up the clue. We have the unlikely scenario that Lydia left the flyer there herself on that night, placing down clues to her own murder. It could be like what Derek explained in the players' earlier interactions online that she was in on the game somehow and believed she was playing the role of victim in a murder-mystery game and not that she

228

was actually about to be murdered. Or as Harrison Lloyd says, someone followed her and put up that exhibition flyer after she'd already been in the store. Why? Putting down my fork, I open the game's website, search through the contents, read through a few of the old threads. Derek has already posted up in one of the chatrooms asking whether anyone has any resources he could peruse on fibre and hair analysis. I go back to the search bar, bring up fresh pages on Greek mythology to see where our little friend, the god of death, fits.

The first article details the story of Sisyphus who cheated Death into trying on his own chains, imprisoning Death in the underworld and creating havoc. As punishment, when Sisyphus was next in the underworld, he would spend eternity working a boulder up a hill only for it to roll away and down when he got to the top. I get the feeling we're being mocked. The detective constantly working, pushing the boulder of justice up that hill, only for them to find themselves at the bottom again with the same task.

At the top of the article, there's a thumbnail image of Thanatos. I click on it and it expands to fill the screen. Then sitting back into my chair, I take up my food. The image shows a winged man, muscular, dark-haired, reaching over a sleeping woman. God of death. I haven't an inkling what it could be referring to or if it's even relevant to our murder game at all.

CHAPTER 19

Baz squints out at the grey sky and the miserable-looking block of flats below it. 'We could still arrest on perverting the course of justice,' he says. 'We'd have them for twenty-four hours at least. Could question, play them off one another.'

I turn off the engine. An entire day and night have passed since the players met up at Ashley Noone's flat. All the players' movements are being monitored but it's been business as usual their end. Going to lectures and returning to their houses after. Once again, I think, Camille Forbes was right on the money. She warned us they'd go quiet. Auto Forensics analysed the photo provided by Derek Cohen. After studying wheel height and shape they narrowed it down to a dark coloured Volkswagen Cargo van but couldn't give us a year and the plates were obscured. Online, Steve has accessed the SD Gaming site Derek said they'd all met on. But either Lydia Callin was never a member or she or someone else deleted all her posts and then her account. The site's admin couldn't find any trace of her but he said that wouldn't be unusual if she left and that there were thousands of members and he couldn't be expected to keep track of them all.

I'm short of tearing my own skin off in frustration. Caught in a feverish kind of obsession between wanting something – anything – to happen and not being able to fully accept how little time we've left before The Murder Box potentially claims another victim.

'Their movements on the outside are worth more to us,' I reply to Baz.

'Shame we've had to pull back, then,' he says. He looks wrecked. Brown smudges under his eyes. Dark stubble over his jaw. We've all had some long hours over the last few days, but I know there's more to Baz's exhaustion. I can see it lurking in the grey of his eyes, pulling at the corners of his mouth.

'I don't intend to pull back but I've to at least appear to be looking after the pennies,' I throw him a cynical smile. 'Besides, if the players have not shot into action after that meeting the other night, I doubt they'll be making any obvious moves now. They'll be squirrelling away behind the scenes for sure. On what? We'll find out soon enough.'

This morning we've been either sitting outside James Mayfield's shared house or tracking him to and from classes but now we've pulled up at the small estate where Orla Flanagan lives. It's a horseshoe of buildings, each pressed up against the other, three bands of concrete balconies across the front, the pebble-dash is that dirty grey, like a white sock that's gone through too many bad washes. The windows are mean and peer out at a meaner strip of red brick paving where two vehicles are parked up. The investigation is stretching time to the max making it difficult for me to believe it's only been days since

Orla gripped my hand as we ran to safety from the explosion on Henry Street.

I reach into the back seat for my jacket, feel over the pockets for my phone and an envelope containing a pair of football tickets for Orla Flanagan.

Baz stretches his body in the seat, zips up his jacket.

'Lookit,' I say. 'You don't need to come up with me, I just want to check in with her, drop these off.' I wave the envelope at him.

'It's grand.' He puts his hand on the door to get out.

'You look tired.' I say.

He stops, turns. 'Well, thanks a lot. You're not looking so hot yourself after the last few days.'

'Alright, calm down. Don't hurt yourself.'

He shakes his head, a ghost of a smile on his lips, and pushes out of the car.

I point up to the third level of the building. 'Think she's in that far one there.'

We walk through the community gates. All three buildings lean over the communal courtyard. Our footsteps announce our presence, echoing up through the residential amphitheatre.

There are potted plants on the pathway outside Orla's home. Lush clusters of pansies. Below the front window a row of tomato plants, dried and brown in their pots. There's a sun-lounger tucked in along the balcony wall, bird droppings staining the cover. Inside, I hear the gentle murmur of a TV. A scrap of black duct tape covers the doorbell, so I knock on the stippled glass pane of the door and it rattles in its frame. Down the way, another door opens and a woman, still in her dressing gown, sticks her head out to watch us.

I see a shadow appear behind the glass. 'Who is it?'

'Orla, it's Frankie Sheehan. Can we come in?'

The door opens and she eyes me cautiously. Her eyes flick to Baz, then back to me again. 'What do you want? We're about to have dinner.'

She's wearing her school uniform, or half of it, the blouse and sweater tucked into a pair of navy trackies. There's a pleasing smell of vinegar-soaked chips emanating from the hall beyond.

'We won't be long.'

She sighs. Opens the door wide then retreats into the flat. I look back to Baz, then follow her into the dull light of her home. On the floor by the door, what looks like her school bag, and another small one with a Spiderman motif on the front. The walls are painted light blue, the floor a pale laminate. I find Orla in the front room, the TV on low, *EastEnders* playing in the background. She puts it on mute.

'Sit down if you like,' she says, pointing to a couple of wooden chairs pressed up against the far wall.

Baz draws them forward, puts one out for me. Orla reaches to the arm of the chair beside her for a spread of paper containing a portion of chips. She plucks one from the pile, drops it in her mouth then holds them out. 'Youse want some?'

'That's alright,' I say. In a chair on the other side of the room, there's a woman, not more than late fifties. She's wearing a pink housecoat, slippers. Her brown hair, streaked with soft grey, is carefully arranged into a neat bun at the top of her head. She hasn't looked up since we entered. Her eyes are fixed on the TV, a tiny crease of concentration between them.

'Your mum?'

233

'Yeah. My brother's out with friends to the cinema. Just me and Mum tonight, living it large,' she says. 'That right, Mum?'

If Mrs Flanagan hears, she doesn't react.

'She's got early dementia. Early 'cause of her age. She's well on with it.'

'I'm sorry,' I say.

'For what?' she says, a shot of challenge in her voice. She lifts her chin, points those blue eyes at me.

Mrs Flanagan raises her head towards us. 'Nurse,' she says, a wobble of confusion. 'Nurse, can you bring me my baby, please.'

Her mother's voice cuts through Orla's glare. The girl puts her chips to the side again, wipes her fingers on her trackies and goes to her mother's side. She lifts her mum's hand as if it were made of the finest glass.

'I will shortly, Mrs Flanagan,' she says.

'I need to get her dressed for when Séamus gets here. Has he phoned?'

'He's on his way,' Orla says. 'Bet he'll be here before *EastEnders* finishes.'

Her mum relaxes at that. Turns her attention back to the TV.

Returning to the sofa, Orla reclaims her chips. 'She gets a bit confused about what year it is, thinks I'm the nurse who helped her when I was born,' she says with a tone that tells me this is all she wants to say about her mum's condition.

I nod towards the TV. 'You think she'll leave with him?'

Orla follows my line of sight to where the TV soap's character, Jean Slater, listens quietly as her love interest holds a bunch of flowers on the other side of a closed door and says goodbye.

234

'Yeah, defo.' She chews through another chip. 'The odd time we're given a happy ending.'

'Nurse,' her mum chirps again. 'Nurse, I need my baby.'

Orla draws in a long breath. 'Sorry about this, could go on a while. What is it youse wanted?'

'Nurse?'

She gets up again, crouches down. 'We're getting her all ready for you now. Finish your programme and we'll bring her in.'

She resumes her seat. Looks over at Baz. 'What the fuck you staring at?'

I turn to Baz. He blinks a few times, pulls his gaze away from Mrs Flanagan. 'Sorry,' he removes his phone from his pocket. 'I just got a call and have to take it.' He gets up and leaves the room. After a few seconds, I hear the click of the front door.

Orla gives me an open-mouthed gawp. 'What's his problem?'

I smile the question away. 'Look,' I say, reaching inside my coat pocket and removing the envelope. I hand it to her. 'These are for you and your brother or whoever he wants to take.'

She licks her fingers free of salt. Eyes me like a bird weighing up a breadcrumb in the palm of a hand. She takes the envelope slowly, slides it open with a thumbnail and removes the football tickets.

'A little something for hanging on back then,' I say.

Pushing the tickets back into the envelope, she secretes them away in her pocket.

When I don't get up to leave, she says. 'Thanks. Fionn'll be delighted.'

'Have you someone to help with your mum?'

'Mrs Birch sits with her when I'm at school. For the most

part, anyways. Depends how the day is going. You probably saw her when you came up. Like a prison warden, only wearing slippers and dressing gown.'

'Sounds like a good neighbour.'

'She's alright, I suppose.'

The end scenes of *EastEnders* are silently building on the TV but Mrs Flanagan is unmoved.

'Has Teddy Dolan contacted you?'

She raises an eyebrow and gives me a look that says I should know better. 'What do you think?'

'I think he owes you a lot.'

Wrapping up the remaining chips, she leaves the leftovers on the arm of the chair. 'People like him don't think they owe anything to anyone. You know, I still have a bruise on my wrist where he grabbed me. I know he'll say he was saving my life or whatever, but he could've just shouted,' she motions a quick pincer movement with her fingers, shoots her arm out straight. 'Grabbed my wrist tight as a terrier's jaws. Told me not to move a muscle or I'd be blown to bits. He looked at me when he said it. His eyes were mad, like. Fucking wide as anything.' She drops her head a little, rubs the heel of her hand against her temple. 'I only remembered that when everything calmed down a bit and I could think about how it happened myself. I go over it a lot 'cause I thought if he moved that much, like, why did I have to stay there?'

I'm not sure I have the answer. Could be that Teddy believed they were being watched and thought she was genuinely in danger if she went off with the phone? But I think the likely scenario is that desperate people in desperate situations do desperate things and he held onto Orla's arm because he took the chance that if it was a remote detonator whoever was threatening to blow him up wouldn't do so if he had a kid at his side.

'I don't know. Sometimes it's difficult to judge these things in the moment.'

'That's what I thought.' She kneads the back of her wrist.

'Nurse,' her mum says.

I leave my card on the arm of the chair. 'If there's any other way we can help, Orla, call me.'

Orla gets up, returns to her mother's side. 'It's okay, Mum,' she says, forgetting the role she should be playing.

Mrs Flanagan squints up at her. 'Who are you?'

Orla closes her eyes briefly, looks over at me. 'Thanks for the tickets, Detective.'

'No problem. Take care, Orla.'

She takes up the remote and turns the sound up. I leave, pull the door closed behind me. My phone vibrates in my pocket. Thinking it's Baz, I answer. 'Everything alright?'

'Frankie, it's Abigail,' Dr James' voice comes down the line. 'I thought you'd like to know that I've got Teddy Dolan's tox report here.'

I move away from Orla's door and lean against the concrete balcony, facing out towards the car park. 'What've we got?'

'Trace levels of flunitrazepam,' she answers. 'Or you might refer to it as Rohypnol.'

A drug known to cause significant memory loss.

She goes on: 'If he was given this throughout his captivity, it might be why he's unable to recall the details of his abduction.'

I take a moment to digest this information. 'Is there a chance his memory will come back?'

She clicks her tongue. 'It does happen with victims who are given one dose, but it's impossible to tell how much he was given. This drug on a regular basis over the period of a month. Honestly, I'm surprised he survived at all.'

'Thanks, Abigail.'

'No problem.'

I hang up. Look out, find Baz's shape in the car below; his elbow pitched against the window, phone pressed to his ear. If the same drug was used on Lydia Callin, there might not have been much of a struggle between her and her killer. She would've been incapacitated. They could take their time. It's another insight into our killer's methods. Another insight into how far they are willing to go.

Even though the pressure of this case is mounting by the minute, there's no avoiding a summons to dinner from Donna Hegarty. An unusual ceremony, the commissioner not one to flatter us with fancy meals out and it grates because time and money are tight. I could tell myself that we've obviously earned some serious head pats for the work we did around her nephew's case, but the evening reeks of manipulation so despite the glass of champagne – we are celebrating, she says – I'm braced for what this is really all about.

'What will you have?' the waitress asks Hegarty who doesn't look up from her menu when she answers.

'What's the fish of the day?'

'Lemon sole, grilled with paprika,' the waitress answers.

'Wonderful,' Hegarty replies, lifting her menu over her shoulder in a dismissive movement, asking her husband, Amos, 'Same?'

He takes a final desperate glance at the menu then relents.

'Sure,' he says, adding a too wide smile in the table's direction. He has the kind of face that suggests, at one stage in his life, he was told that he should smile from the eyes and he's contrived the effect ever since. He's wearing a pink shirt, open at the throat, a darker cashmere sweater tied around his shoulders. Hegarty passes him the bread and, as he reaches across, his shirt sleeve rides up revealing the corner of an old tattoo.

Everyone's coupled up. I derive some satisfaction out of the fact that I don't have to subject a significant other to Hegarty's judgemental stare. Lily, Jack's wife, a retired nurse and never one to hold back, has kept conversation strictly to the restaurant's décor, the weather and how the last time she drank champagne it was to celebrate her daughter's graduation from university. A conversation that dried up quicker than a droplet of water on a hot stove when Hegarty, not thinking, asked her daughter's name and what she'd studied before making the connection and muttering something about 'that Hennessy business' a few years ago. That Hennessy business being a particular thorn in Hegarty's legacy when a TV production company threatened to topple everything for her by creating a documentary around the murder of Hennessy's family.

Hegarty lifts her glass for the second time. 'We may not have all the answers for Teddy, but I for one am more than grateful for all your efforts. It means that when we get whoever subjected my nephew to this terror, we'll have done the groundwork for prosecution. For now though, we can all take a breath and move on.' Then she relaxes into her chair, happier than a cat in a strip of sunlight.

The media have backed off. Teddy held a press conference at his home this morning, Monica, the epitome of the doting and supportive wife by his side, clutching his hand in a show of gratitude.

We all raise our glasses, Jack Clancy his beer. Baz is driving, so clinks a glass of sparkling water. I've been nursing a single glass of champagne from the get-go, not willing to risk being caught out if a call comes through on the case.

'It must be a relief to have him back,' Gemma says to Hegarty, then follows this with a delicate sip of her drink.

'I can't tell you,' Hegarty replies, lifting a wedge of bread from the basket in the middle of the table and pressing a knob of butter into the centre. 'And not only for the reasons you think. Although,' she breaks to take a bite, chews once, twice, then talking out of the side of her mouth, continues, 'obviously, I'm delighted the outcome wasn't worse. Probably helped him in an odd way, you know, public sympathy and all that. But it was bleeding us dry,' she says, meeting each of our eyes to coax agreement.

Jack pats his stomach, as if it were the thing that had suffered the most. 'No debate with that, at all.'

I reach for my glass, wash down a mouthful of distaste. I hate myself for nodding.

Hegarty finishes chewing, swallows. 'Well, no matter. I was pleased with the acknowledgement Teddy gave us this morning. That kind of thing can't be underestimated. And we all know the costs of a murder investigation, so let's be happy that wasn't where this ended up.'

And I'm about to say something, it's on the tip of my tongue – a

240

reminder that Lydia Callin has been murdered – but a sharp glance from Jack serves as the clip around the ear I need and I go for the softer option instead. 'I'm sure we're close to narrowing this down. We have some good leads at least,' I say. I glance down at my bag. It's open, my phone screen up inside, so I can keep an eye out for any updates from the office.

The waitress arrives, arms loaded with plates. 'Steak and peppercorn sauce,' she says, lifting the plate of meat and chips, then putting it in front of Jack.

'Squid-ink pasta?'

Gemma lifts her hand.

'If something comes in, we can look at it again,' Hegarty says. 'We can't afford to keep this going.' Looking up from the table, she says to the waitress. 'Could you bring a bottle of your house sav blanc and a nice cab sav, please?'

Jack raises his empty pint in the waitress's direction. 'A lager when you're ready,' he adds.

I choose my words carefully, hoping that I'm mistaking the suggestion in Hegarty's voice. 'We'll keep some distance between Teddy and the Lydia Callin investigation on the public front. There's no point in dragging this out further for him, but obviously we've to see this through, for Lydia.'

Hegarty bends towards her plate, passes a cupped hand through the steam and inhales. 'Beautiful,' she says, then lifts her cutlery, selects a meaty chunk of fish from her plate. 'The cases should stay separate. There's been no solid evidence that connects them.'

I spear a segment of penne with my fork, turn a raised eyebrow to Jack who keeps his attention on cutting through his steak.

Baz is watching the night sky beyond the restaurant windows. Cowards.

'He was having an affair with her. He last saw her the day before he disappeared. His phone led us to Lydia's body.'

'My understanding is that it was a group of teens who found Lydia Callin's body,' she says. She washes down a mouthful of the fish with a quick gulp of wine. 'This really is delicious. What do you think, Amos?'

He twinkles at her. 'Divine.'

'We're in danger of mission creep,' she says to me. 'A growing issue in the Bureau, I must say. You have to learn when to draw a line, Frankie.'

I turn the fork through my food, reach for more champagne. 'We're due to bring in a couple of suspects tomorrow. I'm sure we'll have something we can use to get traction.'

She shakes her head and my appetite disappears. The noise of the restaurant rattles around us, a piece of cutlery hits the wooden floor a little way off, the screech of a steak knife against a plate.

'I'm afraid that shouldn't happen. The covert op was premature and unnecessary,' she says, darting a glance at me. 'I think you know that. A sledgehammer to crack a nut. I've suggested to Harcourt Street that they should take over Lydia Callin's murder investigation.'

'You can't do that,' I say, louder than I mean to.

'Helen is briefing them as we speak.'

Baz and Jack are frozen, their eyes on me. They didn't know about this either.

I have to hold onto the edge of the table to stop myself going for her. I'm used to some head-butting from above and I'll push back for what I want, and I can step aside when it's needed. But the flippant way Hegarty can move Lydia's case about, like it's a piece on a chessboard, makes my blood scream. For her, it's no bother at all to dismiss the complexities of this investigation, to reduce it down to just another case and put it on the murder conveyor belt. She's not the one who discovered her bedroom stinking and spattered with pig's blood. And I know, if this game claims another victim, Donna Hegarty will still be able to close her eyes and sleep at night. But the creator of this game doesn't intend for anyone to get up from the table. Camille Forbes' stark warning comes back to me. 'The effect of your move has a physical and permanent cost.'

'Donna,' Jack says in the kind of tone you'd use when trying to persuade a stubborn child. 'The Bureau has been with this case from the beginning. We have a feel for it. It wouldn't be a good idea for another department to take over now, we've only just begun to pull in the nets.'

'You don't think Harcourt Street is equipped to handle a murder investigation, Jack?'

He smooths a hand down his tie. Lily sips nervously at her drink. 'Of course they are. Sure, didn't I work with them meself, but we're on the cusp here. We all feel it,' he says, and I appreciate his more than slight nudge of exaggeration. Then, to give Jack his due, he plays this one well: 'And between us now, they've a woeful habit for leaking to the press. Say what you like about the Bureau but we're used to these kinds of cases. We understand the discretion required. If we pass over the case, of course we'll have to let them know about your nephew – and who knows where that story might end up.'

Hegarty continues dissecting her fish, but I can see the tense little lift of her shoulders. After a few moments, she puts down her cutlery, exchanges it for wine.

'I suppose if you say you're close to a solution, then we can give you another few days.'

Jack raises his pint. 'That'll be all we need.'

That's more than we have.

'That's settled, then,' she turns a smile at me. 'Let's not discuss it further tonight. We're here to enjoy ourselves, are we not? Change of subject, anyone?' Her glass goes to her lips where she sniffs the wine then takes a sip.

Baz forces a brief half-smile. Lily reaches for the wine cooler. Jack shoves a mouthful of steak in his gob in order to stop himself from speaking. I am rigid with anger.

Gemma finishes the last of her meal, places her knife and fork on the side of her pasta bowl, then rests her hand over Baz's. 'We've some news.'

A flicker of a frown on Baz's brow, but he keeps his head turned from me. Gemma smiles at him. Her hand tightens over his. The room tilts. My mouth dries.

Hegarty straightens. Smiling wide. 'Let's hear it.'

'Baz and I are moving. Not far. Only to Naas. Sadly, he'll be leaving the Bureau – he'll work out his notice, of course,' she gives me a respectful nod, 'but we've just discovered that he'll be taking up a post at Naas Garda Station.' Her smile opens across her face. She looks at Baz.

He clears his throat. 'My mum is there so—'

I'm speechless.

'He wants a better work–life balance,' Gemma says. Her expression becomes serious. 'We want to thank you, Commissioner Hegarty, for putting in a word and helping him get the new position sorted so quickly.'

'I wish you all the best with your future,' Hegarty says.

I meet Jack's gaze. He's as horrified as I am, but he gathers himself quicker. 'Well, it's a bit out of the blue but sure, good luck and all the best with it, of course.'

'Excuse me,' I take up my bag and head for the restroom.

Leaning over the sink, I run the taps cold, hold my wrists under them. In a way, I knew this was coming. I could feel Baz pulling away. I look up at my reflection, wipe a smudge of mascara away from under my eye. Going to the cubicle, I pull a chunk of toilet paper free and blow my nose. Something clamps tight in my chest and I press the heel of my hand to it. Taking a few breaths, I tell myself that it's okay, it doesn't change anything. I worked alone for years, I can do it again. I ignore the tiny voice that says that's not the point, push away the idea that I'm losing my friend.

Taking a final look in the mirror, I thread my fingers through the ends of my hair then dig my phone out of my bag.

'Helen?'

'Chief? How's dinner?'

'As fun as you can imagine,' I reply. 'Hegarty said she told you to prepare for a handover to Harcourt Street?'

A small silence then, 'Yes but I wanted to wait until I heard from you.'

'Good. We'll be seeing this through. Can you get word out to Ryan and Mullins that they're to pick up Harrison Lloyd and

James Mayfield in the morning. Text me when you've confirmation.'

'You okay? You sound tired.'

'Too much champagne, is all.'

'Nice for some,' she says, but I hear the smile in her voice.
'I'll get that done immediately.'

'Great.'

By the time plates have been cleared and Jack's chewing through
his first antacid, I've more than sobered up. A full jug of water
consumed and a double espresso cooling in front of me. I can
feel Baz looking for me across the table, but I can't even glance
in his direction. I force myself back to the many strands of this
murder investigation. Search for ways to not just pull back the
curtain on The Murder Box but tear down pole and all. Every
now and then Jack gives off a sigh. I know it's because he senses
my plans. Knows that beneath the table, my heels are dug so far
into the ground, nothing will move me.

Back at the flat, I take out my copy of our files on the box
and Lydia Callin. I lay out a copy of the city map. Our biggest
issue with this case is locating where Lydia Callin was murdered,
locating our perp's hiding place.

The geoprofile, taking in the numerous crime scenes across the
city, puts our hotspot over the Rathmines and Rathgar region.
This area of the city allows for easy access to all the crime scenes
relevant to our investigation. Steve has marked out the two
players who live closest to the area: James Mayfield and Harrison
Lloyd. The others are not far out though and geoprofiling is not
always accurate. Our surveillance tells us our suspect is among

the group of players. Add to the fact that they all came together online after asking about gaming groups at the university and Lydia was the only one of their group not attending Trinity, it only points more fingers at them. Lydia was the outsider. I remove the photographs of her autopsy, then phone Helen again.

'Hello, Chief?'

'How's it going?'

'Good, we're all set for tomorrow.'

'Any connections made between Dolan and the suspects?'

'The only connection I can dig up is that last year the college ran an Inspire Me day. Dolan gave a lecture there, titled "From No One to Someone".'

'Cute.'

'It was well attended. I can't find a list of registrations, but going back to Pippa Dunne's Instagram, there's a photograph. A selfie from the event where Dolan's on the podium behind her.'

'Send it to me. What's Pippa's past looking like?'

'No priors. Pretty clean. Some activism for environmental issues. An online campaign against some motorway development. She started out in physics in DIT but changed to engineering in Trinity three years ago.'

I think about whether we should bring in Pippa and Derek tomorrow too. But without charge, each of our suspects will walk out after twenty-four hours. We want to stagger their interviews, gain information to use information.

I look at my watch. In the end, time decides for me. We don't have time to bring in all our suspects, interview and process what we need to in order to get ahead of The Murder Box. We'll have to settle for keeping tabs on the other players until we have more reason to bring them in. And there is also the chance that our killer is outside of the game altogether. It's a small chance, according to our specialist, Camille Forbes, but it's one I can't afford to discount completely. Our best shot is to gather our evidence while this game is still in play.'

'Good work, Helen. Could you get in touch with Camille Forbes, see if she's available to come in tomorrow. I'd like her here for the day, if possible. We might need the benefit of her expertise as we go on.'

'Yes, Ma'am.'

'And keep searching for connections between Lydia and our suspects. We need as much as we can before talking to Harrison Lloyd and James Mayfield tomorrow.'

CHAPTER 20

The doorbell is shrieking. I open my eyes. The flat is cold. The sky still dark beyond the window. I uncurl from the sofa and sit up, rub warmth into my arms. Reaching for my phone, I see two missed calls from Baz.

A text. 'Can I talk to you? I'm outside.'

It's four am.

I get up, press the intercom.

'Hey,' he says.

I release the door. Go to the table, clear up my notes from the case.

He's wearing the same suit as he was at dinner last night. Deep navy, his shirt now rumpled at the collar. There's an evening's worth of stubble around his jaw, tiredness printed under his eyes.

'Come in,' I say. 'I've to be at the Bureau early this morning. I should jump in the shower.' I turn to go to the bathroom.

'Wait! Frankie,' he says, a plead in his voice. 'I'm sorry you found out like that.'

A lump swells in my throat. 'Well. It's done now,' I say.

He winces.

I let out a short sigh. 'It caught me off guard. That's all,' I say, trying to take the sting out of my words.

'I'm sorry. I didn't know Gemma was going to announce it at dinner. In her own way, she was trying to bring some good news to the table.' He pushes a hand through his hair. 'It's all happened very quickly.'

'Is it what you want?'

He looks down at his hands, rubs one over the other. 'I think so.'

'Then it's a good move so.' I turn for the bedroom. 'Can you make some coffee? I need to get ready for work.' Tears are threatening and I close myself away in the bedroom, get a grip on my emotions. I run the shower until it's as hot as I can stand then step under it.

By the time I've dressed, Baz is by the window, watching the dark sky, coffee ready on the counter.

'Thanks,' I say, taking up the mug and going to the sofa to sort through my work documents for the day.

He joins me, sitting cautiously on the edge. 'I guess I needn't be expecting a farewell party?'

I give a short laugh. 'Don't be so sure about that. Helen keeps bunting in her handbag.' I pause, turn to look at him and it takes all I've got to keep my voice steady. 'I'll miss working with you.'

'I know.'

'You're sure of yourself.'

He gives me a tired half-smile. 'Confidence comes easier when you're me.'

I laugh but it chokes in my throat. 'Have to say, never had you down for the local bobby type.'

'It'll be an adjustment.' A long pause, then, 'Listen, I wanted you to know that . . .' he pauses, searches for the right words. 'Gemma and I, we're not moving in together. Or at least that's not what I had in mind. I've been so distracted these past few days, I fucked up . . . I'd no idea that's what she thought.'

I shake my head. Put my hand on his. 'Baz, it doesn't matter. You don't have to explain.'

'We broke up.'

'Again?' I say, giving him a nudge with my elbow.

'Funny.'

'I'm sorry.'

He shakes his head. 'I haven't been fair to her. She's ready to settle down. I'm not there yet.'

I frown. 'Why are you moving if it's not in pursuit of little white fences? Isn't that why you're leaving the Bureau?'

He presses his lips together then: 'No.'

'Then why?'

He doesn't answer straight away. I recall the look in his eyes the day of the bomb and the jab of betrayal I felt when he left my side.

'Look, the last few days have been hell,' I say. 'It'd be understandable if you needed a holiday, a break or something and—'

'It's not that.'

We're both silent.

'I just wanted to say I'm sorry for not telling you first and that whatever happens I'll still be here, you know,' he says.

251

I lie back on the sofa. He does likewise. Both of us stare at the ceiling.

'I knew it was coming,' I say quietly. 'I could feel it.'

'I know.'

His hand moves over mine. I turn my palm up, grip his fingers. A dull headache starts across my forehead. I'm confused. I feel like everything I thought I knew about Baz is crumbling away; the image of our relationship slowly shattering.

'If you've been struggling, you can talk to me?' I turn my head, watch for his reaction. 'Or, I know a good therapist? She's a tendency to believe bonsai trees solve all issues, but if you can overlook that, she might help?'

He smiles up at the ceiling. 'Thanks.'

He struggles with something for a moment, then, 'Myself and Gemma were at my mam's a couple of weeks ago and she started talking about Dad, said that she'd cooked his favourite for his tea. Roast ham. I didn't think much of it, thought it was a slip of the tongue. Then last week, I got a call from Mam,' he says. 'She was at the hairdresser's and wanted me to come get her. I didn't know what was wrong. My sisters have moved away – they've kids and stuff, so Mam usually rings me if she needs something.'

Baz's dad died suddenly last May and I know it's still raw for him. He doesn't talk about his family much but they are close and I know that to him and his sisters, their mother is the sun and they move around her like planets.

He goes on, as if now that he's started, he can't stop. 'I got there and she was at the front of the salon. Those foil strips you use, still in, wouldn't let anyone near her. The stylist said she just got up, didn't know where she was, gathered up her things and wanted them to call me.'

He sits up abruptly, bends over his knees. His palms cover his face. I rest my hand on his back. 'I took her to the hospital and they kept her in for tests. She's got something. They're not altogether sure what's causing it, but there's shrinkage to the front part of her brain. They think she's had a few mini-strokes and it's affecting her memory.' He lifts his face from his hands, takes in a long suck of air.

'I'm so sorry,' I say, understanding now why he left Orla Flanagan's home so quickly.

'The day she was released from the hospital, I went to the house to get the place ready for her. When I walked in, I couldn't believe it. The plates from our dinner two weeks prior were still on the counter. The ham, like rotting, still out. The whole house was a mess,' he shakes his head, looks out at the dark skyline. 'She'd more tests back at the hospital the following day; that's when they said it would get worse and that I should take her home and arrange for some care. I had a nurse stay with her while I came into work.'

'That's when you joined me on Henry Street?'

'Yes.' He gets up, goes to the window. He faces away from me, but the changing emotions on his face are reflected back on the dark pane. 'I shouldn't have been at work that day. It was like I was entering another reality, you know? My head was full of what would happen with Mam and next thing I was standing next to you in the middle of Henry Street, confronted with a bloody bomb. It felt so unreal. I couldn't

253

make the two worlds go together.' He rubs a hand down his face. 'And I left you.'

'Don't do that.'

'I left you. My partner. When you told me to clear the shops. I could see the disappointment in your face. You knew I wanted to go. You gave me that out. And I took it.' He turns from the window. 'It's the one thing a partner shouldn't do, right? We're supposed to be in it together. You could've died.'

I get up. Walk to him. 'And that wouldn't have been on you. Besides, I'm fine.' I put my hand on his arm, give it a gentle squeeze, make sure he hears me. 'I'd no idea what you were going through. I know that on another day, things would be different. I trust you.'

He shakes his head, looks down. 'I shouldn't have been there. I just . . . my head was so full of—' He sighs and I feel the heat of his breath across my cheeks.

'I'm fine. I'm here.'

When we kiss, it's soft, a need. A reassurance. We press into one another and I feel the steady warmth of his hand at the back of my head. Taste the morning's coffee and feel the rough scratch of stubble across the top of my lips.

He draws back and we stand a moment. Not quite ready to pull away but unsure about what's just happened.

Finally, I lift my hand to his face. He leans into my palm. 'Why didn't you tell me what was going on?' I ask.

He meets my eyes, swallows. 'I needed time to sort it out in my head. I don't want to go but this is something I have to do. I knew you'd persuade me to stay at the Bureau and I couldn't deal with that. The new job is on the quieter side, as you've probably gathered, so if I can get the house sorted in Naas, it'll allow me to get some care that would fit around my hours.' He takes a long breath in. 'She's only sixty-six.'

'I'm so sorry, Baz,' I say again. I hug him close and his arms tighten around me.

We return to the sofa. 'What can I do to help?' I ask, meeting his eyes. 'If you need more time off work, Mullins can cover?'

'My sister's been able to step in for two days so I can work. I know it seems odd given the last week, but what I really need is to immerse myself in work. At least while I've my sister to help.'

'Well,' I say, 'if you're not done with the early mornings and late nights yet, we're about to bring in Harrison Lloyd and James Mayfield.' I flick a glance at my watch. 'Ryan will be leaving shortly to retrieve them for questioning.'

He thinks for a second, then, 'I could really do with that.'

'Just flex those interrogation muscles. These kids won't give in easily.' I go to the kitchen, reheat the coffee. Root around in the cupboard, find the box of breakfast bars among the unopened bags of pasta and rice. Shake two free and throw one to Baz. 'Do you think Hegarty's hiding something?'

He raises his eyebrows. 'As in she's covering for Dolan in some way?'

'I don't know. Maybe. Just strange she wants to keep the cases separate.'

'No. I think Hegarty is straight as they come. I've a feeling she'd feed her own kids to the wolves if it meant keeping her rep intact. This is just same old, same old. Hard to win the right budgets from government when your industry's been dragged through the papers all the time. In her eyes, she was doing you a favour, keeping the name of the Bureau clean and passing a giant turd to Harcourt Street.' And it feels good to have this with Baz again. Like someone's kicked the cart and suddenly the wheels have found their groove.

'Where it would get buried,' I add.

'Exactly.'

We both open the breakfast bars, chew through the oversweet oat cakes. I swallow down the dry mouthful.

'Why'd we choose Ashley Noone's gaff to set up?' Baz asks.

'Logistics. Mostly. She's the only one living alone, so we didn't have to deal with extra surveillance issues once we had her on board.'

'You're pegging her innocence on she wouldn't make such a hames of the heart tissue on the slide?'

'Yes.'

'You don't think that could be to throw us off the scent?'

I go to the coffee table, close over my laptop and slide it into my bag. 'Could be,' I concede. 'Her alibi also checked out. But,' I sigh, 'I'm fairly certain, our perp, if they had the kind of skill Ashley has in labs, wouldn't want to forfeit showing that off for the sake of a red herring. In their eyes, they're clever, they're better than us. And they want us to know that.'

'Only a day left on the game's site.'

'We'll get something. I'm sure of it.'

He blows out a long breath. He looks better, like a shadow has passed, the flame of intrigue re-ignited. Whatever happens, I'll miss this. The over and back on the details of our investigation, each of us helping the other put the next piece down. 'I guess we're not the only ones running to this deadline,' he says. 'Players and the killer among them will be readying for the end of this game.'

'Investigations can turn around quickly,' I say. 'We get one sniff of information from Lloyd or Mayfield today and it could be game over. Literally. We get that crime scene, where she was murdered, whether our perp is there or not, it will lead us to them. There's no way they've done that to Lydia's remains, let alone put together everything else without some incriminating evidence left behind.'

'Can we not just go in and search their properties?'

'Ashley Noone is the only one who'd have the opportunity to kill and dismember someone in her flat and we've already had a hunt through there. Clean as a whistle. James Mayfield lives with his mum and the rest of our suspects live in typical five-, six-occupancy student houses. We're looking at a separate property or location within that geoprofile.' I scribble the Lloyd details into my notebook. Tear the page out and hand it to him. 'Here's the address for the pick-up this morning. Give Ryan a shout and let him know you're on the way.' I say. I grab my coat from the hook at the door.

He looks down at the address, nods, then takes my hand. 'Thank you. For everything.'

Beyond the window, Dublin city is waking with the groan and rattle of early morning traffic. The streetlamps are slowly dimming, morning light creeping across the horizon.

I smile at him. 'Just don't be letting on that I'm nice to work with or anything.'

He laughs. 'Why would I tell a lie like that?'

257

CHAPTER 21

You might be forgiven for thinking that Harrison Lloyd wasn't expecting to be brought in for questioning. He shakes my hand at the Bureau door and apologizes for still wearing the top he slept in, a loose-fitting grey T-shirt, saying he'd barely time to sling on jeans and stick his feet in a pair of flip-flops before he was asked to leave. He tells us he was going to call us later today anyway.

We treat him well. No body shoving, no cuffs. Feed into his notion that he's there to help us put together a few gaps in our investigation. We linger at the coffee station. He's grateful, extends profuse thanks at the offer of biscuits as he's not had time to eat yet. On the journey down, he asked Baz only once what we needed to talk to him about. Baz told him he could be a possible key witness in our investigation and Harrison didn't push for more.

When he's ready, I settle him into one of the interview rooms, get him comfortable with tea and more biscuits, then leave him for ten minutes.

Camille Forbes is in the viewing room with Baz and Ryan. Steve's adjusting the contrast on the video feed.

Harrison takes a slow drink of his tea and looks around the room.

'He doesn't seem nervous,' Camille says.

'Relaxed as they come,' I say. 'In a way, this is a dream come true for Harrison. There's no doubt he sees himself working on a crime team or leading one in a few years. From what we've managed to dig up on his studies, he's filled out most of his credits by attending lectures on criminology, reviewing papers on neurological studies of criminal psychopathy, even did a stint, summer before last, with our very own Dr James.'

'Dr James?' she asks.

'Our pathologist. At Whitehall,' I add.

'Interesting,' she says.

Ryan turns over a page in the file he's updating. 'When we got out to his gaff, he'd the box on the table and all, said he was getting ready to turn it in as he was worried it might be related to a real murder. He'd all the true-crime friends at his bedside table. Didn't he?' He says up to Baz.

'Books,' Baz explains, catching my eye over Steve's back. 'Biographies on killers, detectives, non-fiction texts on criminology, forensic psychology. Plenty of gaming stuff as well, figurines, boxes of dice, board games.'

On the screen, Harrison rolls his shoulders, his chest lifts, then slowly drops. He gives his arm a little shakeout. Then he gets up, hands in pockets and walks slowly around the room. He takes in everything, finishing with a lingering stare at the camera positioned on the ceiling.

'If you get him to break from game mode, I'll be impressed,' Camille says. 'I don't think he looks like someone who's used to losing.'

'Neither are we,' I say. Ryan hands me the file. 'Let's see what we can get from him.'

Baz follows me out of the room. 'Can I have a quick word?' he asks, quietly.

'Sure,' I say.

'This morning – if I . . . you know . . . stepped out of line?' He waits for me to help him out. 'What I mean is, I shouldn't have kissed you.'

'I think it was me who made that move,' I say.

There's a lift at the corner of his mouth.

I reach out, squeeze his hand gently. 'I should go. We'll talk later?'

'Charmer.'

'I know,' I say. 'Listen, I'm thinking this guy's too cool. Make sure we've got eyes on the rest of our players, yeah? If they've ironed out their stories, one of them might make a break for it.'

'Will do.'

We're about to move off when Emer comes around one of the desk partitions. 'Ashley Noone contacted us this morning about the surveillance op. She noticed an intermittent buzzing coming from inside the main room in her flat. The lads have already removed all the equipment we used but they went out to make sure they got everything.'

I look at my watch. Not wanting to leave Harrison Lloyd too long. A nervous suspect is a lawyered-up suspect. 'Yes, best to double-check,' I say. 'The assistant commissioner was not a fan

260

of our covert op – we definitely don't want it running longer than necessary.' I turn to head to the interview.

'That's just it. We sent an officer who did a sweep with an RF detector and he found another,' she says.

I double back. 'Another?'

'Another camera.'

She waves me towards the screen, angles it so both Baz and I can see it. And we're back inside Ashley's flat. Only this time from a different angle. Somewhere on the mantelpiece, is my guess. The lights are off in the living area, but the camera must have an infrared setting.

'Where's Ashley now?'

'She's a shift at her aunt's sandwich place.'

I nod towards the screen. 'Is the audio working?'

'I've only been in about five minutes but I'm picking up some background noise from the street outside. As there's already officers at James and Harrison's digs we did a sweep there too and found another hidden camera in Harrison's room.'

'Could it be for personal use?'

'Could be but odd to have it on live record.'

I swallow. 'How about Derek Cohen's and Pippa Dunne's?'

'Not yet, we'll need another warrant for theirs,' she says.

'My flat?'

'We've no access presently but I could try and search for an AV feed remotely.'

I glance at Baz. 'Yes, go ahead please, Emer.'

She switches through windows on her computer asks me the occasional detail about Wi-Fi codes then finally a box opens on the screen. I lean in. The view is of my living and kitchen area.

From the angle, I know the camera is positioned on a bookshelf near the door. The camera must have been put in place when the break-in happened.

'How long have they been there?' I ask.

'We don't know but if we're to assume that all players are being recorded, this is what might be helpful to us.'

I meet Baz's eyes. The same realization on his face: that someone was watching us early this morning.

'There's no camera in Mayfield's house,' Emer says.

'You sure?'

'Yes.'

'Well, that is something.'

Harrison's leaning against the far wall when I enter the room.

'Thought I should stretch my legs. I didn't know how long I'd be here,' he says.

Placing my file on the table, I sit down and he eases away and joins me there.

'Not long,' I say and a flash of disappointment crosses his face.

'I thought there'd be a two-way mirror there,' he says, pointing at the wall and giving a cynical smile.

'We have one in the other room. It's all video here. We'll be recording our conversation today. Is that okay?'

He shrugs. 'Sure.'

'Would you like a lawyer present?'

'Nope. They just slow things down, right?' he says, helpful, like.

'That's great. Alright, we'll begin. It's eight-thirty-four am, Saturday the 14th of September 2013. Detective Frankie

Sheehan interviewing Harrison Lloyd. Harrison, I have to tell you that you don't have to say anything, but it may harm your defence if you fail to mention when questioned something which you later rely on in court. Anything you do say may be given in evidence. Are you okay to continue?'

He puffs out a breath. 'Yeah. I'm happy to go ahead.' I know Harrison will be studying us as much as we are him. Picking through the scraps of our interrogation to see if there is any new information there for him.

'As I said out on the floor, we just want to clear up a few things, then hopefully, you'll be free to go.'

'I'm here to help.'

I open the file and his eyes go straight to it. 'Do you know why we brought you in?'

He collects himself. 'I gathered it was because of The Murder Box?'

'Ah. Okay. That's the mystery game you gave to my colleague.'

'Detective Twoomey, yes.'

'What can you tell us about The Murder Box?'

Wrapping an arm across his middle, he tips his head to the right. 'Have you looked at one?'

'I haven't had a chance to check in with Detective Twoomey yet.'

He purses his lips, then, 'Sorry. For some reason I thought you were sent one.'

'Why would you think that?' I turn over the first page of the file and leave it open on the photographs from Lydia Callin's autopsy.

His eyes flick to the file, then back again.

He swallows. 'I subscribed to it a few weeks ago,' he says,

going back to the previous question. 'I'd seen that kind of thing before and my curiosity was piqued. I'm interested in true crime and this felt like a step up from the usual murder mysteries,' he says. 'Then a couple of evenings ago, we met up in one of the other players' houses and were told that the victim in the game, like in the actual game,' he says again to emphasize his horror, pointing his index finger down towards the table, 'might be real.' His eyes widen and he shakes his head in disbelief. 'I didn't sign up for that.'

'Do you have the names of the other players?'

'I thought you might ask that.' He slips his hand into his back pocket, retrieves a piece of lined notepaper. 'There's the names and addresses.'

Taking the paper, I make a show of reading through the names. I wonder whether they shared their addresses in the end, or whether Harrison Lloyd has spent the last couple of days looking them up. There's the chance he's known them all along.

He continues. 'I'd thought there were so many but now I don't think there are. Just five of us, as far as I can tell. And I guess the victim would make that six.'

I nod to myself. 'Thanks.' I put the list of names into the back of the file. 'Who told you that the victim could be real?'

'Derek Cohen. He said you'd come to talk to him. That you'd also received The Murder Box.' Chancing his arm.

'How did you feel when you heard that the victim could be real?'

'Shocked. I decided as soon as I heard that I'd make copies of the contents of the box for myself, so that I could pass the original over to you.'

'That's very responsible of you.'

'None of us want to get in the way of an investigation. We want to help. That's what we're doing. I mean, we're amateurs, but you hear of armchair detectives blowing cases open all the time,' he says, making air quotes around the term 'armchair detectives'.

'Can you account for your whereabouts on the evening of the tenth of August?'

He thinks for a second. 'Was that a Friday?'

'Saturday.'

'Most likely I was out on the town.'

'Where would that be?'

'Usually, I end up in Club Med in Temple Bar,' he says.

'You're from Berkshire in England?'

'Yes, Streatley, just outside Reading. I head home sometimes when term's over but decided on university here to experience the Irish life and culture so usually try to get some work experience at one of the hospitals or something similar, but I couldn't get anything this year. I travelled around the country a little, hit a few of the festivals, then came back to Dublin, beginning of August, must've been. Yes, that's right. I'd some catching up to do socially, so I'd say I was probably out on the town. I passed my phone to your colleague – there'll probably be texts about it on there. Someone will be able to verify where I was.'

'But you can't?'

'I wouldn't want to take a guess and be wrong.'

'Your parents pay for your upkeep here?'

'I receive funding from the UK government and my parents top up the rest.'

I make small check marks along my notebook as he speaks

and he watches me, growing in confidence as we go, feeling like he's giving all the right answers.

'When was the first time you met Derek Cohen and the other players?'

'Our interactions were strictly online up until a few days ago. We knew we were at the same university but never revealed who we were,' he says. 'I mean, I'd seen Ashley and James at some of the gaming meet-ups but I didn't know them. I wouldn't have been able to tell they were who I was interacting with online. And, of course, Ashley's med like me, but she's in another student group.'

I fear Camille is right and that pulling Harrison Lloyd out of game mode might be next to impossible. He is salivating for information from me – wants to know what I know, how far our investigation has come.

I remove the photo of Lydia from the file, pass it to him. 'Do you know this woman?'

His expression is impassive. 'No.'

I leave the photo on the table for a while longer.

'This is Lydia Callin. Are you sure you don't know her?'

He shakes his head. 'No. I'd remember.' He clears his throat. 'Sorry,' he reaches for his tea, finds it empty, gives it a desperate shake.

'Would you like some water?'

'Please,' he replies.

I look back at the camera, signal for water then look back at Harrison. 'How far did you get into the game, Harrison?'

'Erm, not far. I . . . I worked out that Lydia had gone out on the tenth – there was a copy of a bus ticket, a receipt for some fags

266

and one of those tooth-cleaner things from a newsagent. I went out there. Got talking to the shop assistant. He said that yeah, he remembered her 'cause he couldn't give those tooth things away, that they'd been taking up space on his counter for months.'

Baz knocks once and enters. He places a glass of water down for Harrison.

'Cheers, mate,' Harrison says, smiles.

Baz leaves.

'Where did you go from there?'

He rubs a hand over his face. 'He said she'd left a stack of flyers. On an exhibition at the National Museum. She'd asked him if he'd mind pinning one up on his noticeboard. He gave me the flyer. I probably should have left it there, to be fair to the other players but . . .' he shrugs. 'Anyway, I don't know where I put it, otherwise I'd have given it to your colleague.'

'What was the exhibition?'

'Just Roman history. Nothing special. I checked with the museum, they weren't running anything on that subject. It seems I've hit a brick wall.' He gives a companionable shrug, as if I should relate to that which unfortunately, I do.

'It'd be strange if Lydia Callin was the one laying down clues for her own murder, don't you think?'

He leans forward onto his knee, cups his face in his hand. 'I hadn't thought of it that way. My understanding was that we were being led by certain clues, that whoever put those flyers up was doing so for the game, not because there was going to be a real murder.'

'We spoke to the same newsagent,' I lie. 'He says the flyer was on Greek mythology.'

267

Something that looks like irritation flashes across his face. 'He did? No. I don't think so. I guess the Romans and Greeks are easily confused by people.'

'You're not confused by it?'

'No.'

'Does this phrase mean anything to you: "I am the son of night and darkness, the twin brother to sleep"?'

He straightens, tucks his hand under his leg. 'No.'

'How about the words, Thanatos or Hypnos?'

'No.'

'Okay. Let's get back to The Murder Box. As far as you know, there are five players and the victim, Lydia.'

'Yes,' he says. 'Yes, if we were talking traditional murder mystery here, the victim would be considered another player.'

'So six?'

'Maybe.' He tilts his head. 'Although, I had noticed a number on the outside of the box. The number seven. I thought it could be an issue number.'

'Another player?'

'It's why I thought you'd also received one,' he says.

'Do you drive, Mr Lloyd?'

'I have a licence but I don't drive here. I walk or use public transport.'

'How about other properties? Relatives' homes or friend's houses that you've used or borrowed?'

He frowns. 'No.'

I turn through the file. 'You said you like to study crime? In what way?'

'I hope to work in it in some field eventually. I thought about becoming a pathologist but I'm not sure it's for me. I did some work experience in it with the pathologist here in Dublin. You probably know her. Dr Abigail James?'

Giving him a half-smile, I say: 'It might be difficult to follow that career path once word of The Murder Box gets out.'

'But I've not done anything wrong. I embarked on what I thought was a game. Now, as you say, rightfully,' he presses his palm to his chest, 'I agree with you. It is serious and that's why I'm here. I wanted to come in and speak with you. I want to work with you, to help discover who did this. Whatever you need from me, I'll give.'

'You'd be willing to give a sample of your DNA? Fingerprints?' I say, thinking of the lone print collected from my landlord's house prior to the break-in at my flat.

Fair play to him, he doesn't flinch. 'Sure.'

'Great,' I say. 'Thank you.' I rub a hand against my temple. 'Here's the thing that I keep getting stuck on. We've had a look at the game's website and there appears to be a countdown of sorts?'

A hint of a smile drifts at the corner of his mouth. 'A little *zeitnot*. Adds some more tension to a game.'

I raise my eyebrows. 'It's showing only hours left on the clock?'

'Think midnight tonight is when the glass slipper drops,' he replies with a sickening kind of lightness.

'When you work out your whodunnit, you submit your answer and your process and you win. Is that it?'

He gives me a tolerant kind of smile, as if he wouldn't have expected me to get it. 'That's it.'

'If you're all players and one of you is dead. Murdered.

And there's a clock that runs out by the end of today. What happens if you're not able to feed in those answers in time?' I tilt my head, play the confused card, but there's no mistaking what I'm asking. 'What happens when you lose?'

He answers carefully. 'As you say. It's not about the game any more. It's about a real victim and finding out the answers around what was done to her. I can't speak for the others, but that's what's motivating me. I mean, and forgive me, Detective, if this sounds impertinent, but what happens when *you* lose?'

CHAPTER 22

'What do you think?' I ask Camille.

'He hasn't given you much,' she says. 'But he's lying about the flyer at the shop for one. It being Greek mythology.'

'We'll get a DNA sample and prints for our efforts. If and when we find our crime scene, we'll have that on our system. We can run his prints against the one found at my landlord's house. On the back of that, we'll either have a prime suspect or we'll have one less player on our list.'

'He had a strange reaction to the photos,' she says. 'Barely a reaction to the autopsy pictures but there was something for the photograph of Lydia when she was alive.'

'You noticed that too? Makes it real for him. Could be an angle to pull him out of game mode.'

Camille hooks a shining lock of hair behind her ear. Folds her arms. 'If Lydia Callin was in that shop and she handed over flyers for an exhibition that didn't exist, but turned out to be related to her own murder, how can that be?'

I sigh. 'I don't know, but I suspect Harrison Lloyd is very

271

close to working it out. He went around that question like it was sinkhole that'd just opened up.'

'Could she've been coerced, you think?'

'It's possible, if she was, it still doesn't change the fact that she was murdered by someone. She could have been playing along not knowing what was about to happen.' I hold open the door and she steps out. 'How's Helen doing with James Mayfield?' I ask.

'Not bad at all.'

We head into the second viewing room where beyond the one-way mirror, James Mayfield is adjusting a silver cufflink on the sleeve of a burgundy shirt. At his throat a navy bow tie. His light brown hair is pressed up one side into a peak, giving him a quirky, dishevelled appearance that I know he's spent some time perfecting. 'He's not the most relaxed of individuals,' Camille says. 'A few of the questions from Helen have resulted in short sharp answers but he seems more agitated than angry.'

Helen has an array of photographs laid out between them. Each one showing an item from The Murder Box. We rehearsed this. If there's a suspect who fit our profile, Mayfield is it. He's careful. Tenacious. From the flash of anger we witnessed on his face at Ashley Noone's flat, we know he's not one who appreciates being interrupted or criticized. When we dug about in his exam results from last year, initially his grades sat at a high pass but he'd contested all. Relentlessly. He was rewarded ten extra credits for each module. He has no siblings. His dad died in a car accident when he was eleven. The autopsy results showed high blood-alcohol levels. His mother is an events manager for a wedding company in Kildare and is often away for days on end. When Helen spoke to her, she was able to confirm that she was home on the 10th of August. No work trips away. She said James was home that weekend and when he's home, they usually order pizza and chill out.

Chill out is not a phrase I'd use in reference to James though. He's uncomfortably straight in the chair across from Helen, his expression intense while he waits for the next question.

'Like a tennis player waiting for first serve,' Camille murmurs.

'Yes,' I say.

But Helen is not rushed by the challenge in his eyes. She turns slowly through her notebook, searching the contents with the nib of her pen.

She pauses, brightening. 'Ah,' she utters. Then smiles up at him, shakes her head. 'No, sorry.' She turns another page. And I smile. She's sized up James Mayfield nicely. Knows the buttons to push to make him sloppy.

Mayfield's foot begins a fast tap beneath the table.

'Here we are. Your mum says you were both in on the evening of the tenth of August.'

'Yes.'

'Okay,' she says, more page turning. 'Have you ever been to the Score club in Temple Bar.'

He lifts his chin. 'No.'

'Not even after?'

'After?'

'After you found out that was where Lydia was last seen. I would've assumed you'd visit the scene of the crime, so to speak? Ask around?'

His mouth twists, but he answers. 'Yes, I went after. I knew

273

the manager wouldn't give me anything, but I thought security at the door would be as good as anyone to remember her face.'

'Did they?'

'No.'

'What did you do then?'

He looks down at his hands, his foot stills. 'I didn't know where to go then.'

Helen frowns but she doesn't push him. 'Can you tell us where you were in the days leading up to Saturday the tenth of August?'

'Why?'

'Oh, sorry,' she says, casually. 'You haven't seen these.' She opens the file and places a photograph of Lydia Callin's remains in front of him. 'It's been difficult to date Lydia's death. Her body was not in good shape when we found her. You see?' She slides one of pictures towards him.

His hands tighten into a clasp, small dots of pink appear on the fine arch of his cheekbones. He keeps his eyes averted when he speaks. 'Are you allowed to do that? It's very upsetting.'

Helen waits a few seconds. 'I think it's important that what was done to Lydia Callin is acknowledged. That we bear witness to what she went through. Someone murdered her. Took her life. Then cut up her body. Placed it in suitcases and threw her in a river.'

He raises a closed fist to his mouth. 'I can't remember where I was. I was probably at home on my computer. I don't go out much unless there's college. Anyway,' he says, an imploring note creeping into his voice. 'I think you're wrong on this, if the game says the tenth of August, then you should be looking at the tenth of August.'

Helen collects up the pictures. 'Ah, unfortunately, we're the law, not a board game so we can't work like that. Not as much fun but, I'd say, more effective when it comes to uncovering the truth.' She tidies the photographs into the file, returns to her notebook. 'I don't think it'd be wise for us to trust this game like you seem to.'

He snatches a quick breath through flared nostrils. 'It's the opening move. It's always true.'

She shakes her head. 'But Lydia Callin trusted this game. She was a player, from what I understand, and she's dead. I'd say if you could ask her about truth and fairness and trusting this game, she'd give a very different answer. Don't you?'

His right shoulder shifts beneath his jacket. 'It's a murder-mystery game. It's no secret that someone will be murdered.'

'It sounds like you knew she would be killed?'

'No. Of course not.'

'So, from what you understand, any one of you could have been a victim?'

He wrinkles his nose at that. 'Doubtful.'

'Why is that?'

'This game was planned carefully. Lydia Callin was selected carefully. She had handed in her notice at work, there were no workmates moaning when she failed to turn up. She lives with a self-centred housemate who didn't report her friend missing for days and then made such a half-hearted effort when she finally went to her local station that they weren't arsed to look for her.'

My teeth find the edge of my fingernail. I share a look with Camille.

Helen busies herself with her notebook, tries to work out an

275

angle to get him to reveal how he knows so much. In the end, she settles for direct.

'Do you know Neve Jameson?'

'Not really.' He twists the cufflink again. 'Just observed her, I guess. You know, she hasn't missed a single day at work since her friend went missing. Does she know she's been murdered? That her remains were found?'

We haven't disclosed that information to Neve yet but Helen sidesteps the question neatly. 'People react strangely in times of grief.'

He raises an eyebrow at that. 'She hasn't even called round to Lydia's dad. You'd do that, wouldn't you? If you were a friend. Go round to check on her only surviving parent. See the dog,' he says. 'Charlie, I think his name is.'

'You've been to Mr Callin's home?'

'I didn't stay long. Just wanted to see for myself that there was nothing there. Of course, you guys got there before me. I'm a little behind, but I reckon I'm catching up.'

I see the hint of a smile on Helen's lips before she's a chance to disguise it. We could get him on witness intimidation for that.

'You going to try to charge him?' Camille asks, echoing my thoughts.

'We could. It's odd that he'd say that though, he must know what it could mean for him.'

I'm watching James Mayfield. The quick relentless tap of his foot. He's still bolt upright, the skin over his knuckles strained and white where his hands are once again clasped on the table. And it's then it dawns on me that his tension is not down to arrogance, like I first thought. He is nervous.

276

'What do you know about cameras placed in the homes of the other players?' Helen pushes on, referring to Emer's discovery.

'Only that I assumed they were there. That you had placed them there.'

'Did you install a camera in Ashley Noone's flat?'

'No.'

'Did you install a camera in Harrison Lloyd's bedroom?'

'No.'

She closes her notebook. 'Mr Mayfield, we've located cameras in many of the other players' homes but not in yours. Do you know why that would be?'

'Yes,' he says, simply. 'I realized at Ashley's place, the other night, why she'd offered up her flat to hold the meeting. Thought she'd gotten in your ear and that we were likely being recorded. I found the camera in my room when I got back and removed it.'

'I see,' Helen replies. 'You believe we planted those cameras?'

He chews over his bottom lip. Some of the colour leaves his face. 'Didn't you?'

I pull up in front of the Callin house. There's a group of lads kicking a ball on the green, bundled-up jumpers serving as goal-posts some way off. Three teenage girls are sitting on a wall. Two wearing dark puffa jackets with a black satin sheen, the other braving out the cold September afternoon in a white vest that stops short of her flat stomach. They pass a bottle, each taking a quick gulp before the next. When we emerge from the car, the girls' attention moves from the boys to us and the bottle slips inside one of the jackets.

It's overcast and the porch light is on over the Callin doorway and we make our way towards it. James Mayfield got something here. He found something that he believed put him ahead. Something that has made him nervous. There was a distinct change in his demeanour once he realized that it wasn't us who'd been in his home; it wasn't us playing I-spy. He knew when he was beaten. Or close to it. Such careful answers and then to tell us of how far he'd gone to secure those answers. We would've found out eventually, but to give it up freely like that, forsaking all that effort was not a mistake he'd make easily. I thought we'd gotten all we needed from Joe Callin, and as reluctant as I am to stir up his grief, if it's to find his daughter's killer, then we have to talk to him again.

Jack is with me, more for Joe Callin's benefit, being another familiar face to him. Baz is running surveillance on all our outstanding players.

The doorbell chimes and is accompanied by the loud booming bark of Joe's dog, Charlie. The light in the hall comes on and Joe's shadow grows slowly on the glass panels of the door as he approaches.

'Who is it?' he calls out.

'Frankie Sheehan and Jack Clancy,' I reply.

The chain clicks back and the door opens. He's wearing pale blue pyjamas, a navy dressing gown draped from his shoulders like a cloak. The dog waits patiently to the side, his long golden tail whipping over and back like a metronome.

Joe Callin lifts his nose, his dark eyes searching. 'Has something happened, Detective?' His hand reaches for Charlie's collar.

'Would you mind if we came in, Joe?'

He backs down the hallway. 'No, no. Come in, come in,' he says, as he leads us into the living room. The front window faces out towards the green and beyond the net curtain, I can make out the shapes of the lads as they chase the ball towards the goal. Joe feels for the arms of his chair, lowers himself into it before producing a large white handkerchief from his pocket.

He shakes it out and dabs at his eyes. 'Do sit down now,' he says. 'I was just having a spot of tea. They're due to release Lydia tomorrow. Isn't that right, fella?' He shakes Charlie's collar. 'Yeah,' he answers himself. Shuffling forward in his chair he reaches out, finds the handle of the teapot on the table, then his mug. 'If youse want tea, feel free to fetch another couple of mugs there, Frankie.'

'That's okay,' I say. The TV is on, the volume low. The news playing out. A man telling a reporter how he'd won eight million by accidentally marking the wrong number on his ticket.

'How's the case going, Detective? Did you find him? The person who did this to Lydia?'

I swallow. Look around the room, more smiling pictures of Joe's family. A family that has been slowly erased by circumstance, chance and fucking unfairness. The centre of the sideboard is taken up with a photo of Joe and his late wife on their wedding day. She was a petite woman, 60s slim, her gleaming dark hair swept up and back, a delicate band of pearls and lace holding her veil in place. Her eyes are alive with happiness. Joe has his arm around her waist. He's ducking slightly at the church door against a rain of confetti, his finger tugging at his collar, self-conscious because of the attention. There's no hiding the absolute rapture on his face.

Three children. Lydia the last. I think for a moment that Baz has it right: what's the point in sacrificing everything when a good man loses it all regardless. Nothing we've done or will do can resurrect the Callin family.

'We're still working on it, Joe.'

'That's not looking good, is it?'

'As more time goes on, it can become difficult to develop new leads, but the Bureau are working hard on it.'

He raises his eyebrows. 'I thought for a moment youse were here to say youse were throwing in the towel.'

Jack moves around the room then stops to look at a fish tank in the corner. The water reflects a green background. It's big enough, taking up the whole surface of the wooden dresser it sits on. A filter bubbles away to one side. Other than a single grey rock cluster, and a layer of fine pebbles, it appears empty. Jack is watching something at the bottom of the tank, and it takes me a moment to realize that no, the tank is not empty. There's a fish; a dark, chubby, wide-finned specimen with a large, mournful mouth.

It's lying on its side, motionless. Jack gives me a look that says what the fuck do we do with that. Bad enough the man has lost everything, now his bleedin' fish is dead.

I turn my attention back to Joe. 'We believe a young man came by to visit you recently. A James Mayfield?'

He thinks for a moment. Slurps his tea. 'Ah. Yeah. One of Lydia's friends. Nice chap, a little reserved.'

'Can you recall what you spoke about?'

'We talked about Lydia. What she was like as a child. He was saying how excited she was about getting into teaching. That he always knew she was smart. That's an understatement, says I; she was modest about it, you know, but our Lydia could stand next to any of them with those fancy degrees.'

'He didn't say how he knew her?'

He frowns. 'No, I don't think he did. I thought it was probably from the bar.' A cloud of worry moves across his face. He puts down his mug. 'What's your interest in this chap now? Do you think he might have had something to do with Lydia's murder?'

'We just have a few questions we need answered about his visit here, that's all.'

He wraps the edge of the handkerchief around his index finger, touches it to the corner of his eyes, his bottom lip pushes upwards, and his mouth pulls in as he tries to control his emotions. 'I'm sorry. Gah,' he says. He blows his nose. 'It's all been a bit much.' Charlie collapses at Joe's feet, rests his head between his paws.

'I'm sorry, Mr Callin,' I say, easing away from the subject of James to circle back to later, test the theory that Lydia might have been interested in The Murder Box. That she'd discussed the idea of creating a murder-mystery game with the other players. 'I know we talked about this before, but I wondered given some time, have you remembered whether Lydia mentioned any new friends to you?'

'Nope. No boyfriends that she told me about, like I said before but, and I'm probably dwelling on it a bit too much, she seemed lighter over the last year. I remember thinking there might be someone behind that. A fella or something. She wouldn't be one to tell her da now, not unless it was serious.'

I'm thinking this mood change could have been because of

Teddy Dolan but I need a connection to the other players. 'Even off the cuff, did she mention an Ashley or Pippa?'

'I don't recall, but she didn't really update me on that side of things.' He goes quiet for a minute then, 'You know, that James fella, he was really interested in the pictures.'

'The pictures?'

'Yeah, the family photos. Had a good look at them all, as far as I can tell,' he makes a motion towards his eyes. 'I could sense him moving around the room. He asked me about a few of them. About the one of Lydia's brother next to the bike. What sort of bike it was and whether Lydia ever rode one. I said no. She was against that bike from the start and more so when the accident happened.'

'May I?'

'Work away,' he says.

I get up and peruse the pictures again, searching for what it was that captured James Mayfield's interest. What had he worked out before us? Jack is still guarding the fish tank, now trying the occasional tap against the glass as if he could rouse the creature from the dead.

Joe cranes his neck at the sound. 'How's Agatha doing?' he asks in Jack's direction.

Jack whips his hand away, sticks it in his pocket. 'Grand. Grand. She's doing grand.' He clears his throat. 'What type is she?'

'An Oscar. Had her over ten years now. My wife bought her as an anniversary gift. I can barely make her out in the water nowadays, just a shadow, but she's a character all the same.'

Jack throws a grimace at me. 'She seems it,' he says tightly.

Joe laughs. 'Is she not moving?'

Jack pauses briefly before answering. Then, lowering his voice respectfully, answers: 'I'm afraid not. I'm sorry.'

'Probably been at that as soon as I came in to have my cup of tea. The divil. You're thinking she's dead?'

I put down another framed photograph of Lydia Callin. Nothing leaps out. I can't see what James Mayfield sees. I look around at the gallery of family pictures, frustrated, knowing that the answer is here – or at least part of it.

'She's not?' Jack asks, waving me over in a kind of panic.

I walk over slowly.

In the tank, Agatha remains motionless. Her bulbous eyes are cloudy, her body still as stone.

Joe shuffles upright, eases out of the chair, navigates across the room with impressive efficiency. 'Lydia loved this fish. It's harder for me to enjoy her obviously, but it's kinda nice knowing she's here all the same, even if I can't see nothing but a dark shape in the tank. One of the lads comes round from the pet shop every few months, helps me clean the water. She doesn't like that. She started doing this, playing dead, about a year after we got her. Put the wind up me big time – came downstairs in the morning and thought she was dead. Her lying on her side and not a flicker of a gill. I remember calling Nora in, both of us panicking about how we'd break it to the kids, especially Lydia, then Nora noticed that if she reached for the food, Agatha's eyes followed her. Look,' he says, and feels for a tub from the side of the tank. The shadow of his hand moves across the water and there, a tiny movement of the eye.

He lifts the lid off the tank, and Agatha's eyes follow him.

He takes a pinch of dried flakes and sprinkles them over the surface.

The flakes sink into the tank. A curl of fin and Agatha levers herself upright. Her body pushes through the water. Her wide mouth opens and her tail flicks as she closes in on a particle of food.

'We said it to the pet shop after. Thanatosis,' Joe explains and the word rings through me like a bell. 'Playing dead. That's the fancy term for it. She's a one, alright. Likes a bit of the drama, our Agatha. We hadn't named her up to then, but Lydia gave her the name after that,' he says, dragging the lid back into place.

Thanatosis. Thanatos. Thanatosis. 'After the mystery writer? Agatha Christie?' I ask. Dryness in my mouth. Once again, I look over the gallery of family photos, only now, I see they are not family photos. No group pictures at all. The odd one of Nora and Joe together, of Joe and one of his sons, but every picture of Lydia Callin is of her on her own.

'That's it. She's smart, Lydia. Was smart,' he catches himself. 'Knew all about lots of different subjects, would get a bit obsessed with some of them, you know. She said that this writer disappeared or something and everyone thought she was dead, but she wasn't. Having a time of it somewhere.'

Jack is still beside me, tense. Yet again, I look around at the photos in the room. Lydia sitting in a garden, her hand shielding her face from a band of sunlight. Lydia posing for a school photograph, grey sweater with red stitching along a V-neck and the cuffs. Another, blowing out the candles of a birthday cake; I count seven.

'We heard Lydia liked mysteries?' I ask, comprehending now

284

just how long-standing Lydia's fascination with murder mysteries was. Or is.

'Oh yeah. Always making them up when she was little, read all the books through her teens, couldn't get her nose out of them.'

I walk across the room, take up the framed picture of Lydia in the uniform. It doesn't seem likely that Mr Callin would have an entire sideboard of pictures from his wedding, then babyhood to adulthood of his kids, but none of them together. An uneasy sensation begins in my stomach, pulls at the back of my throat. 'Joe, what was the colour of Lydia's primary school uniform?'

'Oh God, you got me there. Blue, I think.'

I hold up the picture so Jack can see – the implication of what it could mean freezes on his face. If we needed confirmation of what we're dealing with, this is it. Thanatosis. Playing dead. It's exactly what Lydia Callin has been doing. Lydia Callin is not dead at all. And I see her now, on her last visit to her father. Her bag full, but not because she's staying overnight – because she has some prep work to do for her latest project. Her dad opens the door to her. She hugs him, presses a kiss to his cheek. She's glad to see him, but her visits whip up a writhing nest of emotions, few of them good. She allows him to head down the hallway first, chattering to her as he goes, his hand tracing the wall, more out of habit than need. Charlie gives out an excited bark, sits out of the way, near the back door whose wooden panels are swelling beyond white paint, a bright layer of moss growing along the outside window. I see her, as a child, waiting for her mum to return from hospital, hours spent tracing the hand-sized chestnut leaves that are embossed on the pane.

'Joe, do you mind if we take a last look at your daughter's bedroom?'

'Can't say there's much in there now,' he says. 'Think your fellows took most of it.'

'We won't be long. Can I get you more tea?'

'No, no. I've enough here.' A flash of exhaustion moves across his face.

'We'll be as quick as we can.'

He gives the fish tank a little tap and behind his knuckle, Agatha presses her round mouth to the glass.

Out in the hallway, Jack and I walk slowly up the stairs, our hesitation not about air freshener this time but because somehow the atmosphere in the small house has grown thick, like we've stepped through a mist into another reality. On the landing, the sideboard, where now I notice a replica of the framed picture we've seen in the living room. It sends me back to that morning. When she came to the Bureau, she reached across my desk, shook my hand and introduced herself as Neve Jameson. She knew Neve wouldn't be coming back any time soon. I take out a pair of gloves from my pocket, slip them on, then picking up the frame, I lever away the tiny metal clasps that keep the back in place. The picture is a copy, a printout, that Lydia Callin placed there, knowing we'd be looking for more photos of our victim to help with our case. I bring the image close to my face, see the three tiny moles beneath the right eye. Three moles that I now realize were features on Neve Jameson's face, not Lydia Callin's. I put it down, a sick sensation plummeting through me. We cross into Lydia's bedroom.

'Well, I have to give it to her, she's committed,' Jack murmurs.

On the dresser, the incense stick is still there, still burned down only halfway. The hairbrush absent now. I wonder if the brush was even Lydia's or whether she'd stolen that from her housemate too. In my mind's eye, I see her as she drags the brush through her victim's hair. Neve doesn't move as she works, she's sleeping the sleep of the drugged. A sedative slipped into tea, perhaps. Or, like Teddy, flunitrazepam. But unlike Teddy, a crime of revenge and flair, the ex-lover becoming the perfect red herring for her game, Neve won't be waking up. Lydia gathers the hair, examines the strands, ensures she's caught a few with follicles. She needs them to be run for DNA when the crime-scene investigators come looking. She places the hair carefully in a sterile bag. There can't be any risk of contamination for what she has in mind. She knows the hair will be used to identify a body. A body that will take her name.

'Committed is the word,' I say, feeling the vibration of my phone in my pocket.

CHAPTER 23

We exit the house, thanking Joe as we go and apologizing in advance that once again we'll need to invade his privacy for a search. He takes it well, believing that we've had a breakthrough in his daughter's murder case.

It's early afternoon and rain has begun to fall. A slanting rain that stings both skin and eyes. Less than twelve hours remain before Lydia Callin makes her final move in the game. I should feel some sense of relief that we know who we're looking for but the speed at which our victim has switched to suspect brings a sweat out across my back. I'm beginning to doubt we'll know in time exactly who or what Lydia is planning on targeting next.

Jack opens the driver door and I get in. I've asked Helen to gather the team. Explain that we've news they all need to hear.

'Listen,' I say into the phone. 'We've just learned there's a strong likelihood that the body we have at Whitehall is not that of Lydia Callin but of her housemate, Neve Jameson.'

Helen, looking for clarity, asks: 'Lydia Callin is now our suspect?'

'Yes. I believe Neve Jameson was not the person who visited the Bureau to report her friend missing. That it was Lydia Callin. I need you to chase up Neve Jameson's parents. Ask when it was they last heard from or saw their daughter. I suspect Lydia's been using Neve's phone to text them to keep any worries they had at bay and buy some time.'

'You want us to bring Lydia Callin in?'

'Yes.'

'We have a potential problem with that, Ma'am,' Helen replies.

I pull away from the kerb, skid out of the estate and turn back south towards the Bureau. 'What is it?'

Baz's voice comes down the line. 'We've had no eyes on Derek Cohen and Ashley Noone never showed up for her shift at the sandwich shop this morning. I've just got off the phone with their parents, who haven't heard from them either. They've not been into uni, they're not in their accommodation and their phones are switched off.'

'Have they done a runner?'

'Possibly. Although, myself and Ryan went out to Derek's house-share. His laptop and most of his stuff is there. College notes are still in his room. I've a feeling they've been given another clue, possibly fed something into the portal that's called them out. We decrypted a message in one of the private chat rooms on the website. It was sent by Harrison Lloyd early this morning when we'd brought him in. It must've been on the way to the Bureau or before we seized his phone. The message said he'd been brought in for questioning and that he believed he also saw James Mayfield with us.'

Harrison covering his backside. With time tight, and all of

289

the players suspecting that any of them could become the next victim if they don't win, Harrison hinting that James is really the killer might have been enough to get the other players to enter their final solutions into the website.

I change up gear, move into the bus lane and hit the gas. 'Pippa?'

'She's at her house-share. We have a plainclothes team outside. They're about to update her on the situation. Advise her to stay put,' he says. 'I think if we move in now and Lydia's taken the others somewhere or implied that final clues or directions were at another location, we might be stuck with a Teddy Dolan situation – except I doubt they'll be coming out the other side with only a finger missing.'

'Where's Lydia Callin now?'

Steve's voice comes down the line. 'We've been monitoring Neve's – sorry, I mean Lydia's mobile, and cell-site analysis places her at or near the flat on South Circular Road.'

'Okay, get eyes on Lydia Callin. There's only until midnight left on the game. If she's led or holding Ashley and Derek somewhere, she's going to return to them in the next few hours. Hopefully, she'll take us straight to them. Keep Harrison and James at the Bureau. Baz is right. If we don't discover where Lydia's hideout is, we'll have at least two more dead bodies before the end of the day.'

'Chief, Ryan here.' He clears his throat. 'Harwood and I have a suggestion. We could try to use a kind of bait with her.'

I throw an angry glance at Jack, no time for Ryan's flights of fancy. 'What are you talking about?'

'If we went out there, wired up, a GPS tracker on, we shake the tree a little with some questions, she'll make a move. Especially if she thinks there's only one officer.'

I indicate, join the main flow of traffic to overtake a stopped bus. 'Let me get this straight, you're saying we send an officer out there for her to drug and capture?'

'We'd know where they were at all times. She'll take them to wherever she's keeping the others.'

'This is a murderer, Ryan. That's the worst strategy I've ever heard. No.'

Baz's voice is calm and firm when he speaks: 'We're running out of time and options.'

'Listen to me,' I say, sharply. 'Squash that idea. Get eyes on Lydia Callin right now. I want to know if she so much as opens a fucking window in that flat. You hear me? We can afford another few hours to see if she'll move. If she's not left the flat by eight-thirty this evening, bring her in. Do you hear me?'

Jack waves at me to calm down.

'Yes,' comes Ryan's voice.

I hang up.

By the time I return to the office, Helen and Ryan are finishing up with the press conference. They avoid mentioning Neve Jameson's name, focusing the media's attention on our suspect, Lydia Callin. Behind them her picture – the other half of the photograph I was given on the first day of this case – and pictures of both Ashley Noone and Derek Cohen.

Helen does not offer questions but finishes with an urgent appeal for the public to keep an eye out and contact the given number with any information on their whereabouts. Updates are coming in from our man staking out Lydia Callin's flat. I'm hoping she's one for catching the afternoon news. Although part of me worries that Baz is right, that this might send her running, even if it is into our arms. If she is holding Derek and Ashley, and that likelihood is growing by the minute, she could well be the sort to dig in, revel in the power of what she knows and refuse to tell us where her latest two victims are.

'Still can't believe she managed to overpower Dolan,' Baz says.

I frown at him. 'She could have an accomplice but I think this is all too clean for more than one person and something tells me Lydia Callin likes to work alone. Remember, the only strength she'd need is to hold a weapon, to pull a trigger or wield a knife. That's enough to get most people to go along with you. I think she somehow managed to spike Teddy's drink at the exhibition. She waited for him to begin to feel woozy. He went out made the call to Monica and she pulled up at the kerb shortly after. I think he got into that vehicle willingly, even if he can't remember doing so.'

He nods slowly. 'Yeah. I reckon you're right.'

'How are things with your mum?' I ask him.

'My sister's keeping me updated.' He removes his phone from his pocket, glances at the screen. 'Mum's not-so-bad today, a little slow but not bad.'

'I'm glad.'

'A couple of journos have their hands raised at the front. 'Has this anything to do with the body found in the River Dodder last week?' one shouts.

I pause, wait to hear how Helen handles this one.

'We believe there might be a connection to the remains of a young woman found last week and we expect to be able to

292

confirm that soon. Thank you.' She steps down. Ryan moves aside to let her pass, then follows.

'Have you made a decision about home care?' I ask Baz.

'The doctor says she's declining quickly and it won't slow. Whatever we're going to do, we have to do it soon.' He gives a wan smile, draws in a long breath, his chest swelling. 'If this is my last case here, I'll be damned if I'm going to let Lydia Callin wriggle out from under our feet.' There's more than a hint of the old hunger back in Baz's voice and it makes me feel at once excited and anxious. There's a flash of something in his eyes. More than grit, more than drive, but something like need or even desperation. I know what it's like to feel like your world is out of control. And I also know the kind of decisions that result from that feeling.

'For the moment, we sit tight, wait for her move,' I say.

'What if she doesn't move? What if she doesn't see this?' he motions to the press. 'Two more dead?'

'This isn't our only option, Baz. We're ahead of Lydia Callin here. We can still bring her in.'

We walk away from the press, make our way back up towards the case-room floor and cross to the board where Lydia's picture is still positioned front and centre, but now for different reasons.

Baz stares at it.

'Okay?' I ask, trying to feel out where his head is at.

He turns to me sharply as if only now realizing I am there. 'Sure.'

The camera has been removed from my flat. Another signal to Lydia Callin that we're closing in, that she should make her move.

293

Pouring a glass of wine, I sit on the sofa and wait for the update to come through that she's left her flat. I roll out my shoulders, try to make myself relax. Take a sip of wine. It's ten past eight. The game closes in less than four hours. The Chinese I ordered is cooling on the counter. My appetite gone. Mullins has been using the geoprofile in an attempt to pinpoint locations where Lydia might be holding Ashley and Derek. Using Neve Jameson's PPS number we've been able to discover that Lydia Callin has been working in an estate agents under Neve's name.

Our feeling is that she has a property somewhere in the city that's been on the agency's books for so long she's sure there'll be no requests to view it. With the agency closed for the day, we only have Google Earth and the estate agent's website at our disposal until they open again in the morning.

The officer watching Lydia's flat on South Circular feed back through to the Bureau who, in turn, update me every five minutes via text. Lydia exited the flat at four-thirty. We were poised to move in, but it turned out it was a short walk to the shop for a bottle of wine and back again within fifteen minutes. She's not emerged since. Lights have gone on. The TV is flickering against the curtains. We've run the plates on all parked vehicles close to her building. But none have a connection to either Neve Jameson or Lydia Callin. My assumption is that whatever vehicle she has been using is already at this unknown location. The property where Ashley and Derek are likely being kept. If they're still alive.

Mullins is whittling down the list of houses on the estate agent's website, phoning owners and leaving messages on vendors' phones. I look at my watch. Ten minutes, then we go in, whether Lydia moves or not. We can't afford to leave it longer.

I go to the kitchen, plug in my phone. For the third time, check the volume. We've armed vehicles on standby but nowhere to send them. We're pretty sure she's working alone, but we can't be fully sure and we don't want to find two more victims come midnight while we watch Lydia have her evening tea. I'm resigned to bringing Lydia in for questioning, possibly risking not ever discovering what has happened to either Ashley or Derek. I don't like the fact that we have two potential victims outstanding. All the other players have returned to their family homes. Every one of them is being watched until this blows over. If it does blow over. I've a dark feeling that once this knife starts swinging, it won't stop, unless we stop it.

Eight-thirty. It's time. The team will close in on our suspect now as per my orders. Putting the wine to the side, I draw the Chinese towards me and open the paper bag. There'll be a long night of questioning ahead; I need to eat. The chow mein is still warm. Opening the cupboard behind me, I remove a bowl, run it under the hot tap so the cool ceramic doesn't leech what's left of the heat from the meal. I dry the bowl off, then tip the takeaway into it, taking it and a strong coffee to the sofa. A text from Baz saying everything is in hand and I picture the team moving in.

When I've eaten and downed my coffee, I go to the bedroom, change into a fresh pair of trousers and a blouse. Lydia Callin should be in custody soon and I'm going to need my wits about me in order to coax an answer from her. At eight-fifty, I gather up my coat and phone then head out the door. Closing it behind me,

I take the time to double-check the locks. Cedric's door opens slightly and he peeks out from behind the chain.

'Oh, it's you, Frankie. Hey.'

'Hi, Cedric.'

He unhooks the chain. 'I've just let our landlord know that I'll be leaving in a few weeks.'

I hook my hair behind my ear. 'Oh, sorry to hear that.'

'I couldn't get beyond what happened. That he didn't even tell us that someone had the keys to the building. I made a complaint to the Tenancies Board.'

'Good for you.' I pull my bag higher on my shoulder. 'I really have to get going.'

'You should look into it, you know,' he says. 'Getting another flat, that is.'

I give him a smile. 'Maybe I will.'

Halfway down the stairs, I dial through to the office.

'Detective Garvin,' Steve answers.

'I'm on my way in. Is Lydia in custody?'

A pause.

'Steve?'

'I thought you'd said we should hold tight.'

'No. I said if there was no movement to bring her in at eight-thirty. My orders were clear.'

'Detective Harwood said—'

I stop. Reach for the banister. 'What did he say?'

'He said there was a change of plans. That we were going with Ryan's idea.'

I start into a run. 'Steve, is Baz in the office, right now?'

'No.'

'Where is he?'

'He's gone. Out to Lydia's place.'

'Let Jack Clancy know to meet me there. Get those armed units ready. Tell Ryan to kit up, stab vests, sign out firearms. Mullins too.'

CHAPTER 24

I get to my car, slam the door and start the ignition. What the fuck has he done? It takes three goes to dial the officer we stationed outside Lydia Callin's flat.

Finally, it rings. 'Hello Ma'am?'

'Tell me you're at the Callin flat?'

I hear the beep of a car lock. 'No, just got home. Detective Harwood said he was taking over.'

By the time I get to Lydia Callin's, there's no sign of Baz, no sign of his car and no reply from his mobile. I stand back and look up at the building trying to make myself believe that this is happening. Jack grasps my elbow as if he could hold me back from the realisation of what Baz has done. Mullins and Ryan pull up in the Bureau van. They're already trying to get a fix on Baz's location. I swallow a hideous knot of fear. A terrible voice in my head whispers that this game was not built for us to win.

The arms unit enter the building. In minutes they've cleared the house. The neighbours are out, standing in doorways, watching the commotion.

Ryan approaches. Sheepish. He holds out his phone. A message from Baz, sent just before he rang the doorbell on Lydia Callin's flat. It details the strategy he outlined earlier: the GPS activated on his mobile, a tracking device in his shoe. This is a bad idea. Lydia is working her way through The Murder Box. We're two players short and now she has Baz. I've no doubt she'll end them all if we don't find them. And not in a hesitant, reluctant fashion; no, with a triumphant swiftness. You lose.

The lead officer of our armed unit approaches. 'Gerard Worthy,' he says, with a nod. He rolls his shoulders under his protective gear, speaks out at me through the open visor of his helmet. 'No signs of struggle, that we could make out. No sign of either party, I'm afraid.'

Mullins steps out of the Bureau van, laptop in hand. 'We've got activity on the tracker in his shoe,' he says, breathless. 'They're on Sundrive Road. Ten minutes away. The house is a large, semi-derelict Georgian. Our assumptions were right – it's been on the estate agent's books for over a year and it's just west of our geoprofile hotspot.'

'That's the one,' I say, a surge of relief coursing through me.

I signal to Jack that it's time for us to go. This might just be tidier than I imagined. Lydia only has a small head start.

I walk up to Gerard. 'We've a new address. I'll send it to you now. Sundrive Road.'

'I know it.' He turns, ushers his team around him and they move quickly towards their vehicle.

I lean into the Bureau van. 'Ryan?'

'Yes, Chief.'

'Can you send images of the house through to the team and my phone please.'

'Yes, Ma'am.'

Jack drives. And in seconds, the picture of the house comes through on my phone. The agency description includes phrases like 'huge potential', 'in need of repair', 'good bones' the tell-tale language used to describe properties that are shit-heaps. Two floors above ground and a spacious basement where the kitchen used to be. I turn through the pictures on the agent's site. The estate agency where Lydia Callin worked. She slowly usurped Neve's life, then eliminated her altogether. I press a hand to my stomach.

'He'll be okay. We have time,' Jack says, and I don't like the tone, as if he's persuading himself. He hides his anxiety well, but I see his white grip on the steering wheel, the way he leans forward in the driving seat, eyes almost reaching through the windscreen, urging us there faster.

The clock on the dash shows nine fifty-five pm. Time sifting through the glass. I try to make myself relax. Jack is right. We have time. He takes the bus lane anyway, the blue light blinking on the dash, the siren off. Turning my face towards the window, I watch the passing houses and traffic and work on calming my breathing. I need a clear head. I remind myself that we know where Baz is, that the game is not set to end until midnight, but it doesn't help. My heart feels like it's trying to break through my chest.

'How long?' I ask Jack.

'Five minutes,' he says.

I dial Helen at the Bureau. 'Anything new?'

'Our unit is almost there. I managed to get hold of a local officer to do a walk-by. No eyes on anyone inside. She said it looked deserted.'

I think of the pictures of the house. 'Downstairs?'

'She says, there's a lightwell just under the front window that looks down on the basement level. No activity or lights on. The back entrance is up a lane off the main street. She suggested taking a look but I was worried there might be cameras.'

I swallow, try to clear the dryness in my mouth. 'Okay.'

'We did try Lydia's phone. We have Camille here. I thought if she could talk to her—'

'It's too late for that,' I say. 'She's all in. Is Camille next to you now?'

'Frankie, hi,' Camille says.

'What do you suggest? If they're—' I can't bring myself to finish the question.

'We have two hours left. Focus on that. When you get to her, if there is a chance to engage, it could be worth you speaking to her first. The game was sent to you. You are a player. Play to that. Offer her perfection, her own rules, her creation. To someone like her, a game played right, played well, is beautiful,' she adds. 'This is a fantasy she's dreamed up over years – an escape from the difficult, erratic and cruel rules of life. In this, she wants control and that doesn't necessarily mean control over her own fate. There's a chance that if you find her in time, she'll not only confess but come in willingly, almost satisfied.'

'Why do I feel you're about to say but?' I ask.

Jack turns down a quiet residential area and suddenly I see

the dark shape of the armed units' vans snaking up the street ahead of us.

Camille says: 'There's also a good chance she'll decide we've not adhered to the rules. That we've forfeited our right to win and Baz might pay the price for that.'

Silence. An image of Baz crumpled on the basement floor, skin cold, flashes across my mind. Wiping my palms along my trousers, I roll my shoulders and steer away from that thought.

'Okay, we've arrived,' I say. 'Keep your lines free.'

The headlights go off and Jack pulls over to the kerb. I reach into the back seat, take up my stab vest and struggle into it, clipping my gun into the holster at my belt. A yellow taser gun balances out the other side.

We get out of the car in silence. Jack and I follow the road around. Parked a little way up the lane, beyond the opening to the house, is Baz's navy BMW. When Baz called on her this evening, Lydia will have answered his questions blithely. He would have asked to use her restroom. A tactic that will have raised a red flag in her mind. Then he would have accepted her offer of tea and stupidly drank it all down. Too much faith in the belief that we'd get to him in time. It wouldn't have taken long for the drug to take hold, that much I know. Lydia Callin has her dosage wrapped up tight.

Gerard waves his team on and they filter up the garden. I hold back with Jack, waiting for the okay to move forward. The security lights over next door's garden flick on, spill yellow light down over the fence. Our officers move closer to the bushes. The back door is open. Wide open. An invitation. And the sight wakens a feeling of certainty that Lydia has been expecting us, that this is exactly how she wanted her game to go. Three lives in the balance.

The first officers slip through the open door, the white flicker of torchlight dances across the back windows of the house.

'Gardaí! If there's anyone here, make yourself known,' a male voice calls out.

The neighbour's upstairs light goes on.

Jack nods at it. 'I'll go,' he says and retreats back towards the street to ask the neighbours to remain indoors.

More shouts. 'Gardaí! If there's anyone here, make yourself known.' I wait for a follow-up. A different callout. 'Target found!' But still the same commands come squeezing in around me like pinches on my skin. 'Gardaí! If there's anyone here, make yourself known!'

The thought that we've got it wrong worms its way into my brain. That we've got the wrong house, that this is yet another red herring from Lydia Callin.

The torchlights appear in the top-floor windows, then Gerard is at the door, waving me forward. I enter the house and darkness envelops me. The air inside is cool and smells damp. Unclipping my gun, I remove my torch from my vest and move further inside. The other officers have relaxed and are searching cupboards, checking every crevice for any hint on where our perp has gone.

The floor is bare, ripped free of carpet, right down to concrete. Above, the plaster has loosened from the ceiling. I've studied the layout and know where I'm going. Downstairs, to a room that in many ways matches Teddy Dolan's description. Underground, where life felt but a finger's stretch away, traffic noises and foot-steps overhead. A basement.

I find the stairs off to the left, knowing before I descend onto the last step that Baz isn't here. But I have to see for myself. See if I can pick up any indication that tells me what's happened in this room.

The room is cavernous, wrapping around the sloping ceiling of the stairwell. I move the beam of my torch over the walls, search the corners. In an alcove to the right is a trestle-top table. Scraps of paper litter the surface. The beam picks up a flash of red card. In the opposite corner, there's a tiny black object on the concrete floor. It could be a piece of rubbish, a pebble or a flake of dirt but even before I move to examine it more closely, I know exactly what it is. The tracking device from Baz's shoe. My hands drop to my side.

Outside, Gerard's talking into the radio at his shoulder, ordering his team to spread out, search the neighbouring gardens. I wipe the sweat from my eyes.

'Frankie?' Jack comes up behind me. 'What's happening?'

I can't hide the terror in my voice. 'They've gone.'

CHAPTER 25

'What do you mean?' Jack asks.

I point back at the house. 'They're not in the fucking house, Jack,' I say.

He pales.

'They were supposed to be here. This is where the game led us,' I say.

He meets my eyes. 'Could we have got her wrong?'

The Murder Box flashes in my mind. She's spent too long sourcing the right materials, finding the perfect shade of red for the box, painstakingly putting it all together. It's been months in the planning.

'Her profile,' I say, 'her desire to make this game work. It's made for someone to win. They should be here. We played along. They should be here.'

'Okay. Okay,' he says quietly. 'We got it wrong, then. If, as you say, all the information is there, then we took a wrong turn, missed something. We look again.'

'We don't have much time, Jack,' I say.

'Well then, we look quick,' he says. He turns to Gerard. 'Anything turns up, no matter how small, you let us know but be prepared to move out as soon as we have another location.'

Gerard looks up from his radio. 'Yes, Sir.'

Ryan and Mullins are parked up down the street. We knock and the door slides open.

'Tell me we have something.' I thought I'd find both of them slack-jawed and defeated but I should know Mullins better by now.

'We spoke to Lydia Callin's neighbour on South Circular Road,' Ryan says. 'She said she thought she saw a man leaving the property with a young woman sometime before nine. The neighbour thought they were drunk, said they both looked worse for wear. They got into a navy BMW, the man crawled into the back, the woman was driving. The neighbour thought about phoning in because she reckoned neither should be driving but her sister called and she forgot all about it. We managed from that time frame to get Baz's car on the traffic cams after that. The tracker was still sending signals at this point. We've had a look through CCTV, searched over the past few weeks for vehicles parking up on this street. A black van, similar to the one we've been searching for, turns up this back lane, out of shot unfortunately, so can't see the driver, but a scan of the plates shows that it's a stolen rental under Dolan's name. We've already put out an APB on the plates, nothing so far.'

'How about the website? Any more entries on it?' I ask, desperate to narrow this down. A sick clenching sensation in my stomach.

'Nothing. Not since Harrison's message this morning.'

I drop my head into my hands, curl my fingers in my hair. There is no doubt in my mind that if we don't get to Baz before midnight, he won't survive, along with Ashley Noone and Derek Cohen. Somehow, my hands have slipped from the boulder and in my mind's eye, I watch as it rolls out from under my grasp and crashes down that hill.

Mullins holds out a map of the city; he has highlighted the route. 'I've been looking back over every fork in the case.' He traces a finger around the geoprofile we created. The red hotspot in the centre covers this street. 'If we remove the other scenes, the break-ins,' he crosses them off as he speaks, 'we remove them because they're not real murder scenes, right? They're red herrings. Distractions. We mark down where the victim's body was discovered,' he puts a circle around Clonskeagh, 'Lydia Callin's workplace under her pseudonym as Neve Jameson – and I think we might be looking much further south.'

I stare down at the two points in the map. Not enough to give us any specific information about where Baz might be. Removing my phone from my pocket, I hope that crime scene are still with Joe Callin, knowing that he might struggle to get to the phone or have switched it off for the night. But we need something. A toehold. And I hope that he can give it to us.

'Y'ello,' Keith says. I hear the crackle of his face mask as he pulls it down. 'What's up?'

'Keith, I need to speak with Mr Callin, urgently.'

'No bother. Hang on,' Keith says. 'The poor man's shattered.'

I wait, watching the seconds pass on my watch.

Joe Callin's voice comes down the line. 'Hello?' Hesitant.

'Joe, is there somewhere south of the city that Lydia would've been particularly familiar with? Somewhere between,' Mullins holds out the map to me, 'Donnybrook, Dundrum or even near UCD?'

'Frankie, is that you?'

'Yes, Joe.'

'They're saying that Lydia might be alive, after all?' he says, a spark of joy in his voice.

I close my eyes, blink away tears. 'Yes. We believe she might have revisited an old haunt, perhaps. Can you recall anywhere?'

'Let me think. Well, yeah, she was awarded a scholarship for St Margaret's secondary. That's around there. The school wasn't her thing. She said she was bullied a bit, you know how teens can be. She left when her mum got ill. It's derelict now, as far as I know.'

Mullins is feeding the information into our system. He turns his laptop around and shows me a picture of what would once have been an elegant, sprawling building but now the windows are dark, smashed like broken teeth, slates missing from the lower half of the roof. For Lydia, her time in this place would've marked the moment her life began to change and not for the best.

'Thank you, Joe,' I say. 'That's very helpful.'

He raises his voice. 'Let me know if you find her.'

I swallow. 'We will.' I hang up. 'Let's go,' I say to Jack.

Jack nods, heads over to let the armed unit know to follow us.

I look at my watch. 'How long will it take for us to get there?' I ask Mullins.

He brings up the route. 'Roadworks here but if you take this road, you might be able to get there in twenty. I could see if there's another armed unit in the area that could get there quicker.'

I weigh up the risks on letting another team get to Lydia before we do and find myself shaking my head. 'I don't think so. This box was sent to us. To me. I don't think we'll get Baz back if someone else shows up.'

He nods. 'Thought so.'

'Meet us there,' I say to both him and Ryan. 'Keep looking for other locations, warehouses, abandoned buildings, even bloody Airbnbs. In case we've got it wrong again. Send me the access points to St Margaret's.'

Mullins reaches out to the handle of the sliding door. 'Yes, Ma'am.' He pulls it closed.

I don't wait for Jack, head for the car and have the engine running by the time he returns. As soon as the door closes, I speed away from the kerb.

The streetlights whip by overhead. The dark sky spills down rain. I concentrate on the road, not wanting to look at the neon clock that's ticking down on the dashboard. My bladder gives an uncomfortable squeeze, nausea twists in my gut. Sweat is building down my back, along my hairline. I feel the sting of it in my eyes. I need to focus. Pressing my lips together, I make myself breathe slowly, in and out through my nose.

Jack is quiet beside me. The walls that border the roads at Donnybrook reach around us, broken up by the occasional tree; the shadows from their bare branches passing overhead. I feel my ears pop. The car sweeps around a bend and the school appears. A lumpen, dark shape, the faint glow of light flickering in a downstairs window. I ease my foot from the accelerator and the arms unit passes and follows the stone wall boundary that surrounds the school.

I slow to a stop. Rain thrums down on the roof of the car. Jack removes his coat, pulls a stab vest over his head, tightens it at the waist and finds his torch. He checks the battery against his palm. We get out and immediately, I feel a give at the back of my knees. I get to the rear of the car just as my stomach empties. Jack waits. I wipe my mouth. Once more the armed officers slide out of the van like seals into water. I count four; the rest are still behind securing our previous location. I hope it's enough.

I nod to Jack, then squinting against the rain, we follow the team towards the building. The old school is big and consists of a central area comprising of two floors, flanked by two annexes, three floors in height. The roof tiles have long since been stripped, the supporting beams naked and curving inwards like a crushed ribcage. Overhead, I hear the whir of a helicopter. Gerard is on the radio and a beam from above lights up the school as if it were a lost boat at sea.

Jack and I press close to the rest of the team. Firearms drawn, the white light of their torches pointing in at the dark. The school opens out into a wide corridor. The floor is littered with beer cans and broken glass. They're everywhere. Even to the last, Lydia Callin is planning. If the helicopter had failed to signal our arrival, she would have heard us coming. My stomach gives another lurch. The team pick their way across the floor. Two go right, the others left. Jack and I glance at one another before I follow one pair and he the other. I cast my beam around and above, following a stairwell ahead. Flecks of water hit my face.

The ceiling and the floors above have fallen through. The black sky scratched white with rain. A shadow moves across a gap in the floor overhead. I blink my vision clear. Raise my gun towards the night.

The first call out from Gerard makes me jump. 'Gardaí! If there is anyone on the premises, make yourself known.'

An echo of the same from the left. I step over the leg of a broken chair. Pass what must have been a science lab at some point, the wooden cupboards that line the room sagging from the wall. The workbenches where students once sat on hard round stools in front of Bunsen burners are strewn with broken ceiling tiles. Ahead, the flickering light we saw from outside moves beneath the bottom of a classroom door. I want to call out to Jack. I swallow. Hold my nerve. Try to hold myself back. Resist pushing by Gerard.

He calls out again. 'Gardaí! Is there someone inside?'

I grit my teeth. Drag in a breath and count down from five. Another glance at my watch.

'Gardaí! Make yourself known.' His hand is on the door.

He opens it, gives the wood a push so that it swings wide, the beam of his torch making sweeps of the room. It's a canteen. I move forward slowly, trail light over the walls. A row of broken windows look out on a deserted basketball court. A couple of the food counters have been removed, the silhouette picked out in grubby lines on the wall. Two tables have survived. The standard school affair, skinny metal legs and formica. But where once their easy-clean surfaces would've shone, they're now covered in dirt and grime. Across the middle of one of the tables is a large, dark mass. At first, I think it's part of the ceiling that's come down but as I pass my beam over it, I see that no, it's not one single mass but two people, sitting across from one another.

Wind snakes through the empty window frames, combs cold fingers through the room and lifts a strand of golden hair from Ashley Noone's smooth brow. She sits across from Derek Cohen, The Murder Box laid out between them. Ashley could be watching me; her blue eyes don't move from my face as I approach. Her head is turned, lying on her folded arms, as if she'd only needed to rest a little. I know before I touch them that they're dead.

There's a scuffle of feet from somewhere down the hall and Gerard's radio clicks.

'Target in sight. East wing, room 15A on map,' a voice scratches down the line.

'Copy that.'

Gerard is telling me to get behind him. Get in line. But I'm already halfway down the hall. Torchlight bouncing on the ground ahead. He catches up. Stops in front of me and pushes me back.

I try to get a grip on my emotions. Blink through the panic.

'Focus, detective. We proceed carefully. Your partner's life depends on it,' he says, his voice a hiss of warning. 'Can you do this?'

It takes a moment to settle the noise in my ears. Every cell in my body is urging me to rush towards Baz.

Gerard looks at me expectantly. I nod. He waits a second, weighing me up and I pull myself straight.

'I'm okay,' I say.

'Frankie Sheehan!' a woman's voice shouts, and my body is half-moving towards her before I stop. Gerard is right. We are

312

not on strings here to be pulled and made to dance to Lydia Callin's melodies.

Gerard extends a hand back towards me, pats the air. Stay back.

A low voice on his radio. 'Target is armed with a knife. Hostage is conscious but badly injured. We don't have a clear shot.'

Baz's face rises in my mind, the memory of his cheek under my palm, the touch of his lips. I try to think what he would do, how he came through for me, got there when I needed him to; the hand in the dark that knew when to hold back. And when to swoop in.

'Frankie!' The woman's voice screeches. 'Are you there? I know you are.'

Gerard moves towards the door of the room. I peer over his shoulder. It's an old staff room or office. There's a long single window at one end that once looked down at students in the grounds but now shows only a row of jagged shards clinging to the frame.

The other three officers and Jack are spread out against the inside walls; the beams from their torches aimed at the other end of the room, where in a corner Baz is on his knees. His arms are extended above him, hooked on a rusted metal bracket; his hands limp over a set of handcuffs. There is a person huddled behind him, their body tight to his back and shielded by the walls on either side.

I whisper to Gerard. 'It's me she wants to talk to. Keep looking for that shot. Take it the second you can.'

He moves to the side, then into the room, walking forwards slowly. I keep my weapon trained on Lydia Callin but feel the tremble in my shoulder. Lydia's arm is wrapped around Baz's chest, tight against his collarbone, the knife clasped in her hand. In every way, she is surrounded, but none of us can act without hitting Baz.

Gerard stalks the room, looking for an angle, but Lydia has positioned herself well. This ends the way she wants it to end. She holds Baz against her, one hand in his hair, keeping his head up. The blade of the knife is dirty, the tip already breaking skin. He's bleeding somewhere in the chest or abdomen. His grey shirt soaked dark. His face has a greenish hue that makes me cold with fear. His breath comes in tiny gasps; his chest rising and falling rapidly. He's lost a lot of blood.

'You made it,' Lydia cries. I can't see her face but her voice is filled with an anguished sort of joy. 'You made it.'

'Lydia, please drop the knife,' I say.

'You have to make me,' she says, her voice shaking. 'The winner has to do it,' she follows that with a short choke of laughter. I catch a glimpse of her cheek just behind Baz's temple. Her face is pink with emotion, wet with tears. 'I wasn't sure how I'd wrap it up,' she says. 'At one point, I thought you'd managed to drag us all out of it. But then your partner appeared at my flat. And I saw what you were doing. So clever. And I felt relief. Pure relief. Everything was unspooling as it should. I gave it my best, but in the end, you did work it all out. I knew you would. I hoped you would. You are the detective, after all.' She sniffs, a spike of energy, and I see the narrow strips of muscle in her shoulder flex. The hand around the knife tightens. 'You won this one, Frankie. Now, you have to finish it.'

'Lydia, if you drop the knife and step out, we can finish this game how you imagined.'

'With an arrest?' she says, irritated that I'm not getting it. 'That's not how I imagined it. It deserves better than that.'

And I know she means for me to kill her. I've won, after all.

'Let me help you,' I say. 'Please.'

Silence. I hear the shuffle of feet behind Baz as she adjusts her posture, her eye flicks down and I realize she's checking the time.

'There's only minutes left,' she says, through gritted teeth.

I tighten the hold on my gun. The others in the team are unwavering. The weapons stay trained on Lydia. On Baz. I consider pulling the trigger, sending a bullet through her forearm, severing muscle and nerve tissue, the knife loosening from her hand and falling to the floor. But her arm is crossed over Baz's chest. I shoot her arm, I shoot my partner.

She senses my hesitation. 'I'll kill him.'

There is a darkness in her voice that rings true. I've heard that darkness before. And experience tells me to believe her.

'You know I will,' she continues. 'I studied you for weeks before sending you The Murder Box. It meant everything when you logged on to the site. I was worried you wouldn't take the case, thought I'd gone too far with that lying piece of scum, Teddy. I guess I should thank him for something: he brought me to you. Your doggedness on his case. On all your cases made me realise you would make the perfect player. I know you, Frankie. I know your training. Your passion,' she sighs through the last. 'I have the same passions. And I knew when I showed you that picture of Neve and I, you'd take one look at your victim and not be able to help yourself. That you'd elevate The Murder

Box to where it is now. You get it. The game. The beauty of it. In another life, I would have stood by your side,' bitterness thickens her tongue, 'but my path was full of holes and what could I do with that?'

'Lydia, please, drop the knife.'

'I won't do that. You have to finish it. That's how this game ends. I know what you'll do when I kill him. I know what he means to you.'

Baz coughs, his head jerks and she tightens her grip on his hair. A red trail of blood rolls down the side of his neck. His eyes strain towards his chest. He wants me to chance it. To take the shot at Lydia's arm and hope the bullet lodges there or that its deadly path is somehow slowed. That it won't tear through his organs like the knife that's threatening to tear across his throat.

It's barely a sigh but I hear him rasp. 'Shoot.'

I swallow, make the decision and lower my weapon. I hold up my free palm. 'Lydia, I'm putting my gun down.' Squatting slowly, I lay the firearm on the floor and slide it away with my foot. I straighten. 'Your dad—' I begin, but Lydia's voice rises over mine.

'Ten seconds,' she shouts. 'Finish the game, Frankie. Finish it!' The knife trembles at Baz's throat.

'Your dad told me how much he loves you—'

'Five seconds.'

I unclip the holster at my waist, tears catching in my throat. A voice in the back of my head, begging, pleading, beseeching whatever gods are up there to make this work. To bring Baz out alive. 'He and Charlie are hoping to see you soon.'

'Two—'

I draw the taser from my belt, hoping at least one of the probes finds Lydia's arm. It goes off with a bang and a shower of blue confetti. The fine metal threads unwind in the air as they travel towards their targets. Baz's body arches. Lydia's fingers tighten, the knuckles flexing hard. Then, slowly, they slacken. The knife falls. The team are a blur of movement. They swoop in on Lydia, drag her out from behind Baz.

I run to Baz. Make sure he hears me when I tell him, he's going to be okay. I reach up towards the wall bracket.

'Help me get him down.'

CHAPTER 26

I pull up outside Joe Callin's house. The porch light is on, only now there is a square of plywood in one of the front windows. Obscenities are scrawled in red paint on the door, over the walls.

When Joe opens the door, he reaches down, as before, and hooks a forefinger through Charlie's collar.

'Detective,' he says. 'It's good of you to come round.'

'Hey, Joe.'

'Come in. Come in.'

A woman is drying her hands with a tea towel in the doorway to the kitchen. Late sixties, wearing a pair of jeans and a cream roll-up sweater.

'This is Audrey,' he says. 'Audrey, Frankie.'

'Can I get you a tea?' Audrey asks.

'No, thank you, I can't stay too long.'

I follow Joe into the living room where he eases himself into his armchair with a sigh. 'Lydia tells me her trial date is set.'

'Yes. For the new year.'

'She sounded well.'

'I think she's doing okay,' I say.

I wasn't there when they brought Lydia in for questioning. No detective would trust themselves with a perp who's done what Lydia has to my partner. But I replayed the video afterwards. Helen rolled up the sleeves of her blouse, laid out her notes and conducted the interview. Gradually, she teased out Lydia's story, smoothed over all the questions we wanted to ask but none of the answers brought any kind of comfort. Lydia showed no remorse. Her voice remained as light and chilling as a late autumn breeze. The only thing it promised was more coldness to come.

'Was it because Teddy ended your relationship?' Helen asked. 'Was that why this started?'

A withering look from Lydia. 'Oh, please,' she said. 'This was coming a long time before Teddy Dolan came to his senses. I slept with Teddy Dolan because I could. End of. The nation's sweetheart and he's no different to you or I.' She leaned in. 'When you cut him, he bleeds. Imagine that.' She took a long breath. 'I suppose I should be grateful. I needed a detective for the game, someone to push it firmly into the real world. When I saw Detective Sheehan making a statement about his case on TV, I knew I'd found the right person.'

Helen nodded then, as if it was the most reasonable explanation in the world. 'When did you start planning the game?'

Lydia pursed her lips at this, thinking. Her lawyer tried to tell her she didn't have to answer that but she ignored him.

'Months, six? Longer – most of my life,' she said. 'Here's the beauty of a murder-mystery game: you have the world of the game, the players at the table, the rules are set, you have your selection of clues to work on.' She raises a finger, 'Some might not be clues at all. A red herring here or there. But that's fair. You know to expect that. You play or you bend those rules, whatever way you want, and you win or lose by those choices.'

In her eyes, she'd played – her family had played – by the rules and still everything was stripped away. A working-class family, good, loving, supportive. I can sense that, as I stand here next to her dad. But slowly, little pieces of that life broke away and there was nothing Lydia could do to stop it. So, eventually, she broke away too. As for The Murder Box, she said she felt the beginning of the idea as quietly and as certainly as the first drop of rain on the back of a hand. As years progressed, somewhere in her mind, the idea did too. It became a sanctuary. A place to retreat, to draw around herself when the bitter pill of life became too painful to swallow and her anger threatened to spill over. When it came down to it, when the moment arrived, when she knew it was time, she was surprised that the plan was already there, her subconscious putting all the pieces together for her, from beginning to end.

Although Joe Callin is holding on to the Lydia he thinks he knows, my feeling is that she left many years ago. As I watched her answer Helen's questions, I heard her try to suppress the disdain in her voice when she talked about the other players. I saw her smile as she described how, on the SD Gaming forum, she'd seen the question about gaming clubs at Trinity. 'If I'd had their shot at life, I would've been there and I would have been better than any of them.'

In a small back room in the school where she'd held Baz by the throat, they found a narrow camp bed, the mattress still bearing the stains from where she'd killed or dismembered Neve.

But it took half a day and help from the canine unit before they discovered her kit shoved far beneath the floorboards in the canteen. There they found a laptop, Neve's mobile phone, knives, keys to my flat, remote camera devices and everything she used to set her plan in motion. The history of her online searches revealed thousands of visits to sites on forensics and, more recently, homemade explosives. They found documents that detailed how her game could work, rough drafts, some ideas shelved for later, others scrapped. And she did plan it well. She pored over police procedure, documented the various directions her clues would point us towards. She used our own methods to send us straight down the wrong path from the beginning.

I glance through the Callin living-room door, towards the stairs, recalling the hiss of air freshener over our heads as Jack and I walked up on that first visit and then Lydia's room, the incense, Jack examining the hairbrush on the dresser.

'Her lawyer seems good,' Joe says, pulling me out of my thoughts. And there's too much hope in his voice.

'He is,' I say. I touch my tongue to my lips, 'Mr Callin, I just wanted to warn you—'

'You don't have to say it, Frankie. I know what she's done and my heart aches with sorrow for it. Every night I lie awake, combing over the past, searching for the moment it went wrong. But even now, when I talk to her, I can't hear a hint of it in her voice. I'm not able to see that in her. And only now I'm realizing, it isn't my place to see that. That's for people like you. She's my daughter. I love her.' He stretches out a hand and I take it. 'That's the only way I can deal with this. I don't know how else to get through it. Don't mistake me. I'm not waiting for her to come home. I'm not. For Lydia's sake and for those she hurt, justice has to be done. I can live with that.'

Back in the car, I rest my hands at the top of the steering wheel and let my head drop forward. The tentacles of this case reached wide, tightened around so many lives. Neve Jameson. Neve was a quiet person, her mum told us, undemanding and trusting. She'd two younger siblings, so she was used to putting others first, helping out when she could. Her dad said she'd really cared for Lydia. Had known about her background, encouraged her to try for her exams again. She'd been ecstatic for her friend when she'd won a place in teaching college. He'd shaken his head, reached for his wife's hand and asked the question none of us were able to answer. 'I don't understand it. Why?' When Helen questioned Lydia about it, Lydia's answer was matter-of-fact. Neve provided her with an adequate doppelgänger. Lydia had access to her phone, her identity and eventually, her life. No other victim would've worked for the game.

Ashley Noone, a promising med student, gone. Her family broken. Derek Cohen's mother collapsed to the ground when she was informed by Ryan that her son had been murdered. Harrison Lloyd, confronted with the reality of what happened to the other players, couldn't deal with his own guilt, and was found unconscious by his flatmates in his room some days after Lydia Callin's arrest; an overdose. Harrison's message that final morning, prompted both Ashley and Derek to enter the wrong answer into the game's portal. They lost, Lydia said to Helen, and so in order to extract her cost she told them they were close to a solution, that the evidence they needed would be found at the deserted school. Derek got to the school first, he'd barely stepped across the threshold of the building before the knife found the back of his neck. Ashley arrived only an hour after.

James Mayfield and Pippa Dunne have been hounded on social media. James, unable to deal with the attention, has not returned to his studies. And when I checked back in with young Orla Flanagan, her doctor had prescribed her sleeping tablets to help her deal with night terrors.

And then there's Baz. Those last moments in that room rise in my mind. The seconds counting down. Lydia's hand tightening. I straighten, pull in a ragged breath and turn on the ignition.

The sky is washed clean. A light blue that'd make you believe there was never such a thing as darkness. A wind, sharp and fresh, breathes coolness on my face. Above, the last leaves of the oak Jack and I stand under rustle and loosen from their branches. The murmurs from the priest stop. He makes a final shape of the cross over the grave, cutting his hand through the air, then stands, head bowed. People begin to move away from the graveside. They're quiet at first, their voices respectful whispers, then growing slowly louder as they near their vehicles. How many strides is it to moving on? The wind picks up again. I catch the scent of freshly turned earth and feel Jack's arm at my back.

'I'm sure it used to be simpler,' I say to him.

'It was never simpler,' he replies after a bit. 'You get better at the job and it makes you think the results should be better, but they never are. We begin at the wrong end of this game.'

Lydia Callin's prosecution will be swift. Swift like the blade she wielded on her victims. In some ways, I marvel at her determination, her strength to make sure it all played out. She told

Helen it took her two days to dispose of Neve's remains. She wasn't Neve any more, she'd said, and her face had taken on a chilling clinical expression as she explained her process. I'm not sure whether the detail she offered so freely was so that we could close our case or whether it was a need to show us, in her own words, the magnificence of The Murder Box.

Around the grave, the family gather. The priest raises his book to his chest, then, with a final nod, walks away, his robes lifting in the breeze.

Baz is alone.

Jack and I follow the narrow gravel path to stand at his side. I step up beside him and reach for his hand. His fingers close around mine.

'Mam would've liked that,' he says, looking down at the green covering that's been laid over the grave.

'It was a grand turnout,' Jack says.

Baz shifts his weight a little, leans harder on the walking stick. 'My sisters are having a few over to Mam's house now, if youse fancy it.'

'Sure,' I say.

He looks out towards the street where mourners are huddled in small groups. 'But I'd love a quiet pint somewhere.'

'There's a place just up the road.' Jack says, always with an eye for a pub.

We turn, walk away from the grave. We move slowly, letting Baz choose the pace.

He looks at me. The colour not quite back in his face, a bit too much of a shadow beneath his eyes, but he makes an effort at a smile. 'I never thanked you for tasering me.'

'You know, I'd been longing to try that out,' I say.

'Glad I was in the right place, then so. Suppose I should be grateful you didn't try for the shot, after all. You've a dreadful aim.'

'You know, next time I think I will.' And that wins me a laugh, and the sound is like a warm drink on a cold day.

I draw the neck of my coat closed. I have all my people with me. This time we came out all right. Bruised. Changed. But whole. And the relief of that brings water to my eyes. In the end, this time, we won.

ACKNOWLEDGEMENTS

Thank you to all the readers and booksellers who continue to support my books. Thank you to my wonderful agent, Susan Armstrong and all the team at C&W Agency.

During the writing of this book, the coronavirus pandemic began and I am hugely grateful to my publishers for adapting and for their patience while I finished this novel. Special thanks to my editor, Stefanie Bierwerth, to Jon Riley and Jasmine Palmer. Thank you to all the riverrun and Quercus team, particularly Milly Reid, Lipfon Tang, David Murphy and to my copyeditor Anne Newman.

Thank you to all those members of law enforcement who have generously given their time and advice on the certain elements of procedure.

Thank you to friends and family who have listened, read and offered advice on my writing, especially to my talented sister, Ann Kiernan.

Thank you, as always, to Matthew, and to Grace, for everything.